# JOURNEY of PEACE

Wings of Hope

# JOURNEY of PEACE

*a novel by*

# CONNIE STEVENS

Published by Wings of Hope Publishing Group
Established 2013
www.wingsofhopepublishing.com
Find us on Facebook: Search "Wings of Hope"

Printed in the United States of America

Stevens, Connie
    Journey of Peace / Connie Stevens
    Wings of Hope Publishing Group
    Print ISBN: 978-1-944309-42-8
    eBook ISBN: 978-1-944309-43-5

Cover artwork and typesetting by Vogel Design in Wichita, Kansas.

To John

*The steps of a good man are [a]ordered by the Lord,*
*And He delights in his way.* PSALM 37:23

*In all things showing yourself to be a pattern of good works; in doc-*
*trine showing integrity, reverence, incorruptibility.* TITUS 2:7

# ᥫ CHAPTER ONE

*Raleigh, North Carolina 1888*

Margaret Fellrath cringed under the scathing glare of the sheriff at the county jail. Yesterday afternoon, the judge had pounded his gavel and declared the jury found her brothers guilty of robbing the Griswold Freight Office. The fact that she worked as a shipping clerk for Mr. Griswold threw the light of suspicion on her, and despite the jury declaring her innocent for lack of evidence that she had anything to do with her brothers' crime, many in the court room had still cast judgmental stares in her direction. Even now, as she asked if she could see her brothers, the sheriff narrowed his eyes and warned her the visit would be a short one, and he would be listening.

He rattled the key in the lock, and the door leading to the cell area swung open with a clank and *thunk*. She followed him down a short row of cells to the end where both of her brothers occupied the same space. The light of early dawn from the tiny, single window barely illuminated the cell enough to see her siblings. The sheriff took a few steps back and stood with his feet spread apart and his arms crossed.

Brock, the younger of the two, was sprawled on a cot, his greasy brown hair tangled and stringy. The eldest of the three siblings, Ned, stood looking out the high, bar-reinforced window. His stocky build, full face, and thick eyebrows always put Margaret in mind of their father. She wrinkled her nose. The place smelled of dampness, unwashed bodies, and human waste. How would her brothers survive being locked up in such a place for the seven years the judge had ordered?

"Ned? Brock?" She was afraid to speak much louder than a whisper with the sheriff hovering close by, although she wasn't sure why. Her brothers had already been convicted.

Ned turned. A slight smile tipped his lips.

Brock raised his head from the cot. He snorted. "What're you doin' here?"

"You're my brothers." Margaret divided her gaze between both men. "I came to see how you're doing and find out if you need anything."

Brock sneered. "How we're doin'? How do you think we're doin'?" He sat up and swung his legs around to the floor. His brooding expression made his dark eyes appear deeper. "After you snitched to the sheriff about our plans and sold us out? Yeah, I need somethin'. I need out of here."

Margaret sucked in a sharp breath and took a step backward. "I—I—"

"Shut up, Brock. Margaret didn't sell us out." Ned approached the bars and reached out his hand to her.

"No touching!" The barked order rang from over her shoulder. She risked a glance behind her where the sheriff stood glowering.

Ned gave the man a withering look and pulled his hand back. "Thanks for comin', Margaret." He cast a glance at his surroundings. "Sorry you have to see us like this."

Brock stood and pointed to his sister. "She's the one put us here. Only way old man Griswold and the sheriff woulda known our plans was if she told them. You get paid for snitchin' on your kin, baby sister?"

Ned spun around. "You either shut up, or I'll shut you up. Go back to sleep." He turned back to Margaret and curled his fingers around the bars. "Don't pay him no mind. You all right? The fancy lawyer was pretty rough on you."

She stepped closer, but halted, not wishing to raise the ire of the sheriff. "Yes, I'm all right. I'm just heartsick, like I know Mama would've been. Why, Ned? I begged you to stop."

He hung his head briefly. "I know. I shoulda listened. You always were the good one, the one who never got into trouble." He angled his head. "You remember all them Bible verses Mama tried to make us learn?"

"Of course, I remember them. I found it amazing that even though Mama couldn't read, she still memorized scriptures by listening to them being spoken." Pain sliced through her heart. Mama was with Jesus now, and Margaret sure hoped she couldn't see her sons from where she was. "I learned to sing the hymns Mama sang when I helped hang all the laundry."

A noise came from the direction of Brock's cot that sounded like a grunt of disdain. Brock always hated that Mama took in laundry for all the rich folks. Margaret didn't much like it either, but Mama never complained, even when she was worn to a frazzle at the end of the day.

"Ha! You did more than hang laundry. You took over doin' everything else so Mama could wash and iron all those clothes for people." A rueful grin split Ned's face. "Took you a while to get the hang of cookin', but you finally turned out some fair biscuits." The smile fell from his face, and his expression turned serious. "What you gonna do now?"

Margaret lifted her shoulders. "What I've been doing. Working for Mr. Griswold. Living at the boardinghouse. Trying to save a few pennies once in a while."

The sheriff stepped around beside her. "Time's up."

"Oh, please. Just another minute." Tightness in her throat threatened tears. "My brothers are the only family I have."

"Hmph. That's not much to brag about, young lady." But he stepped back and waited.

"I have to go to work now, but I'll be back. Can I bring you some supper?" She peered over her shoulder at the sheriff for permission. The man shrugged.

Ned licked his lips. "Supper would be great. The food here ain't much good."

Margaret gave him the brightest smile she could manage. "I'll go down to the café and get you some chicken and dumplings. I know it's your favorite." She took a few steps toward the door, the sheriff right behind her, but looked back at her brothers. "I'll be back tonight. I promise." She lifted her fingers in a gesture of farewell.

As she made her way down the street toward the Griswold Freight Office, people eyed her with suspicion. Didn't they hear the jury state there was no evidence to indicate she had anything to do with the robbery?

She approached the front door of the freight office and fished in her reticule for her key, but when she inserted it in the lock, the door swung open easily. Mr. Griswold stood just inside the door. Surprised to see him so early, she hesitated after she closed the door behind her. "Good morning, Mr. Griswold."

Her boss simply grunted. She glanced at the clock. Five minutes early. Mr. Griswold wasn't known for his amiable, pleasant personality, but he generally wasn't rude. She hurried to the cramped corner where her desk and files were located. Her footsteps halted. She always tidied her desk before she left for the day, but this morning the only thing on her desk was a small box. Inside was a collection of a few of her own items, things she had brought to work for her personal use. Everything else had been cleared away.

She turned and found Mr. Griswold standing with his arms folded across his chest. "Mr. Griswold, I don't understand..."

"Don't need you workin' here no more. That's all you need to understand." He huffed. "You might've pulled the wool over the judge and jury's eyes, but you won't never convince me you didn't let those brothers o' yours in with your key. Weren't no broken locks, no broken windows, they didn't bust a hole in the roof. Only way they coulda got in was with a key. Your key." He held his hand out. "And I want it back."

She couldn't have been more shocked if he'd slapped her. Heat rose up to choke her and she struggled to gulp air. "Mr. Griswold, I assure you—"

"Nothin' to talk about. I can tell you, everyone up and down this block, and this whole street, believes the same way. Nobody in this town thinks the judge did right by you. You oughta be on your way to prison along with your brothers." His fingers beckoned. "Gimme the key."

Her hand trembled as she reached into her reticule and fumbled for the key. Nausea gripped her belly. Mr. Griswold had trusted her, but now— How could she change his mind? Her fingers found the key and she almost dropped it when she handed it over.

Her boss—her former boss—reached into his vest and pulled out her pay envelope. "Here's what I owe you, and not a penny more." He tossed it on the desk beside the small box, and then he stepped aside, indicating the door. She stuffed the thin pay envelope into her reticule, picked up the meager collection of her personal items, and walked out the door on numb legs.

The morning sun blinded her when she stepped onto the brick street. Confusion tugged her one way, and then another. She didn't want to go back to the jail, unwilling to tell her brothers she'd lost her job. Brock would laugh, telling her it was her own fault, but Ned would fret, worrying about how she would take care of herself. Not that they ever took care of her after Mama died. She'd been on her own since the moment the preacher pronounced the benediction over Mama's grave. But Ned liked to think he "looked in on her" once in a while. More like they wanted a place to hide out for a few days. That changed when a storm tore the shack apart. Margaret had taken all her worldly goods to the city where she could find a job and a room to rent. Is that where she should go now?

She trudged back to the boardinghouse, thankful she heard clattering coming from the kitchen where Mrs. Porter, her landlady, was occupied. She tiptoed up the steps, not willing for Mrs. Porter or anyone else to learn she'd lost her job. She closed her door and leaned against it, finally allowing the tears to seep from beneath her eyelashes. She set the box down on the bed and picked up Mama's Bible from the rickety chair. If what Mr. Griswold said was true, that everyone believed her to be guilty despite what the judge and jury declared, she'd have a hard time finding employment.

She sat down on the chair, careful that it didn't creak or squeak, lest Mrs. Porter hear. "God, I never could understand why Mama had to work so hard. She was a believer, and You said You'd take care of her. Just like I can't understand why everyone thinks I'm guilty, even though the court said I'm not. If You really do take care of the people who believe in You, why is this happening?"

She leaned her head back until it pressed against the wall behind her. Was she waiting for an answer? There didn't appear to be one forthcoming. She opened the Bible where Margaret kept a bit of ragged lace from her mother's church dress. The scripture marked by the piece of lace was underlined.

*For You have been a shelter for me, a strong tower from the enemy. I will abide in Your tabernacle forever; I will trust in the shelter of Your wings.* Mama's favorite psalm.

She read all afternoon, and apparently Mrs. Porter never knew she was there. If she didn't find a job soon, she'd no longer be able to pay her rent. She looked at the money in the pay envelope. As Mr. Griswold had said, it was only for the days she'd worked, and did not include the days she'd had to appear in court. She added the paltry amount to the small purse in the bottom of her reticule.

She pushed aside the frayed curtain and checked the position of the sun. As she had promised her brothers, she would go to the café and bring them chicken and dumplings. It would use a bit of her precious coin, but she'd promised. Tomorrow morning, she'd start looking for a new job, hoping Mr. Griswold's prediction was faulty.

As the sun hung low in the western sky, Margaret stepped into the sheriff's office. The deputy sitting at the desk hastily lowered the bottle he had tipped up to his lips and hid it under the desk. She raised her eyebrows at the man's action, but said nothing. "The sheriff said it was all right if I brought my brothers some supper." She held up the small pot of chicken and dumplings.

The deputy shook his head. "He didn't tell me no such thing, little lady, and I ain't lettin' you take that back there." His ample belly hung over his belt. "Just leave it here on the desk while I check with him to see what he says. I ain't losin' my job over the likes o' you an' them brothers o' yours."

More likely he'd lose his job for drinking on duty, but pointing that out wouldn't convince the deputy to allow her to see her brothers. "But I promised to bring them supper, and I hoped I could spend some time with them."

The deputy crooked his thumb toward the desk. "You heard me."

Besides bringing Ned and Brock their supper, she'd wanted to share with them what she'd read in Mama's Bible earlier. Brock might not wish to hear it, but Ned would listen. She sighed and plunked the pot and spoons on the desk. "Please make sure my *brothers* get this, and nobody else mistakes it for their supper." Did the man catch her meaning?

The deputy hissed out a laugh and the odor of alcohol reeked on his breath. "Don't you worry none. I'll make sure they get it." He lifted the lid from the pot and drew in a deep, appreciative sniff. "The wagon is supposed to be here sometime tomorrow to transport those two to Central Prison. They'll get fed real good there."

"Please let me at least go see them and talk to them. If they are being taken someplace else tomorrow, I might not be able to see them for a long time."

The deputy shooed her away from him toward the door. "Go on, now. Git."

Resolved to be at the jail first thing in the morning before the prison wagon arrived, she walked back to the boardinghouse with a heavy heart. "Oh, Mama. I wish I could talk to you."

She picked at her own supper, a scoop of greasy beef stew and a cold biscuit, hoping Ned and Brock were feasting on chicken and dumplings, unless the deputy had gorged himself. The other folks around the table barely spoke to her over supper. Did they all believe as Mr. Griswold did?

She excused herself and retired to her room. As she changed into her nightdress, she made a mental list of all the places she might go tomorrow to look for work.

The following morning, she dressed carefully in the dress she usually wore to church. She descended the stairs, but before she reached the bottom, Mrs. Porter stood there and thrust a newspaper at her.

"Reckon we know why you wanted to go back to your room so early last night." The woman fairly snarled at her.

She took the newspaper and stared at the headline screaming across the top: *Fellrath Gang Escapes.*

## ❧ CHAPTER TWO

The sheriff scribbled a note on a scrap of paper while Margaret sat across from him in the boardinghouse parlor, twisting her fingers and biting her lip. After a dozen or more questions about the pot of chicken and dumplings she'd left at the jail for her brothers, he looked over at her with eyes of steel and repeated questions she'd already answered.

"What all was in that pot besides the chicken and dumplings?"

Margaret glanced over at the arched doorway where Mrs. Porter stood, chaperoning she'd said, but Margaret was convinced her landlady was more interested in eavesdropping than chaperoning. "I already told you, I got the chicken and dumplings from the café on Fourth Street. We aren't allowed to use the kitchen here."

Mrs. Porter piped up. "I can attest to that, Sheriff. My boarders don't come into my kitchen."

The heavy-set man glanced back and forth between the two women. "What did you tell the cook at the café to put in the chicken and dumplings?"

Margaret wanted to scream, but was certain the sheriff would view any emotional display as a sign of guilt, so she reined in her temper. "I told you that, too. I merely stopped by the café and told the serving girl I wished to take a pot of chicken and dumplings to my brothers. She didn't know who I was or who my brothers are. She went to the kitchen and came back with a pot that was covered with a lid. I didn't even take the lid off. I paid for the food, thanked her, and told her I would bring the pot back in the morning. That was all."

The sheriff lifted his chin and shot an accusatory stare at her. "Then what do you think caused my deputy to fall asleep so soundly, he didn't hear a thing?"

She interlaced her fingers and drew in a measured breath. "You are asking the wrong person, Sheriff. You should be asking your deputy. While you're at it, ask him what he was drinking. I saw him with a bottle, and I smelled alcohol on his breath."

"And you're telling me you have no idea how your brothers unlocked the door of their cell." Sarcasm dripped from his tone.

"That is what I am saying. I don't know. Believe me, had I known, I would have tried to talk them out of it."

A smirk pulled one corner of the sheriff's mouth into an unnatural curve. "Sure you would've." He rose and stuffed the paper he'd been writing on into his pocket along with the stubby pencil. "Well, we'll find them. When we do, they won't see the outside of Central Prison until they are old men."

He gave Mrs. Porter a brief nod. "Ma'am."

When he was gone, Margaret covered her face with her hands, trying to hold back the tears, until Mrs. Porter cleared her throat. Margaret lowered her hands and found her landlady eyeing her and rubbing her chin.

"Your rent is paid through Saturday, and that's when I want you out." Without another word, Mrs. Porter turned so sharply, her skirts had to catch up with her, and she strode back to the kitchen.

First her job and now her place of residence. Mr. Griswold was right. Everyone in town believed her to be guilty of aiding her brothers. Even her landlady and the sheriff. She was running out of choices. Even if she moved into another boardinghouse, everyone in Raleigh knew the name of Fellrath now. She had no more options. Leaving Raleigh was the only thing left to do.

She returned to her room and packed her things. All her clothing, save the dress she would wear in the morning, fit in her worn satchel, and her other personal things went into a canvas drawstring bag. The only thing she left out was Mama's Bible to keep her company tonight.

She sat up late into the night, reading Mama's favorite scriptures, weeping, praying, and reading some more. In the early morning hours when dawn had barely streaked pink stains across the sky, Margaret tiptoed down the stairs with her satchel and canvas bag before anyone else was up. She eased the front door open, praying it wouldn't squeak. Once she was beyond the front porch, she released a pent-up breath and prayed the ticket window at the train depot was open this early.

No breeze stirred yet as she walked the fourteen blocks to the depot. The streets were empty except for a wagon delivering milk. Here and there lamps glowed from inside a shop or an upstairs window. Were her brothers somewhere in the city? Were they captured? A chill ran through her, and she breathed a prayer for their safety despite being quite convinced they needed to pay for their crimes. Maybe prison would finally convince them to remember what their mother had tried to teach them, and embrace it. But they had to be found and recaptured first, and fear of over-zealous posse riders stirred within her.

The train depot loomed ahead, but she saw no sign of a train waiting for people to board. Just as she stepped up onto the platform, the ticket window slid open. A wizened old man with wisps of white hair poking out from the visor around his forehead peered out at her.

"Mighty early for a young lady to be out by herself." Disapproval rang in his voice. He shifted his focus back and forth around her. "Travelin' alone?" His eyebrows dipped and he clucked his tongue. "Where to?"

After assessing her funds and spending a few minutes in indecision, she finally chose one of the small mountain towns where nobody likely had ever heard of Ned and Brock Fellrath. The westbound train wouldn't arrive for another hour and a half, so she made herself as comfortable as possible on the platform's hard bench.

She wrapped her arms around her bags and held them close, and leaned back against the depot's clapboard siding. Maybe she could catch a bit of a nap, seeing as how she hadn't slept all night. But sleep didn't happen. Every few minutes she looked down the street expecting to see the sheriff coming to question her further or, worse, throw her in jail. He and everyone else thought her to be as guilty as her brothers, no matter the lack of evidence.

A train whistle finally sounded in the distance. Minutes later, the huge iron beast squealed its wheels and belched steam as it came to a halt at the depot. With one last glance around to see who might be observing her, she boarded, finding a seat near the rear of the car in the corner. She was doing the right thing. She couldn't continue to live here, nor could she find work, if nobody believed in her innocence.

A couple of other people boarded and sat well away from her. She should have purchased a newspaper to hold up and hide behind, but the headlines proclaiming her brothers had escaped would draw unwanted attention.

The conductor hollered, "All aboard," and the train lurched forward. As Raleigh slid past the windows and out of sight, she heaved a sigh of relief, and she looked forward to starting over in a new place. She pulled out her ticket when the conductor came around, and after he punched it, she studied the itinerary the man at the ticket window had written there. Eleven stops and three different trains. She prayed she could lose herself in the crowds of such big cities.

An hour into the journey, doubts assailed her and her stomach churned. There was no guarantee she'd find a job or a place to stay. Was the little mountain town where she was headed far enough from Raleigh? Her purse limited how far she could travel. Did they get the big city newspapers there? Maybe this wasn't such a good idea. What if she got on the wrong train in Salisbury or Asheville?

Two days and eight depots—or was it nine?—later, the train reached Asheville. People disembarked the train at the depot, Margaret included. She dodged people and luggage carts on the platform, weaving her way to the ticket window to inquire when her next train was scheduled to arrive. Every person who glanced her way appeared to judge her. Did they all know why she'd left Raleigh? It was too late now.

*Hot Springs, North Carolina*

Cullen Delaney angled his head to scrutinize the row of rose bushes he was pruning. Because they lined the entrance to the Mountain Park Hotel and Resort and were one of the first things their wealthy clientele noticed upon arrival, they had to be manicured to perfection. Mr. Greeley, the head groundskeeper, accepted nothing less because Horace Fairchild, the manager of the place, accepted nothing less. Cullen clipped a few more stems before he heard the train whistle in the distance. Once the train pulled into the depot, they could expect a new batch of tourists to begin arriving within fifteen minutes.

Cullen hurried to rake up the rose bush clippings and toss them into his wheelbarrow to ensure the well-groomed appearance to the grounds. Mr. Fairchild didn't like for the groundskeepers to be visible when the guests arrived. Cullen pushed the wheelbarrow down past the thick hedgerow, out of sight of the tourists, to the tool shed. Glad he was to be working outside and getting his hands dirty rather than carrying baggage for the elite and holding his hand out for tips.

Becoming what Mr. Greeley called a horticulturist required some training, but the old man often didn't share his knowledge. Cullen wondered if the gentleman feared losing his position if a younger man possessed the same skills. Maybe that was why Mr. Greeley didn't explain many of his gardening methods. Being the assistant groundskeeper didn't pay much, nor did it keep him busy. His idle hours found him more and more often down at the sheriff's office, until Sheriff Grant Harper declared if Cullen was going to spend so much time there, he might as well be Harper's deputy on a part-time basis.

The hiss of steam and screeching of steel on steel announced the train's arrival. Cullen dumped the wheelbarrow into the waste pile behind the tool shed and put his equipment away. Before emerging from behind the hedgerow screen, he stopped at the pump, washed his hands and smoothed down his hair. After a quick perusal checking for stains on his clothing, he walked back toward the hotel to see what Mr. Greeley had for him to do next.

A young woman carrying a shabby carpetbag and cloth sack walked up the hotel drive. She couldn't possibly be a tourist—the wealthy always arrived in fancy carriages. Her clothing, while clean, was wrinkled and threadbare. Her footsteps and posture bespoke of discouragement. But there she was, heading toward the front door of the hotel like she was a paying guest.

Judging by her appearance and her baggage, Cullen calculated her goal was likely employment, but if she committed the faux pas of walking in the front door, she'd be rejected before she could even inquire. He glanced about, hoping to intercept her before anyone else noticed her.

"Excuse me, miss."

The young woman halted and turned, and Cullen smiled at her. She dropped her gaze almost immediately.

"Good afternoon, and welcome to the Mountain Park Hotel."

She peered up at him for a moment before turning partially away. "Thank you."

He could barely hear her, and he stepped closer. As he did so, she stiffened and shrank back. What could possibly cause her to react with such timidity?

"I—I—" Her chin dipped and her neck muscles convulsed as she swallowed. "I'm looking for work. The man at the train depot said I might check here."

Despite the fact she wasn't looking at him, he smiled anyway. "I'm an assistant groundskeeper, so I don't really know whether or not they are hiring inside, Miss ..."

Her head jerked up and her eyes widened. She stammered. "Uh, uh, M— M— R-Rose. Rose...Miller."

Goodness, but he'd never encountered anyone so shy. She could barely spit out her own name. How did she think she was going to ask for a job?

"Pleased to make your acquaintance, Rose Miller. I'm Cullen." He stuck his hand out but she again drew back, so he turned and pointed around the side of the building to the employee entrance. "Go on down that way, just past the stone wall, and turn left. You'll see the gray door that says 'Staff.' Go in there, and ask to speak with Miss Templeton." He lowered his voice. "Miss Templeton can be a bit...intimidating, but don't let her scare you." The truth was Miss Templeton could frighten Goliath into surrender, but he hoped Miss Miller would be less timid once she got inside.

A shudder visibly shook Miss Miller's shoulders. He almost asked her if she wanted him to accompany her, but he sensed the offer might embarrass her, and his presence wouldn't impress Miss Templeton.

She rearranged her grip on her bags and straightened her shoulders, as if fortifying herself to face a formidable adversary. She cleared her throat. "Thank you—" She seemed to have forgotten his name, but Miss Templeton's name was far more important.

He tugged on the brim of his hat. "Good luck."

She started down the side drive toward the employee entrance. Cullen watched her go. Her extreme shyness and hesitant stammering when he asked her name piqued his curiosity. Speculating what kind of life she'd led before arriving at Hot Springs arrested his thoughts. Had she been abused? Was she in trouble? Cullen raised his eyebrows. Was she running from something or somebody? Working with Sheriff Harper, even part time, had increased his awareness of odd behavior in people. Harper had taught him to be watchful. For sure, he wouldn't mind watching Rose Miller.

# ✒ CHAPTER THREE

Margaret followed the directions the man—she couldn't remember his name, but he'd said he was a groundskeeper—gave her to find the employee entrance. He'd done her a favor by telling which door to use, but even now she almost choked, remembering the way her stomach had clenched and her throat went dry when he asked her name. Why hadn't she anticipated people wanting to know her name, especially when she looked for work? When one met new people, they introduced themselves, and she should have planned accordingly. She couldn't use her real name. Even up here in this sleepy little town that felt a world away from Raleigh, they had newspapers. Her middle name, Rose, and her mother's maiden name went well together. Miller was such a common name, nobody would suspect. It wasn't really a lie, was it? Rose *was* part of her name, and Mama was a Miller before she was a Fellrath. Separating herself from her brothers' notoriety was the prudent thing to do. But she'd have to remember— *My name is Rose.*

Just past the stone wall, she looked to the left like the groundskeeper had told her. There was the Staff door the man told her about. She walked up to it and hesitated. Should she knock? Should she just go in? She glanced back to see if the man was still there, but he'd already turned away. She returned her focus to the door. She could stand there and wait for someone to come in or out, but that seemed silly.

*Marg—Rose, you're an adult. You can do this.* She took a deep breath, raised her hand, and gave a tentative knock. A few moments later, the door opened. A woman who appeared a bit older than she, wearing a crisp white apron over a black shirtwaist and black skirt, smiled a greeting.

"Hello. Are you here to see someone?"

Margaret nodded. "I'm looking for work. I was told to ask for Miss Templeton."

The woman's smile faded a bit. "Yes, Miss Templeton is here. Do you have an appointment?"

The glimmer of hope she'd enjoyed only a moment ago dropped into the pit of her stomach. "Appointment? N-no, I just got off the train." Margaret bit her lip. "I didn't know I needed an appointment. A man at the train depot said I might inquire here about a position."

The woman glanced over her shoulder. "I understand. Come in and wait right here on this bench. I'll go ask if she can see you."

Margaret sat and smoothed her blue skirt the best she could and made sure her shirtwaist was properly tucked in. The skirt was old and somewhat faded, but she didn't own any new, fashionable clothes. She ran her fingers over her hair and rearranged a few of the pins while she waited. Wishing she'd taken the time to freshen up and don a clean dress, she could only pray her appearance didn't cancel her chance for employment. Besides, she had no place to belong, not yet, anyway. So unless she wanted to use the outhouse behind the train depot as a private place to change her clothes, what she was wearing would have to do.

The hallway was a hive of activity. The aromas coming from what had to be the kitchen made her mouth water, and she realized how hungry she was. Uniformed men with white gloves carried large trays laden with fancy silver serving dishes and platters, while others pushed carts bearing stacks of plates, bowls, and silverware. Just inside the arched doorway, the women in the kitchen moved around each other in a sort of frenzied dance, deftly executing their duties with efficiency as well as an odd kind of grace.

She marveled at the number of people, all going different directions and performing different tasks, but the entire operation ran as smooth as ice in winter. The young woman who'd met her at the door returned and beckoned. "Leave your bags here, and follow me. By the way, my name is Nellie."

*My name is Rose Miller. My name is Rose Miller.* "I'm Rose Miller." She stood and followed Nellie down the hall and around a corner to another hallway with less activity. They stopped in front of a door that bore a brass plate stating this was the office of the head housekeeper.

Nellie gave her an encouraging wink. "Good luck, Rose." She rapped on the door and waited until a voice on the other side bid them enter. She opened the door and announced to the woman sitting behind the desk, "This is Rose Miller." Then Nellie, whom Rose had known for a total of five minutes, was gone.

Several seconds elapsed as the woman made some kind of entry in a record book. She finally laid her pen on the tray with her inkwell, blew on the page to hasten the ink drying, and closed the book. When she looked up, her stern expression reminded Rose of a schoolteacher she'd had as a little girl. Every student in the room, including the older boys, was afraid of the woman. For the space of several heartbeats, Rose was transported back to that one-room schoolhouse, trembling in her shoes in the presence of this woman.

*God, I should have prayed before I came in here. Please be with me now. I pray I will honor You like Mama taught me.*

The housekeeper's narrowed eyes appeared to see all the way through her. The thin, grim line of her lips suggested the woman never smiled. Frown lines formed parentheses around her mouth and carved deep crevices between her eyes. Her nondescript brownish hair was pulled tightly back, revealing a few streaks of gray, as if she had no time to fix it in an attractive way. Rose jumped when the housekeeper cleared her throat.

"I am Miss Templeton, the head housekeeper. My staff is made up of the chambermaids, kitchen staff, scullery maids, hall boys, laundresses, and those serving in the dining room. Here at the Mountain Park Hotel and Resort, we strive for excellence and tolerate nothing less. Our standards are high, and the goal is to exceed them in every aspect of the service we render to our guests. Any staff member who does not meet our expectations is dismissed."

Rose pulled in a rattled breath. Moisture beaded on her forehead and dripped through her hair while a shiver shuddered through her. She longed to turn tail and run out the door, but she needed a job.

Miss Templeton raised one eyebrow and nailed Rose with an unblinking stare. "Well? Speak up."

Rose opened her mouth, but all that came out was a muffled croak. Her tongue stuck to the roof of her mouth. She tried to swallow, but a wad of cotton took up residence in her throat. She squeaked around the lump, and rasped, "I'm Rose Miller." She dragged in another breath. "I'm inquiring about a possible position."

Miss Templeton sniffed and lifted her chin. "Well, at least you can manage to put a few words together." She interlaced her fingers. "All of the kitchen positions are filled. We currently employ seven chambermaids. However, because our busiest season is about to be upon us, there is an opening for an extra chambermaid."

Rose gave a shaky nod. "Yes, ma'am. I can do that."

Miss Templeton's countenance suggested skepticism. "I will be the judge of that." She stood, stepped to a file cabinet, and withdrew a booklet. "This will outline the standards and guidelines, the rules to which all staff members must adhere, and a description of the duties of a chambermaid." She handed the booklet to Rose and checked the timepiece hanging from her neck by a black ribbon. "You have just over two hours to read this and report back to me if you still feel you can perform this job and follow the guidelines of the Mountain Park Hotel and Resort." She closed the file drawer and stood as stiffly as a mannequin. "I will interview you at that time."

"Th-thank you." Rose hugged the booklet to her middle. She stepped backwards toward the door. Was she dismissed?

Without another word, Miss Templeton took her seat at the desk again and reopened the ledger in which she'd been working when Rose entered. Rose slipped out the door and retraced her steps to retrieve her bags. If she could absorb everything in the booklet in two hours, and pass the interview to Miss Templeton's satisfaction, she might have a job. She settled herself with a slow, deep breath. Leading a quiet life hidden away in this tiny mountain town might mean an end to her nightmare—as long as nobody found out Rose Miller was actually Margaret Rose Fellrath.

The fuzz on the coiling stems poked Cullen's fingers as he dropped one last handful of baby squash into one basket. Another basket overflowing with fresh green beans sat nearby. The memory of his mother humming while she pulled weeds from her garden and coaxed seedlings to grow pulled his lips into a tiny smile. Ma always seemed at peace in her garden, even though he knew his mother had experienced her share of trouble. He picked up the baskets and sighed. How long had it been since he'd known peace in his soul?

He stopped by the kitchen to drop off the fresh garden produce for Mrs. Keegan—the best cook in the world, except for Ma. She greeted him with her usual smile and tilted her head toward a platter at the end of the work table. "Take a cinnamon scone with ye, Cullen, me boy."

He grabbed a scone and leaned to give Mrs. Keegan a peck on the cheek. "Thanks, Miz Keegan."

The cook flapped her hand at him. "G'way with ye now."

He took a bite of the scone and cast a blissful look heavenward as he was exiting the kitchen. "Mmm—*oof!*" He nearly choked on the crumbs of the scone when he collided with one of the maids coming around the corner. The young woman he met yesterday, Rose Miller, flinched, and then widened her eyes.

In unison, they both exclaimed, "I'm so sorry."

"Are you all right, Miss Miller? I shouldn't eat Mrs. Keegan's pastries without watching where I'm going." He brushed cinnamon sugar off his chin.

Miss Miller ducked her head. "Pardon me for being so clumsy."

Cullen laughed. "I was the one who plowed around the corner." He noted her uniform and white apron. "So, Miss Templeton hired you. Congratulations."

Her cheeks turned a delightful shade of pink, and the inclination to get to know her better held him in place.

"We get people visiting here from all over the country. Where are you from? Do you think you'll like working here? Have you done this kind of work before?"

The pink drained away and she stiffened. Just like yesterday when he'd first met her. He only meant to put her at ease by striking up a casual conversation. But his attempt to talk to her had the opposite effect of what he intended. She pulled into herself, arms wrapped around her middle and fear in her eyes. She mumbled something inaudible and scurried away.

He watched after her, an uneasy feeling in his gut. Perhaps she simply wasn't very friendly, but he couldn't help wondering if she was hiding something.

When he turned, Miss Templeton stood in the doorway. "Mr. Delaney, is it not?"

Since he was part of the outdoor maintenance staff, the head housekeeper wasn't his supervisor, but he didn't wish to get on the wrong side of her. "Yes, ma'am." He hid the half-eaten scone behind his back.

Her gaze followed the path his hand had taken, and the permanent frown on her face deepened. "Miss Miller has work to do and does not have time to socialize."

Cullen nodded. "Yes, ma'am, I know that. I was just telling her congratulations on getting the job."

The housekeeper's expression did not change. "I see. She won't have the job long if you keep distracting her."

"I'm sor—"

Miss Templeton scowled and pointed to the dirt stains from the garden on his shirt. "Go put on a clean shirt if you're going to be in view of the hotel guests."

He resisted the urge to salute and headed up the narrow back stairs to the staff hallway. While he was glad Miss Miller had gotten the job she sought, he felt a little sorry for her working under Josephine Templeton. The woman could strike terror in a grizzly bear. He'd heard the gossip among the employees about the turnover in staff managed by the housekeeper. Many new hires left after their first week. He hoped that wouldn't be the case with Miss Miller, although he had no reason to feel that way. He'd barely met her, and she wouldn't even talk to him. He admonished himself not to speculate over her shyness.

His room was all the way at the end of the staff hall. At the time he was hired, there were no spaces available to bunk with another male employee, and he'd been given two choices. He could sleep in the back of the tool shed, or he could have this tiny space meant to be an upstairs broom closet. It was barely big enough for a single cot, a lamp stand, and a chair. Some of his clothing hung from a few pegs while the rest was folded and stacked on a single shelf. A tiny window let in minimal light. The place wasn't much bigger than one of the jail cells over at the sheriff's office, but it was better than the tool shed.

He peeled off his dirty shirt and reached for his last clean one. He'd need to remember to take his dirty clothes to the laundry building located behind the tool shed. The ladies who worked in the laundry didn't mind doing his clothes since he always paid them a small amount for their trouble. As he buttoned the fresh shirt, his mind skittered back once again to the new maid. Rose Miller was a puzzle. Something about her intrigued him—exactly what he couldn't say, but when he had a chance to spend some time with Sheriff Harper, he planned to ask to go through some of the sheriff's reports.

# ～ CHAPTER FOUR

Josephine Templeton stood as rigid as a flagpole watching Nellie and Rose go through the long list of tasks required in cleaning a room after the occupant had checked out. Training new girls in the role of chambermaid was always a tedious process. Some of them worked well, and others didn't. Which category Rose Miller fell under remained to be seen.

Rose glanced back and forth between her and Nellie as she attempted to put fresh sheets on the bed. The girl showed not an ounce of self-confidence or efficiency, and moved like a sloth. At this rate, she'd never get past her first few days.

"Rose, those corners are all wrong." Josephine pointed to the mattress. "This corner isn't straight, and you've done the other one backwards. They should be mirror images of each other. Remove the sheets and start over."

When she stepped over to the bed, Rose shrank back. Josephine had seen timid girls before. They usually didn't last long under her supervision. She should have known this one wasn't suited to such exacting standards. "Didn't you read the section in the booklet on the proper method of bed making?"

She could barely hear Rose's response. "Y-yes, ma'am, I did."

Josephine pushed out a harsh sigh. "Then you should know you've started all wrong. You spread the first bed sheet, and tuck the bottom edge, except for the corners. Then you take the loose end of the sheet precisely twelve inches from the corner, at the head of the bed. Where is your ruler?"

Rose's hands shook as she fetched the ruler and laid it at the top end of the mattress.

"Now pull the edge of the sheet straight out and form a flap." She watched as Rose performed the task. "No, no, no, pull that flap at the twelve-inch mark so it lays perfectly flat. Now tuck in the part that hangs free."

Josephine *tsked*. Didn't girls receive any guidance or instruction in the proper running of a home as they grew up? Teaching a fully grown young woman how to make a bed shouldn't be her responsibility.

"Now pull the flap out toward you, bring it down over the side of the bed, and tuck it in. Make sure it's smooth and flat." She tapped her foot, waiting for Rose to accomplish the simple step. "Now move on to the bottom of the bed and repeat those steps."

She hovered over Rose's shoulder, measuring every fold and tuck with her eyes. The girl drew her arm up and dragged her sleeve across her forehead, despite the breeze coming in the open window. *Pfft*. She acted as if this was strenuous work. Rose wouldn't last the day.

Josephine continued dictating step by simple step what Rose should have memorized from the booklet. "Now spread the second sheet, wrong side up, from the edge of the mattress so it is precisely centered. Lay the duvet six inches lower than the second sheet." She huffed out a loud breath. "Use your ruler, girl. Six inches."

She glanced over to check Nellie's progress. The more experienced chambermaid's lips were pressed into a thin line and her jaw muscle worked back and forth. "Nellie, have you finished those windows yet?"

Nellie responded without raising her head. "No, ma'am." She rubbed the glass with more vigor.

Josephine returned her attention to Rose. "Now spread the third sheet over the duvet. Fold the second sheet above the duvet and third sheet, and fold precisely to eight inches."

Rose positioned the ruler without being told, and executed the step with no further correction.

"Now tightly tuck the sheets under the mattress along both sides first, and then at the foot of the bed. Tightly tuck the second sheet, duvet, and third sheet together, and miter the corners."

The girl looked ready to burst into tears. Josephine continued directing Rose in each pain-staking step, until the bedspread lay evenly spaced and hung flawlessly. "Remember this instruction. Now, gather up the soiled linens and begin wiping the baseboards."

She turned back to Nellie who had moved on to cleaning the windowsills. Irritation held Josephine in its grip. She had yet to find a maid who could adequately serve in the role of trainer for the new hires. Nellie should be able to do the training after being employed here for nearly two years, but Josephine still found flaws in her work. Did the woman not know how to properly clean a window?

"Nellie, did you not pay attention to what you were doing? There are streaks on these windows. You cannot daydream while you're working. If you cannot keep your mind on what you're doing, you will no longer work here. Do them over."

As Nellie hastened to comply, Josephine continued to upbraid her. "You should be able to perform your duties according to the exacting standards Mr. Fairchild requires. You've been here almost two years. I should not have to look over your shoulder to ensure you are accomplishing your tasks properly."

"Yes, ma'am."

"And your hair is coming loose from the pins. We cannot allow our appearance to become sloppy and unkempt."

"Yes, ma'am."

Josephine checked the time. "I will be back in exactly forty-five minutes. I expect this room, as well as the next, to be finished to my satisfaction, or you will both work through your noontime break to get caught up."

She turned and strode out of the room, toward the stairway at the end of the hall. Several of the rooms on the second floor were assigned to one of the newer chambermaids. At seventeen, Cora was the youngest maid in her employ, and had yet to develop a work ethic that produced the excellence required. Cora learned quickly and could do the work, but sometimes took short cuts if not closely supervised, and often acted petulant when Josephine stood and watched. She'd been tempted more than once to fire Cora for her attitude, but it wasn't easy to find chambermaids. However, Cora didn't need to know that. If threats of termination could motivate her to improve, Josephine knew how to wield that stick.

Josephine had hesitated when assigning Rose Miller to the staff accommodations, but Cora's room was the only one with a vacancy. So, like it or not, Rose and Cora were roommates. Certainly not the best arrangement, and if it proved problematic, reassignments might be necessary, assuming Rose remained employed there. Josephine made a mental note to watch Rose for signs that Cora influenced her in a negative way.

She'd barely reached the stairs when she encountered Mr. Fairchild. The man was never in a good mood, but today he appeared especially peeved. She could always tell, because he had a vein in the side of his neck that twitched when he was angry. As he approached her, the vein stood out and fairly throbbed.

"Miss Templeton." He pulled back his shoulders and drew himself up, as if trying to make himself appear taller than her, a feat that would only be accomplished if he grew two inches.

"Good morning, Mr. Fairchild."

He ignored her greeting and pointed up the stairway. "I just found one of your maids standing in the guest room she was supposed to be cleaning. She was primping in front of the mirror."

He pronounced his words with such forceful agitation, a droplet of spittle landed on Josephine's cheek, but she dared not wipe it away.

"I will not tolerate employees that waste time and dawdle."

"Yes, sir. I'll take care of it, sir."

"See that you do." He barked out the command before stalking off in the opposite direction.

Josephine frowned, and hurried up the stairs to find Cora.

While Rose bent to collect the soiled towels and bundle them with the bed linens, Nellie instructed, "Let me reposition the windows, and then I'll show you what to do with the dirty linens. We open the windows wide when we enter to air the room, but partially close them when we are finished. They should be open one and a half inches, to allow enough air in so the room does not become stuffy."

Rose nodded. Nellie sounded as if she was reading from the booklet Miss Templeton had given her. After a final sweep of the room, Nellie pulled the door closed and locked it with her master key. Nellie showed Rose how to sign off a completed room from their daily list, and directed her to a well-camouflaged trap door that, when opened, revealed a large bin.

"We drop the dirty linens here as we move from room to room. At the end of our shift, it's our responsibility to gather them and take them to the laundry building, which is located out behind the hedgerow. You can't see the laundry building from the hotel, but if you follow the gravel path, it will lead you there."

As Rose deposited the linens and made a note to find the laundry once they were finished, Nellie lowered her voice and leaned close to her. "I'm sorry Miss Templeton was so hard on you. You'll get used to her."

Rose wasn't convinced she could ever get used to the woman's criticism and demeaning tone. She whispered back. "She was hard on you, too. Is she always like that?"

"No." Nellie grinned over her shoulder at Rose. "Sometimes she's worse." She consulted the list. "Our next room is 172. Here it is." She unlocked the door and pushed it open. "You take the bed, I'll open the windows and begin wiping down the walls and the woodwork."

Rose stripped the bed and Nellie set to work with a dust cloth. Without slowing her pace, Nellie continued their conversation. "If you do your work, and do it according to the book, you'll be all right. Miss Templeton is hard to work for, but I think if she can see you're trying your best, she won't fire you. Just don't ever cross her."

Trying her best and not crossing the head housekeeper was already her plan. She only wished she could stay out of the woman's line of fire. "How long do you think it takes before she leaves you alone and lets you do your work?"

Nellie snorted. "In July, I will finish my second year of employment here. She still hangs over my shoulder, pointing out mistakes." She fetched the bottle of furniture polish. "In the time I've been here, I've seen more than a dozen girls come and go. Some were fired for repeated infractions or insubordination. Others quit because they hated working for Miss Templeton." She dabbed her cloth with the polish.

Rose got the distinct impression from Nellie's tone that she also hated working for Miss Templeton. "I can understand quitting for that reason. Why have you stayed here for two years?"

Nellie buffed the mahogany armoire to high luster. "My husband was part of the building crew for this hotel when he was injured in an accident, and he can't work anymore. So we have switched places, in a manner of speaking. I work to support the family, and he takes care of the children and does some of the cooking, from his wheeled chair."

Rose's hands halted mid-activity. "Oh, my. I'm so sorry." From the time she was a little girl, she remembered Mama working to support the family, but it was because her father was rarely there. She was nine years old the last time she saw him, and Mama worked from dawn to well after dark every day. She couldn't imagine her father taking care of children or cooking like Nellie's husband. "How many children do you have?"

A smile glowed on Nellie's face. "Four. Two boys and two girls."

Rose straightened with a jerk. "How old are you?" The question blurted out before Rose could stop it. She covered her mouth with her fingers. "I'm sorry. That was rude of me."

Nellie laughed. "It's all right. People have told Wade he must have robbed the cradle. I'm twenty-eight."

Rose released a relieved breath that she hadn't offended her working partner. "I thought you and I were close to the same age. I'm nineteen."

She pressed her lips shut. She'd just broken one of her own rules not to share any personal information about herself with anyone. "We better hurry. Miss Templeton will be back soon."

In her diligence to make perfect folds and tucks and measure the flaps, she'd not yet finished the bed, but every detail was perfect. Perhaps Miss Templeton would be pleased with the quality of her work instead of making her do it over. She and Nellie worked in silence for a time. Once she measured the hang of the bedspread on both sides and satisfied herself it was even, Rose started pushing the carpet sweeper over the ornate rugs in the room, while Nellie made the windows sparkle and the windowsills shine.

"You two should have finished this room over ten minutes ago." The strident voice startled Rose, and she nearly dropped the handle of the sweeper.

Miss Templeton stepped into the room, casting a scrutinizing eye around her. She lifted the corners of the bedspread to inspect the corners of the sheets, and then did a slow turn, sweeping her gaze around the room. Not a speck of dust, fingerprint, or streak anywhere. Surely the housekeeper would compliment them on their work. Instead, she checked the timepiece dangling from her neck.

"Rose, you are working too slowly and are behind schedule. You will forfeit your noonday break and work to catch up. Nellie, let Rose finish the floors in here. You move on to the next room, and both of you stop dawdling."

Nellie murmured, "Yes, ma'am," and hurried past the housekeeper with her head down. But the young wife and mother didn't escape Miss Templeton's criticism. "Nellie, you have a stain on your apron. You know I will not tolerate a slovenly appearance. Go change."

# CHAPTER FIVE

ullen had spent hours chopping up the fallen leaves and stuffing them into old burlap sacks last October. He hadn't understood why at the time. He only remembered thinking what a useless chore it seemed—almost as if Mr. Greeley assigned him anything he could devise to keep his assistant occupied. He'd like to learn some of the old gentleman's secrets and hints of becoming a skilled gardener. If he decided to pursue this line of work, and hoped to advance to a higher position one day, he needed to know more than chopping up leaves and pruning roses and pulling weeds.

Over the winter, old Mr. Greeley had instructed Cullen to collect potato peelings, egg shells, coffee grounds, and vegetable scraps from the kitchen. It became his job to add the bags of chopped leaves to these buckets of garbage and stir the smelly mixture in barrels. This morning, a wagonload of sawmill chips was delivered and dumped into a small mountain on the far side of the tool shed. Mr. Greeley handed him a pitchfork and told him to start dumping those barrels of compost into the chips.

"Pay attention, boy. This makes a fine mulch to hold the moisture in the ground around the plants." The two of them turned over forks of compost and wood chips until they were combined. "You load up the wheelbarrow and bring it over to the rose bushes along the drive."

Mr. Greeley picked up an armload of newspapers and a water bucket. By the time Cullen arrived at the rose bushes with the loaded wheelbarrow, the old man had soaked a roll of newspapers in the water bucket. He directed Cullen to get down on his hands and knees and layer the wet newspapers all around the bushes, and then spread the mulch in a thick blanket to cover the newspaper.

"Newspapers keeps the weeds from spouting. That means less work to keep the beds looking nice." Mr. Greeley sent him a sharp look that made Cullen wonder if the head groundskeeper could read his thoughts. "You learn things better if you do them instead of me just telling you about them."

Cullen sat back on his heels and wiped his dirty hands on his pants. He didn't think Mr. Greeley had paid him any mind last year when he complained about the old man not teaching him any gardening secrets. He understood the man's motives better, now. "I appreciate you sharing this with me."

"Hmph. Why do you want to be a gardener? Seems to me a strapping young fellow like you could do something better with his life than planting flowers and pruning hedges." Mr. Greeley moved down to the next set of rose bushes, and Cullen followed him.

The question, though a fair one, gave Cullen pause. Odd that Mr. Greeley sounded as if he belittled his own occupation. While Cullen did enjoy making things grow and held on to comfortable memories of hours spent in his family's garden, Mr. Greeley's insightful question shined a light on the true desire he'd held onto for so many years. But he'd let go of it a few years back. To say he'd set his sights on becoming a gardener wasn't being honest, not completely. He knelt and began to peel the wet newspapers apart and lay them down, overlapping them the way Mr. Greeley had instructed.

"When I was a boy, I enjoyed helping my ma in the garden. It was probably my favorite chore, certainly more so than mucking out the barn or splitting firewood."

Mr. Greeley chuckled. "Don't know too many boys who enjoy mucking out a barn."

Cullen reached for another roll of wet newspapers. "Maybe it's because putting my hands in the soil reminds me of my ma. Helping her made me feel good, because I felt like I was doing something to help take care of the family." He patted the newspapers in place and stood and stretched. "My pa died when I was twelve. I was the oldest. Had two younger sisters and my ma, so I had to be the man of the family."

Mr. Greeley's thick white eyebrows knit together and his jowls waggled as he shook his head. "At twelve? You weren't even shaving yet."

"No, but I had to grow up in a hurry. Pa would've expected me to take care of Ma and my sisters. My pa was my hero. I looked up to him. I respected him. I wanted to be like him." The tightness in Cullen's throat wouldn't let him say more.

A tender expression softened Mr. Greeley's features. "I like hearing about a son who looks up to his pa. Never had a son of my own, but I have a grandson who means everything to me. How did your pa die, if you don't mind my asking?"

Cullen swallowed back the thickness that threatened to choke him. "He was trying to stop a bank robbery."

Mr. Greeley's eyes widened, and he stared at Cullen over the top of his spectacles. "Oh, my. I'm sorry, boy."

Cullen nodded. "I'm going to go get another load of mulch." He grabbed the wheelbarrow handles and headed for the far side of the tool shed.

Yes, Pa was his hero. Pa was a special man, a wonderful father, a loving husband. But there was more he didn't tell Mr. Greeley. Cullen gripped the handles of the wheelbarrow so tightly, his fingers hurt. It wasn't only because Pa was good father that Cullen wanted to be like him. His pa was the sheriff in the town where they lived in Missouri, and he'd wanted to follow in Pa's footsteps from the time he was a little boy.

He set the wheelbarrow down beside the pile of mulch and dragged his sleeve over his eyes. Oh, how he wanted to be just like his pa, but he would never be like Pa. Shame burned his face as he tossed shovelfuls of mulch into the wheelbarrow. A sheriff's son was supposed to be tough and strong and courageous. Like a preacher's kid was supposed to be righteous all the time and never do anything wrong. Neither one of those descriptions applied to him.

The wheelbarrow full again, he pushed it back in the direction where the head groundskeeper waited. Mr. Greeley's question forced him to confront his own weakness. Working as a gardener carried him back to a time when his life was predictable, when the things he did for his family mattered, and he felt important. He thought he'd be satisfied with that. But even though he'd let go of his childish dream of following in Pa's footsteps, something still drew him. Maybe it was his love for his pa, maybe it was sorrow over knowing what a disappointment he'd be to Pa. Or maybe it was something else—regret so bitter and so deep, he'd wished a thousand times he could turn back the clock and relive that awful day. If God gave him a second chance to redeem himself, would he prove to be worthy of the office of sheriff, or would he fail again?

The sun was already dipping behind the mountain, throwing long shadows, when Miss Templeton gave Rose directions to the laundry building—*Go past the hedgerow. The first building is the tool shed. The laundry is behind the tool shed. And don't dawdle! There is still work to be done.* The load of sheets and towels mounded in such a tall heap in the laundry cart, she could barely see where she was going. Bone-weary and feet aching, she thanked God for giving her a friend in Nellie. When Miss Templeton took away Rose's noontime break, the young woman had sneaked her a sandwich, which Rose had slipped into her apron pocket. Knowing

Miss Templeton would come around without warning to check on her, she grabbed a quick bite and chewed quickly between rooms. She still had mopping to do in the staff hallway, but since she'd not been to the laundry before, she thought it best to take the linens out while it was still light enough to find her way.

She identified the tool shed by the equipment she could see through the window. The odor of lye soap hung in the air. She followed her nose and found the board and batten building tucked back behind the tool shed, like Miss Templeton had said. Over a dozen rows of drying laundry hung, flapping in the breeze. Even with the door propped open, the building was positively steamy. One girl still worked, even though most of the housekeeping staff had already finished their shifts. Rose lifted an armload of linens from the cart. "Where should I put these?"

The girl turned, and Rose almost dropped the linens where she stood. "Cora! What are you doing working out here? Why are you crying? What happened? Are you all right?"

Cora glared at her and stabbed her finger through the air. "Put them in that corner." She wiped sweat from her face and pulled a wet sheet through the wringer of the washing contraption. Steam dampened Cora's hair, causing tendrils to stick against the side of her face.

Rose dumped the linens and stepped over to her roommate. "You didn't answer my question. Why are you working out here?"

Cora let loose with a fresh torrent of tears. "Don't act like you don't know."

"I *don't* know. That's why I asked."

The girl fed another sheet into the wringer. "Miss Templeton hollered at me because *somebody* told her I was lollygagging. I tried to tell her I wasn't, but she said *somebody* saw me. She demoted me to the laundry." Animosity sparked from her blue eyes.

"You think I am the somebody?" Rose gasped. "I haven't seen you since breakfast. You were working on a different floor."

Cora grabbed a large paddle and agitated the soapy water before depositing more sheets and swirling them around in the huge steaming vat. "I hope you're happy, now that I'm stuck out here."

"I'm not hap— Who is going to clean the rooms that were assigned to you?"

Cora threw the paddle into the tub and hot, soapy water splashed over both of them. "You are! Isn't that what you wanted? To get me out of the way so you could take over the second floor?"

Rose's mouth slacked open, but she had no words. Her jaw worked up and down like a fish flopping on the shore. She stared at Cora without blinking. Weariness already dulled her senses to the point she could hardly think, and a throbbing headache pulsated at the base of her skull. She put both hands to her ears and tried to understand how she was the target of Cora's accusation.

"Cora, this is only my second day working. I'm still being trained. I can't take over a floor. I got into trouble with Miss Templeton today, too. She said I was working too slow. Why would you, or Miss Templeton, or anyone else think I'm ready to take over a whole floor?" She shook her head, grasping for reason. "Cora, I'm sorry this has happened, truly I am."

Cora spun toward Rose so hard, her pieces of wet hair slapped her face. "You don't expect me to believe that. After you lied to Miss Templeton about me."

The headache climbed up the back of Rose's skull and escalated to the top of her head. She held out her hands. "Whether you believe me or not, I never said a word to Miss Templeton about you."

The housekeeper's warning about not dawdling rang in her aching head. "Look, I have to get back, because I still have work to do, but I hope we can talk about this later tonight."

"Pfft." Cora returned to her drudgery and Rose scurried out the door.

The sun was no longer visible, and looming darkness fell like a cloak. She made her way around the corner of the tool shed only to come face to face with the groundskeeper. She still couldn't remember his name.

His face registered his surprise at seeing her. "Hello again, Miss Miller. You're still working? Kinda late, isn't it?"

She tilted her head. Was he trying to be funny? If he was, she failed to see the humor. "I suppose I'm a slow learner. If you will excuse me, please—" She started to go around him, but he stopped her.

"Wait, please." He put his hand out, but pulled it back immediately. "I wanted to ask you how you're getting along, but it sounds like you've had a hard time. I'm sorry. Miss Templeton isn't easy to work for."

"So I've been told. She is going to be even harder to work for if I don't get back in there and finish my duties."

She continued on back toward the hotel, leaving the man standing in the gathering darkness. Mama would frown at her rudeness, but she had not the time, nor inclination, to stand and chat. As she approached the staff entrance at the rear of the hotel, she had to admit the groundskeeper was simply being polite. It was friendship that frightened her.

# ❧ CHAPTER SIX

J osephine left the kitchen with a steaming cup of Earl Gray tea and returned to her office. It was past 7:00, and most of the hotel guests were enjoying supper. But she still had next week's schedule to complete, and Mr. Fairchild expected it on his desk first thing in the morning.

She reached her office and unlocked it with the key that hung from her belt. Leaving the door ajar so she could keep an eye and ear on what was going on out in the hall, she settled into her desk chair and looked over the schedule for what felt like the hundredth time. With Cora working in the laundry for the past three days, and Rose barely broken in, dividing up the work to make sure all the rooms were attended properly was a challenge.

She took a sip of tea. The bracing Earl Gray revitalized her when the day was well-spent but work remained. She had yet to inform Mr. Fairchild that she'd moved Cora to the laundry. It was a disciplinary action she'd chosen to take rather than firing the girl and having to hire another new maid. Training one maid at a time was quite enough. Besides, she would only work in the laundry for a week or so. Aggie Prescott, the head laundress, had taken time off to help her daughter during the birth of a child, and was due to return by the beginning of next week. Mr. Fairchild would assume moving Cora to the laundry was simply to fill in for Aggie.

The light coming from her west facing window was fading. She reached across her desk for the lamp and turned up the wick. Her office had an electric light, as did the entire hotel, but she found the illumination harsh. Besides, indoor electricity made her nervous, no matter if it was quite the prestigious amenity.

The sound of footsteps in the hall reached her, and out of habit, she glanced up to watch through the gap of the partially open door to see who was passing. Rose Miller hurried past her door.

"Rose."

The footsteps halted.

"Rose Miller."

After a moment, the footsteps returned back to her door, more slowly than they had passed. A tentative tap on the door frame.

"Come in, Miss Miller."

The new maid stepped into the office. The first thing Josephine noted was her wet and stained apron. "Rose, why are you still working? Even with the additional assignments, you should have finished over an hour ago."

Rose dipped her head and clasped her hands together. Her fingers trembled as she tried to interlace them. She mumbled a barely audible response.

"Speak up, girl. Stand up straight. Chin up. Stop hunching your shoulders."

Rose complied, her eyes wide with apprehension. "Yes, ma'am."

Josephine raised her eyebrows and sent her gaze up and down Rose's dirty apron, wet sleeves, and messy hair. "Why have you not finished? And why on earth is your uniform wet? What is going on?"

Her voice tremulous, Rose explained. "Nellie and I finished our work, and Nellie went to help the girls in the west wing, and I—" Her breath caught.

Josephine nailed Rose with a stern look. "You what?"

Rose pulled in a deep breath. "Well, even though we were finished, Cora wasn't. The other two laundry ladies had already left, but Cora still had another pile of laundry to do, so—" Rose swallowed visibly. "So I helped her."

"I see." Josephine frowned and pushed back from her desk a bit. She fixed her gaze on the girl for a full minute before speaking. "You have overstepped your bounds. We all have our work to accomplish. I have mine, you have yours, and Cora has hers. You are not doing Cora or yourself a favor by going behind my back to help her."

Rose's eyes widened and the color drained from her face. "Oh, no, ma'am, I didn't—"

Josephine silenced her with an upraised hand. "Cora must do her own work or she will never learn the work ethic required here at the Mountain Park Hotel. Furthermore, Miss Miller, you have only been employed here a few days and I have had to admonish you several times already. You are not getting off to a good start. You are still in your new hire probation period, and if you earn too many black marks on your record, it will result in termination."

Rose wrapped her arms around herself and lifted her shoulders as if struck by a sudden chill. Her voice sounded thin and frail. "I am trying to do what I'm told, and I'm trying to do my work well. And…and I need this job. I promise I'll try harder."

The girl was actually a fast learner, and after only three days, Josephine found fewer things about her work that needed correction. But helping Cora to get by with doing less than her assigned work bordered on insubordination.

"Trying harder will mean letting Cora do her own work." Josephine tapped her fingernail on the desk. "I warn you not to listen to Cora's complaints. Slackness will not be tolerated, and Cora has no one to blame but herself for her demotion. I will have to consider long and hard whether or not this incident will go on your record."

"Yes, ma'am."

"Go upstairs at once and get out of those dirty, wet clothes." She shooed the girl from her office with a flap of her fingers.

Josephine stared at the empty doorway where Rose had just exited. The girl may have meant well, but she had much to learn about how to choose her friends. Partnering with a petulant, immature snip like Cora was not a wise choice. The fact that they shared a room didn't require they become friends. But it was the discouragement in Rose's eyes that haunted her.

She picked up her teacup and took a sip, but the tea had grown cold.

After three days of raking, weeding, and mulching every shrub, rose bush, and flower bed on the property, Mr. Greeley told Cullen he wouldn't need him for a day or two. Cullen did what he always did when he had time away from the hotel grounds. He headed for the sheriff's office.

Sheriff Harper was leaning back in his chair with his booted feet propped up on the desk, reading a newspaper when Cullen walked in. "Look at you. Is this what the sheriff does all day?"

Harper snorted. "Sheriffin' is a hot and cold business. Some days there ain't nothin' to do, and other days I'm runnin' to catch my own tail." He lowered the paper. "How you doin'?"

Cullen grabbed one of the rickety slat-back chairs, turned it around backward, and straddled it. "Doing all right."

The sheriff tossed the newspaper on the desk. "You workin' for me part time has been all right up to now, but y'know with that hotel bringin' in more and more people, sooner or later, I'm gonna need a full-time deputy. You interested?"

Cullen shrugged. The offer sent restless indecision rattling his insides. At one time, he might have jumped at the chance to work full time with an experienced sheriff. But now…"I don't know. Maybe."

Harper wrinkled his brow. "You really like what you're doin' over there at the hotel? Plantin' and growin' stuff?"

An uneasy smile tugged at Cullen's mouth, and he told the sheriff what he'd told Mr. Greeley. "I like working in the dirt, making things grow. It reminds me of when I was a boy helping my ma in her garden."

The older man scratched his head, a dubious expression in his eyes, as if he didn't quite believe Cullen's reply. "If that's what you feel called to do, then I suppose it's kinda like bein' a farmer. But I don't aim to hire another deputy till you make up your mind. You're my first choice."

Cullen gave him a mute nod. The sheriff paid him a compliment. Being wanted felt good. But there were things the sheriff didn't know. Things Cullen wasn't ready to share.

"You got anything you need me to do?"

Harper looked around the office. The place wasn't exactly neat and tidy, but it wasn't overly messy either. It was somewhere in between. "Reckon you can go through those posters and compare with the latest arrest reports. See who is still on the Wanted list. I already cleaned all the guns this mornin', but I s'pose you can sweep out the cells, just in case we get overnight company this weekend."

"You expecting trouble?"

Harper tipped his head and connected his gaze with Cullen's. "Son, you always expect trouble in this business. You always prepare."

"Guess I'll go through the posters first." Cullen sent a wicked grin across the desk to Harper. "Maybe while I'm busy doing something important, the sheriff will sweep out the cells."

"That's the deputy's job, son."

The sheriff's dry tone made Cullen laugh.

Cullen rolled his head from side to side to work out the kinks in his neck. Of the thirty-seven Wanted posters, nine of the suspects were reported to have been apprehended, six were killed in shoot-outs, three were hanged, and eight were in the penitentiary. "I'm putting these in the apprehended file. These other eleven are still on the loose, or we can only assume they are."

"This month's arrest report should come in any day now." Harper folded back the newspaper. "Hey, Cullen, look at this." He held the paper out and pointed to an article. "This newspaper is over a week old, but I haven't gotten any wires tellin' me these two have been caught. Raleigh is about two hundred eighty miles from here, but we still need to be watchful."

Cullen grinned as he took the newspaper. "You've taught me to always be watchful."

He scanned the article about a couple of convicted thieves who escaped county jail before they could be transported to state prison. "I've never heard of these men. Ned and Brock Fellrath?"

"I have." Sheriff Harper pulled out a toothpick and chewed on the end. "They're brothers. Known mostly for petty crimes, but once in a while they do somethin' that gets the attention of lawmen all over the state. Nobody ever caught up with them, until—" He gestured to the newspaper. "They got caught robbin' a freight office. They've been known to hang around saloons, watchin' card games. When the games break up, they follow the winners and waylay them. They're also suspected of holdin' up a stage near Greensboro."

Cullen yanked his attention from the newspaper. "Anyone hurt?"

"No, but they thumped the driver in the head and robbed all the passengers." Harper got up from his desk and crossed to the file cabinet. "Seems to me I have somethin' in here on those two." He thumbed through the files for several minutes.

Cullen read to the end of the article. "Says here their sister is part of their gang. Margaret Fellrath."

"Mmm." The sheriff kept searching the files. "Wouldn't be the first time a woman got tangled up with ne'er-do-well kinfolk." He muttered under his breath until, finally, he pulled out a piece of wrinkled and creased paper. "Here it is. The Fellrath gang is suspected of tryin' to rob a bank in Asheville. A bank teller was hurt. Seems he tried to tell the Fellrath brothers he couldn't open the safe 'cause only the bank manager had the combination and he was home sick. Some shootin' happened—the report goes the bank teller pulled a gun out of his cash drawer, but there's no mention of anyone bein' shot. Doesn't say nothin' about a woman bein' with them." Harper held up the creased paper. "This happened back in March. That newspaper article you got there is a week old, and it's out of Raleigh, so it appears they've stuck close to North Carolina."

"The newspaper article didn't say if the sister is traveling with them or not." Cullen tried to imagine the role of a woman outlaw. They weren't common, but when one came to light, the newspapers usually made a big deal about them. He'd read about the notorious Belle Starr being convicted of horse stealing and serving time in prison in Michigan. She must not have learned her lesson, because just two years ago, she was arrested again for the same thing.

Harper returned the note to the file. "Tell you what—since you're workin' over there at the hotel, you keep an eye out and watch as the tourists come and go. These Fellrath brothers could try to pass themselves off as tourists and rob the rich folks that come to soak in the hot springs."

Cullen stroked his chin. "Kind of hard to know what I'm watching for. We don't have any posters on these Fellraths. You have any information about them? Their ages? Height? Hair color?"

The sheriff's mouth stretched into a wide grin. "You're thinkin' like a lawman. Nope, we don't have that. Just watch for anyone who looks out of place. If someone checks in that makes the hair stand up on the back o' your neck, come and get me."

"What are you going to be doing in the meantime?" Cullen returned the newspaper to the sheriff's desk.

Harper stood at the window and looked through the dusty glass. "I plan to spend time at the train depot, watchin' folks get off the train. Like you, I don't know what they look like, but after you've been in this business as long as I have, you get to where you have that feelin'."

Cullen remembered his pa saying the same thing.

# CHAPTER SEVEN

After three days, Rose gave up trying to get Cora to talk with her about the night Rose found her working in the laundry. If the girl refused to speak to her, there was nothing Rose could do about it. Mama would have encouraged her to pray for Cora, so she did. Silently when she slipped into bed at night, so exhausted she could barely stay awake more than a few minutes, she tried to spend those minutes praying for Cora before sleep claimed her. Sharing a room with so much animosity in the air wasn't easy, but Cora wouldn't believe her when she denied saying anything to Miss Templeton about her. Even going out to the laundry building to help Cora that night after all her own work was finished didn't change the girl's mind. Instead, she accused Rose of feeling guilty over what she'd done and trying to make up for it.

Rose battled returning the hostility, but every time her thoughts turned to resentment or getting even, Mama's voice whispered through her dark contemplations. *Do not render evil for evil, daughter.* She was right, of course, but observing Mama's teaching—which in truth was God's teaching—was still hard.

Until Cora discovered for herself that Rose had nothing to do with her being moved to the laundry service, Rose decided not to pursue further attempts to sway Cora's opinion. Arguing didn't solve anything. She'd learned that truth when she argued with her brothers every time they came home from weeks of wherever their exploits took them. They never heeded her advice or her warnings. Cora likely wouldn't either. For the life of her, however, Rose couldn't remember acting so childish at seventeen. That was likely due to the fact that she'd had to grow up much earlier than most girls. Not only did she need to help Mama with all the laundry they took in, she also took over most of the household chores by the time she was fourteen.

Even at such a young age, she began to notice Mama struggling to keep up with her work. She should have known something was wrong then, but Mama never complained. Oh, how she wished she'd insisted Mama see a doctor. When she was Cora's age, she'd already had to bury her mother.

There was a positive side to Cora's petulance. Rose came here with the hope of hiding away where nobody would ever make the connection between her and her brothers. The best way to avoid recognition or association with the Fellrath name was keeping to herself, not talking too much, and avoiding situations where people gave her more than a passing glance. Maybe having a roommate who didn't want to talk to her was a good thing.

Maintaining distance from people and keeping to herself was becoming an art, a dance of dodges, ducks, and sidesteps. If any of her coworkers noticed her aloofness, they didn't mention it. Her other goal—appeasing Miss Templeton—was a much more complicated waltz.

The small dining room set aside for the staff to eat their meals tended to be crowded, forcing Rose to sit with people she didn't know who wanted to strike up a conversation. She replied with polite words, but wished for a place of solitude. Mrs. Keegan in the kitchen told her employees were not permitted to go into areas reserved for hotel guests, but pointed out a few secluded spots near the far back of the property where the guests did not frequent. The prospect of escaping the clusters of employees, even for thirty minutes, lent an air of peace to her heart. Privacy, however temporary, meant she could let down her guard for a while, so she celebrated the discovery of a few large rocks far enough behind the work buildings they offered a place of isolation. It was there she took her lunch every day, weather permitting.

After working indoors most of her life, helping her mother with cooking, cleaning, and ironing, later working in a stuffy little corner of the freight office, and presently cleaning hotel rooms, she relished the freedom of being outside. As long as Miss Templeton didn't object, it was her respite each day.

She settled on one of the rocks and took in a deep, easy breath. The shady spot where she could enjoy a soft breeze off the mountain and listen to the concert of the birds soothed her spirit. She unwrapped the cloth napkin in her lap and took a bite of her ham sandwich.

"Mama, I wish you were here to talk to me. I need your advice. You always knew what to do." Remembering how Mama quoted scripture always filled Rose with wonder. Even though Mama loved her Bible, the Bible Mama's mother had handed down from her mother, and the very Bible Rose now owned, Mama couldn't read. But she sure listened. Every Sunday in church, Mama soaked in every word the preacher said, so that every Sunday afternoon as she worked washing and ironing other people's clothes, she repeated the scriptures over and over.

"Hello?"

Rose startled and nearly dropped her sandwich in the dirt.

"Rose?"

Cora stepped past the hedgerow and glanced around. "I thought I heard you talking to somebody. What are you doing out here, anyway?"

Rose swallowed back disappointment at Cora's presence. "I was talking to...myself. I like coming out here where it's quiet."

After days of not speaking to her, now her roommate plunked herself down on a rock beside Rose. Cora reached into her apron pocket and pulled out two cookies and handed one to Rose. "I heard you tell Mrs.

Keegan oatmeal cookies were your favorite."

Puzzled, she accepted the cookie with a soft 'thank you' and waited to see why Cora had followed her out to the secluded lunch spot.

Cora took a bite of her cookie and looked past Rose to where a bluish haze graced the mountaintops. "I couldn't figure out why you came out here. I'd rather sit in a chair than on a rock, and have people to talk to instead of talking to myself. But I suppose it is pretty."

And up until a minute ago, it was quiet.

"I was talking to Nellie, and she told me it was Mr. Fairchild who told Miss Templeton I was wasting time. He had seen me stop for a moment to fix my hair. You know how Miss Templeton is always badgering us about making sure our hair is pinned or our uniform is tidy. That's all I was doing, checking my hair to see if it looked all right before she came and hollered at me, and Mr. Fairchild saw me looking in the mirror. Don't you think that's unfair? I was only doing what Miss Templeton harps about all the time." She stuffed another bite of cookie in her mouth. "Anyway, I'm sorry I thought you lied to Miss Templeton about me." With her mouth full of oatmeal cookie, Cora's apology was barely discernible.

"It's all right, Cora. I understand how upset you were." She took a nibble of her own cookie.

Cora swallowed and poked out her bottom lip. "But now I'm stuck working in the laundry."

Mama's gentle admonition came to revisit her, and she passed it on to Cora. "The best way to change that is to show Miss Templeton she can trust you to do your job. When she knows she can depend on you, maybe she will make you a chambermaid again."

Cora shrugged and began to whine. "But it's not fair. Miss Templeton is—"

Rose held up her hand. "Cora, complaining is not going to help you. I admit I've been intimidated by Miss Templeton, too, but she has a hard job making sure everyone on her staff upholds such high standards. I'm just trying to do my work in a way that satisfies her, and then maybe she won't feel that she must look over my shoulder all the time."

Cora mumbled begrudging acquiescence and hopped down from the rock. "See you later." She strolled back toward the laundry building.

Rose stood and brushed the crumbs off her skirt and apron. Her own advice lingered in her mind. Miss Templeton's scrutiny made her more than a little nervous, and not because she feared the woman's criticism.

Josephine went over next week's schedule again. Logistically, it didn't make sense to keep Cora in the laundry any longer. Aggie Prescott was back from helping out when her daughter gave birth to twin boys, and when Aggie was in the laundry, Josephine didn't have to concern herself with it. The woman was dependable and beyond efficient. Cora's presence would probably drive Aggie to quit.

She would inform Cora tomorrow morning of the change in assignments. The girl would think she was being reinstated to her former position because she'd found favor in Josephine's sight, but that wasn't the case. She was just being practical, and Cora was still on probation.

She picked up the timepiece that hung from her neck on the black ribbon. Her meeting with Mr. Fairchild was scheduled for half past eight, and she would arrive at his office precisely on time. She refused to give the man any cause to think of her as anything but organized, capable, and competent. Each of her reports—supply orders, quarterly expenditures, anticipated expenses, employee schedules, new hires, maintenance of facilities, and notations of needed repairs or changes— was written up in meticulous penmanship without so much as a tiny smudge. She committed the figures to memory so she could report each line while Mr. Fairchild followed along from the documents she'd prepared. Was it too much to hope Mr. Fairchild would be pleased with the efficient way she handled the staff, carried out the operation under her supervision, and came in under budget? Well, he wouldn't be *pleased*. Mr.

Fairchild was never pleased. In the four years she had worked for the man, she'd never seen him smile.

Then, she never smiled, either. Smiling was for people with nothing to do. Besides, with whom would she share a smile? All of her staff disliked her, but she wasn't doing this job to be liked. She was merely doing what Mr. Fairchild expected of her. Did she expect a raise? A compliment? She tried to imagine the hotel manager paying her a compliment, and her mind would not bring the concept to bear. Not that it was important. In all the years she labored for her aunt and uncle, nobody had ever so much as told her she'd done a good job. But she didn't lessen her effort, she didn't become lazy or sloppy in her work ethic. Why would she have need of a compliment from Mr. Fairchild now? What foolishness. If her staff held to a different opinion, they'd be disappointed.

She arranged the reports in alphabetical order and tapped the ends on the desk to perfectly align them before sliding them into a spotless new folder. Reaching down to the bottom desk drawer, she retrieved a small mirror she kept for self-inspections before attending meetings. She couldn't berate her staff for having an untidy appearance if she didn't maintain her own. Her fingers slid over her hair to ensure there was not a strand out of place. Each pin placed just so, and the tight bun at the nape of her neck twisted evenly. The random strands of gray were a surprise, however. When had they made an appearance, and why had she not noticed before? She scowled at her reflection. There was nothing she could do about a few gray hairs. At least her collar laid flat against the pristine white, pin-tucked shirtwaist which was, in turn, tucked neatly into her freshly ironed brilliantine black skirt. A soft rag put one last polish on her shoes.

But when she stared at her face reflected in the mirror, the dark shadows around her eyes gave her a hollow look that even her spectacles could not hide. Sleepless nights did that to a person, and there was nothing to be done to remedy it. She couldn't remember the last time she'd slept for more than an hour or two at a time. When she did sleep, she never slept deeply. She'd trained herself to disallow restfulness, knowing what waited for her within the shadows of slumber. At least sitting up, awake at two o'clock in the morning, was better than the nightmares.

The timepiece hanging from the ribbon lay backwards against her bodice. Slovenly! She could not allow that. She quickly corrected it, making sure the ribbon wasn't twisted and the knot was centered exactly at the back of her neck. She opened the watch with the soft cloth, so as not to leave any fingerprint to smudge the shine. Three more minutes. She would be precisely on time.

# ๛ CHAPTER EIGHT

The flower beds were planted, the outbuildings painted, the driveway raked, and the planter boxes thinned out and weeded. Cullen cleaned the gardening tools and stored them away. When he stepped out the door of the tool shed, Mr. Greeley looked up from the potting bench where he had some saplings in pots.

"Everything done for the day?"

Cullen dusted off his trousers. "Yes, sir."

Mr. Greeley removed his broad-brimmed straw hat and fanned himself. "There's nothing else that needs doing. Go ahead and take the rest of today off. Maybe tomorrow, too."

It wasn't even lunchtime yet. "Are you sure you won't need my help?"

Mr. Greeley waved his hat in Cullen's direction. "No, no. I'm going to graft some of these young trees."

Cullen smirked. When it came to giving away his techniques and methods, the older man was still rather secretive. He wanted Cullen around to do the dirty work—not that Cullen minded doing those things, but he thought he'd hired on to learn the trade. "I wouldn't mind watching you."

Mr. Greeley gave him an intuitive look over the top of his spectacles.

"Cullen, boy, I know you like puttering in the garden, but if I believed you truly wanted to make this your life's work, I'd be happy to teach you everything I know. But I can see in your eyes, boy, your heart isn't in this. It's just a job to you." He ran his hand through his sparse white hair and put his hat on. "Now, when you tell me you're heading over to the sheriff's office, that's when I see your eyes light up."

The old man patted Cullen's shoulder. "Go on."

Guilt needled Cullen. He hated disappointing old Mr. Greeley, but the old man's wisdom and insight was exactly right. As much as he enjoyed putting his hands in the soil and seeing seeds sprout and grow, he'd been forcing himself to pursue it as a vocation. "I'll check with Mrs. Keegan to see if she needs anything from the kitchen garden."

Mr. Greeley nodded and turned back to his saplings, and Cullen jogged over to the staff entrance. He poked his head in the kitchen. "Mrs. Keegan, you need anything from the kitchen garden today?"

"Ah, Cullen, me boy, I already sent young Patsy out to pick some radishes and cucumbers. But happy I am to see ye. I made some cinnamon spice cookies today. I know they're your favorite." The cook bustled over to one of the work tables where racks of cookies were still cooling.

Cullen laughed out loud. Mrs. Keegan said the same thing every day. Whatever kind of cookies she made, she assumed they were Cullen's favorite. He accepted the bundle of still-warm cookies and gave Mrs. Keegan a peck on the cheek.

The cook's face flamed red. "*Woosht!* Off with ye now."

He turned to leave and came face to face with Rose Miller carrying a large tray loaded with dirty dishes. "Whoa." He set aside his cookies. "Let me get that for you. Are you working in the dining room now?"

She dropped her gaze and murmured something about dishes left in the rooms. Why wouldn't she look at him? She turned to leave, and Cullen called to her. "Do you have a minute to talk?"

She shook her head. "I have work to do, and Miss Templeton doesn't like for the maids to loiter in the hallways."

Cullen caught up with her in three strides. "Have I offended you in some way?"

Her shoulders lifted slightly. "No. I just don't have time to talk."

"I'd like to talk with you, when you have time. Maybe when you take your mid-day break."

Even with her face turned partly away from him, he watched her eyes widen and she stiffened. "I'm sorry. I have to go." She fairly ran up the back stairway, and he got the distinct impression she was escaping rather than going back to work.

More puzzled than ever, he determined to ask Sheriff Harper today if he had any records on a Rose Miller. He retrieved his napkin-wrapped bundle of cookies, waved to Mrs. Keegan, and strode out the door and down the drive toward the sheriff's office.

When he arrived at Sheriff Harper's office, the man shoved a broom at him. "Good, my deputy's here. Sweep out the office."

Cullen gave him a withering look, but grabbed the broom and started stirring up a dust storm. Harper coughed and scowled, and grabbed a chair to sit outside. A minute later, Cullen swept the pile of dirt out the door and the sheriff waved the dust away from his face.

"I'm done sweeping. You mind if I look through some of your files?"

Harper brushed dirt from his shirt sleeves and trousers. "What are you lookin' for?"

Cullen rubbed the back of his neck and told him about Rose. "When I try to talk to her, she turns away, won't talk to me, always hurries off."

The sheriff chuckled. "Maybe she's just shy, son. Or maybe she thinks you're ugly."

Cullen rolled his eyes. "Why did she stammer and hesitate when I asked her name? Doesn't she know her own name? Every time I try to start a conversation with her, she acts...I don't know...secretive." Maybe it was the wariness the sheriff had drilled into him and he was chasing nothing but his own imagination.

He and the sheriff searched through files and records for over an hour without turning up anything on anyone named Rose Miller.

"Has this woman done anything, other than not talkin' to you?" Harper smirked. "Anything that caused you to be suspicious?"

Chagrin warmed his face. "Not really."

The sheriff pressed his twitching lips together and returned the files to their place in the cabinet before turning around to face Cullen. "Son, you have to base your suspicions on somethin' more solid than the fact that this girl don't want to talk to you."

Cullen plunked his hands on his hips and shot a contentious look at Harper. "You said a few days ago that you 'get a feeling' about people."

Harper mimicked Cullen's stance. "I also mentioned somethin' about bein' in this business for a long time." He put his hand on Cullen's shoulder. "Son, it's experience that sharpens those instincts. I believe you have the ability, you just need the experience."

Cullen stuffed his hands in his pockets. Just because his ego was bruised over failing to engage Rose in a conversation didn't mean she had anything to hide. "You're right."

The sheriff slapped him on the shoulder. "You'll learn. That's what deputies do."

"Anything going on you think I should know about?" He craned his neck to peek in the direction of the cells. Both were empty.

"Not right now, but I'll send you down to the telegraph office later to see if any messages have come in." Harper settled behind his desk while Cullen unwrapped Mrs. Keegan's cookies.

While they munched, Harper regaled Cullen with the story about the two neighbors up the mountain who couldn't get along, until he became so exasperated, he threw them both in jail—in the same cell. "Told 'em they'd sit there until they could learn how to be civil to each other. Took 'em four days to finally shake hands and call a truce. Then they was mad at me 'cause I told 'em they could o' walked out any time. The cell door was never locked."

Cullen laughed, but he caught the lesson. Sometimes a sheriff had to execute the law in a creative way to get folks to comply. "You heard any more about those Fellrath boys who escaped jail?"

Harper shook his head and stuffed the remainder of his cookie in his mouth. "Nope. Been watchin' folks comin' and goin' at the depot. Have you seen anyone new show up at the hotel you wanted to keep your eye on? I mean, other than Rose Miller."

Cullen forced a laugh, and brushed cookie crumbs from his shirt. He had a feeling the sheriff planned to tease him about Rose for a while.

Harper crossed to the small stove in the corner and poured a cup of coffee. He held up the pot. "You want a cup?"

Cullen pursed his lips. If the lawman could tease him about Rose Miller, Cullen could shovel it back. "Who made it?"

Harper snorted. "You see anyone else around this office? I did."

Swallowing back a chuckle, Cullen shook his head. "No, thanks."

A growl rumbled from the sheriff's throat, and he returned to his desk, mumbling something about a young whippersnapper. He leaned back and plopped his feet on the desk. "Have y' given any more thought to what we talked about the other day? Acceptin' the full-time deputy job? Or are you still playin' with flowers?"

It was a fair question. Cullen knew the job was a hard one and the pay wasn't great, but that wasn't why he held himself back from the opportunity. Sooner or later, he'd have to confront the incident from his past that had changed everything.

"Son, if bein' a lawman is what you really want to do, there's nothin' like bein' a deputy and shadowin' the sheriff to learn. Call it goin' to school." Harper took a noisy slurp of coffee.

Cullen slumped in his chair, assailed by fiery arrows shooting memories of the day his goals and desires turned upside down. He remained silent for long minutes, trying to figure out how to answer the sheriff's question. But Harper didn't press. He was a patient man and understood how sometimes a fellow needs to work through his thoughts. The man reminded Cullen a lot of his pa.

After several minutes, his memories and emotions weren't any less tangled than they were before, but Cullen pulled in a deep breath and began to voice his thoughts the best he could. "There's something I should have told you a long time ago." His stomach soured, and he wished he hadn't eaten the cookies. "My pa was a sheriff."

Harper's expression remained even. No surprise registered. "You said your pa died when you were a boy."

Cullen nodded. "He got killed trying to stop a bank robbery."

Harper waited for him to continue.

Vivid memories of the man his father was rose in his mind. "I always wanted to be like him. My pa was my hero—he was the best man I ever knew. By the time I was six years old, I knew I wanted to be a sheriff some day, just like Pa." Cullen swallowed back a lump in his throat. "I was twelve when Pa got killed. I knew he'd expect me to step into his shoes and be the man of the family for my ma and my younger sisters, so I had to grow up in a hurry. I must have asked myself the question a thousand times—'How would Pa handle this?' Pa's death didn't scare me away from wanting to be a sheriff. It was my all-consuming goal. I was determined to become a sheriff and make my pa proud of me."

Sheriff Harper templed his fingers under his stubbly chin. "Somethin' tells me your pa was already proud of you. If he was the man you say he was, then I expect he raised a pretty fine son." Harper's ice blue eyes studied him. "When you've been a sheriff as long as I have, you learn to be a good judge of character, and I had a feelin' you were cut out for this kind of work from the day I met you. Learnin' about your pa and how you wanted to follow in his footsteps just proves I was right." He gestured around the office, taking in the gun rack and the Wanted posters on the wall, all the way around to the cells. "All this...this is in your blood, son. So I don't understand why you're draggin' your feet about the deputy job. This doesn't have anything to do with that gardenin' job, does it?"

"No." A half-hearted smile pulled at his cheeks. "Even old Mr. Greeley thinks I'd be happier working here than there." He surely was grateful to

God for the mentors He'd put in his life. Their support and encouragement was a gift. If only he could live up to their expectations.

The sheriff tilted his head. "So why are you hesitatin'?"

The question was the one he had dreaded to answer, but here it was, and Harper deserved to know the truth. "Because I've changed my mind about being a sheriff—or a deputy for that matter. I don't have what it takes."

Harper's eyebrows raised up. "What makes you say that? Other than bein' able to drink strong coffee and go without sleep for days at a time, live on short pay and eat cold rations, what do you think it takes?"

Cullen tried to force the words, but they wouldn't leave his lips. Needle pricks ran down his neck, and he unconsciously tried to rub them away. "I'm wasting your time. You need a deputy you can depend on."

"Hold on just a minute here." The sheriff held up his hand, fingers splayed. "Why do you think you ain't dependable? Are you tellin' me my instincts are wrong?"

"No, sir. I would never do that. You're a man worth listening to." Cullen wished with everything in him that he didn't have to expose his own weakness to this man who had grown nearly as close to him as Pa. "There are more important things to consider than strong coffee, sleepless nights, and short pay."

The sheriff leaned back in his chair and folded his arms across his chest. "Then answer my question. What do you think it takes?"

Cullen dropped his gaze to the toes of his boots. The single word answer stuck in his throat, but he pushed it out. "Courage."

The man sitting behind the desk didn't reply, but even without looking, Cullen could feel him staring a hole all the way through him.

# ✒︎ CHAPTER NINE

The days blurred together, each filled with establishing habits for working efficiently. Rose studied the booklet Miss Templeton had given her until she could almost quote it from memory. Cora was still aloof, which was all right with Rose. Nellie showed her helpful hints to make some of her tasks go more quickly, and Rose settled into a routine.

"Before your shift is over each evening, set up everything you will need for the next day." Nellie pointed to the compartments in her supply box. "It saves time in the morning to have your dusting cloths, scrub brushes, polish, ammonia for the windows, baking soda and borax for the bathing rooms, and lye for your scrub bucket all prepared and ready."

"Thank you, Nellie. I believe that will help get me started more quickly in the morning." A brittle part of Rose's defenses broke off and crumbled away. If circumstances were different, she and Nellie could be good friends. But friendship was a luxury she couldn't afford.

Rose entered her first room of the day and lined up her supplies in the order in which she would use them, and then dove in. While no longer working side by side with Nellie, her would-be friend who helped train her was only a couple of rooms away. Knowing Nellie wasn't far lent an air of comfort in case she needed help, but determination filled her with grit. She pushed herself, working quickly, but thoroughly, to complete her rooms to Miss Templeton's satisfaction.

The head housekeeper came around every hour, appraising Rose's work. Every time the woman stepped into one of her rooms and ran her fingers over every piece of furniture, examined the windows from every angle to look for streaks, and bent to check the baseboards, Rose's stomach churned. Was she annoyed because she couldn't find so much as a speck of dust? Shouldn't she be pleased at Rose's efficiency? After she couldn't find any task for Rose to do over, she sniffed and opened the watch hanging from her neck. "This is only your third room this morning, Rose. You are working too slowly. Speed and efficiency. Expeditious accuracy." She snapped the watch closed and moved next door to the room where Nellie worked.

Poor Nellie was the target for Miss Templeton's criticism today. Nellie's fine hair simply would not stay pinned, and her slightly plump figure tended to tug her shirtwaist out from her skirt waistband whenever she bent over. After listening to Miss Templeton berate the maid in the next room, Rose waited until she was certain the housekeeper had departed to check on the other chambermaids.

Rose poked her head into the room where Nellie worked. The girl had her back to the door. "Psst. Nellie."

Nellie dragged her sleeve across her face before she turned around. A pasted smile graced the lower half of her face, but her eyes were damp and red. Rose's chest tightened.

"Nellie, I remember hearing a couple of women talking in a store one day. They said they used laundry starch, diluted much more than for laundry use. They rinsed it through their hair, so when they twisted and pinned it, it stayed in place."

Nellie's expression brightened. "Laundry starch?"

Rose smiled and nodded. "Mix it with twice as much water as you would for laundry, and pour it over your hair after you wash it."

Nellie's shoulders sagged. "Thanks. I'll try it."

Rose scurried back to her duties with a lightness in her heart that she could offer Nellie some helpful advice in return for the way the woman had helped her. She moved on to her fourth room, finished it in record time, and was nearing the completion of her fifth room when Miss Templeton made her next appearance. She walked around the room with her critical eye trained on every corner. After only a minute, she looked at her watch as usual.

"That's more like it." And she left without another word. It was as close to a compliment as Rose would likely hear from Miss Templeton, but joy still swirled within her.

Rose gathered up her cleaning supplies and stowed them in the cleaning closet on that floor before heading downstairs for lunch. The staff dining room was already filling up, but Rose simply picked up a sandwich and a couple of cookies and headed out to her favorite spot. The fresh breeze coming off the mountain bathed her uplifted face with a soft caress while it soughed through the trees. Escaping to the outdoors eased the tension of Miss Templeton's inspections and the fear of her coworkers becoming too friendly. Closing herself off from the others might help ensure her privacy, but loneliness was a high price to pay for it. She settled onto one of the large rocks, said a short prayer over her lunch, and unwrapped her sandwich.

As she chewed her first bite, a masculine voice intruded. "Mind if I sit down?"

She startled and jerked her attention in the direction of the voice. That gardener—the one whose name she couldn't remember, the one who kept trying to talk to her. Truth be told, she *did* mind if he sat, but saying so was rude. Mama never abided rudeness. She scooted over as far as she could without falling off the rock.

"Thanks." He sat and sucked in a deep, noisy breath. "Nice day."

He bit into his sandwich and munched. The silence between them was thick, but with no inclination to fill it with conversation, she remained silent and concentrated on her own lunch.

"I don't think we were ever properly introduced the day you arrived. I'm Cullen Delaney."

She gave a short nod. He'd introduced himself that day. Maybe he guessed that she couldn't remember his name. Did he expect her to remember it from now on?

He cleared his throat. "How do you like working at the Mountain Park?"

She swallowed the bite of sandwich in her mouth. "It's a job."

A few more quiet minutes stretched out between them.

"Is there anything I can do to help you get acquainted and settled?"

She was as acquainted as was needful, and there was no point in settling too comfortably. She only planned to stay as long as it took to save enough money to move farther away. "No, thank you."

The stilted conversation grew more awkward. Cullen shifted around on his side of the rock. "You know, there is a room set aside for the employees to take their meals and socialize a bit."

Was he hinting he wanted to socialize? Every muscle in her body stiffened. "Yes, I know."

He finished his sandwich and shook out the napkin that had wrapped it. "But you come out here nearly every day and sit by yourself."

Alarm gripped her and her breathing became more shallow. The only way he could know that she came outside everyday at lunchtime was if he'd been watching her. Her stomach tightened and dread thickened her throat.

"Why do you come out here? Don't you like the people you work with?"

She turned her head toward him for only a moment. Was he truly curious, was he nosy, or was he trying to start a conversation? She wasn't interested in any of those things. She fastened her gaze on her half-eaten sandwich in her lap. "I like being alone."

Would he take the hint?

He leaned back on his elbows and crossed his legs at his ankles, the picture of a man getting comfortable for a while. "Well, it is nice sitting out here. It's peaceful."

Peaceful? She hadn't known a moment's peace since the day her brothers were arrested and charged with the freight office robbery. Now all of Raleigh thought her to be guilty of not only aiding her brothers in the robbery, but they somehow believed she had something to do with their escape. Peace? Not likely.

Cullen still appeared determined to get her to chat. "What kind of cookies did Mrs. Keegan make today?"

She rewrapped the remainder of her sandwich and reached in her apron pocket and handed him the cookie she withdrew. "Molasses."

He accepted the cookie. "Mmm, my favorite. Of course, Mrs. Keegan thinks every kind of cookie is my favorite. But I really do favor molasses cookies." He smiled as if he thought she cared.

Josephine bit her lip as she stood at the narrow window of her office, looking out across the expansive grounds. Nearly every day, she'd watched Rose Miller walk out and sit on the large rocks behind the tool shed to eat her lunch…alone. The girl had the right to eat where she liked, provided she wasn't in sight of the hotel guests. But if her reason for preferring solitude was discord among the staff, it could lead to greater issues. Mr. Fairchild didn't like discord.

Today, however, Miss Miller was not alone, and Josephine wasn't sure which worried her more, the girl's reclusiveness or seeing her keeping company with that handsome Cullen Delaney. He was a charmer, that one. A nice enough fellow, she supposed, as long as he didn't interfere with Rose getting her work done.

She studied the pair sharing the rock. The distance between her office window and those large rocks was sufficient that she couldn't discern their facial expressions, and thus determining whether their conversation was pleasant was impossible. Rose Miller didn't seem the flirty type, but Josephine had to admit the newest chambermaid was hard to read. She was a serious girl, willing, capable, an adequate worker who took instruction well, learning quickly how to do her job. The past couple of days, Josephine had been hard pressed to find anything about Rose's work to criticize. But it was as if there was no other side to her outside of her work.

"Her personal life is of no concern to me, as long as she performs her job well and stays out of trouble." A tiny, unidentified niggle elbowed Josephine, which she promptly pushed aside. Why should she care anything about the girl as long as she did her job to Josephine's satisfaction and the Mountain Park's standards?

Still, something unspoken about Rose Miller prodded Josephine. She'd tried over the past couple of weeks to figure out what made Rose so standoffish. Josephine rubbed her finger over her chin. "A person who is lonely doesn't go out of her way to be alone."

The words startled her, as if someone else in the room had spoken. A thousand accusations pointed at her. She, herself, went out of her way to be alone, even though loneliness haunted her. How often had she pretended she needed no one? How many times had she lied to herself, saying her position precluded her from forming friendships? A shiver rippled through her, and time faded backward.

Thirty years ago, she'd shared a rock with a young man. A romantic picnic, stolen moments of privacy. Even now, the memory of the flutters in her stomach drew heat into her face. If her aunt and uncle had ever found out, she shuddered to think what they might've done.

Spencer Lombard claimed to love her. Bitterness pulled her mouth into a bow. "He lied to me. Why did I ever believe him?" She glanced over her shoulder to see if her office door was ajar, as she sometimes left it. Relief whooshed from her lips. No one overheard her talking to herself, but who else was there to talk to? Spencer had promised to take her away from the life of drudgery, servitude, and abuse she'd endured at the hands of her aunt and uncle. He'd promised he'd come for her late at night. He told her to be ready, and they'd run away and get married. Promised …

She clamped her teeth together and swallowed. Spencer's promises evaporated like the morning mist over the mountain, and he disappeared right along with them. He never came for her that night. Or the following night, or the night after that.

Her throat burned, and she shook her head to drive away the foolish memories. Josephine blinked away the moisture from her eyes and instead, fixed her stare on Rose Miller and Cullen Delaney again. Was he making promises to her he didn't intend to keep?

A surge of protectiveness swelled through her. Was she not responsible for those in her employ? Her fingers curled and tightened. Should she intervene to ensure Rose didn't end up like she had, a lonely spinster nobody liked? An old maid?

A soft snort escaped. That was precisely what she was. What irony. She'd trusted Spencer to take her away from a life of servitude, and here she was, head housekeeper in charge of a staff of servants. God certainly had a twisted sense of humor.

She pulled her focus away from the pair and instead shifted her gaze to the neat stacks of paper arranged meticulously on her desk. She had work to do and didn't have time to indulge in pensive recollections. Such musings were a waste of time. Rose was an employee, nothing more.

"I am her supervisor, not her mother." Why did that statement sound so hollow?

# CHAPTER TEN

Rose pushed the mop back and forth, side to side the length of the third-floor hallway in the staff wing that housed the female employees. With every swab, her muscles ached and her shoulders cramped. Miss Templeton declared now that she was getting all her rooms done in a timely manner and according to the high standards set by the Mountain Park Hotel and Resort, she was ready to take on added responsibility. Mopping the hallway and sweeping the stairs at each end of the hall were now added to her list of daily tasks.

While she was glad Miss Templeton found her work satisfactory, the additional duties contributed to her weariness at the end of the day. She wondered if the extra work came with an increase in pay, but she dared not ask. The head housekeeper appeared to have eased off her scrutiny of every move Rose made, but she still feared incurring the woman's disapproval.

She dipped the mop in the scrub bucket again and twisted the strings to wring them out. The pungent aroma of the lye soap reminded her of helping Mama with the baskets of laundry every day. She couldn't recall ever hearing Mama complain about being tired or the work being too hard, so Rose wouldn't either.

*Think about something else.*

The memory of Cullen Delaney coming and sharing her rock today crept into her thoughts. She scowled and pursed her lips, trying to dismiss the picture, but it wouldn't cooperate. She'd not allowed herself to look at him for more than a few seconds, but those short glances were enough to fix his image indelibly in her mind. She couldn't decide if his attempt at coaxing her into a conversation was annoying or amusing. Either way, he was just being nice—something Mama had always told her to do.

*"Doing something nice for somebody else gets your mind off your own troubles."* Mama never acted like she had any troubles, although she had plenty. How Mama found the time to do nice things for others was more than Rose could comprehend. She worked such long hours, bent over a scrub board, her hands red and raw from the hot water and lye soap. Despite working seven days a week and only taking a couple of hours off on Sunday to attend church, once or twice a week, Mama took a pot of soup to a neighbor, or a bunch of wildflowers to one of the widows at church. She even cared for the children of one of her laundry customers for several days when the woman was ill, refusing to take any extra payment. Rose could still hear Mama telling the woman's husband it was the least she could do for his wife, seeing as how Jesus had done much more for her.

After Mama died, Rose learned the real reason she worked from before dawn until long after dark. Mama had never told her about Papa's debts. All she'd ever said was how blessed she was to be able to work hard. Was she trying to forget the long hours, or her aching back, or that Papa had left his family with a long list of debts owing all over town?

Did Cullen Delaney have troubles he was trying to forget? Is that why he was trying to be nice? She shrugged. What difference did it make? She had no plans to become friendly with anyone, least of all someone like Cullen Delaney who kept asking nosy questions.

Nellie was nice enough, and the helpful suggestions she offered did make Rose's job easier. A shaft of guilt poked her. Nellie's situation wasn't unlike Mama's. The poor woman worked so hard because of her husband's injury. Nellie said her husband took care of the children the best he could from his wheeled chair, but Rose couldn't imagine working all day at the Mountain Park, and then going home to cook and clean there as well. Maybe she could do something nice for Nellie—as a thank you, not as an offer of friendship. A bunch of wildflowers didn't seem adequate. She'd have to give it some thought.

Cora was another story. Her roommate complained daily about somebody or something, and she gossiped about the hotel guests whose rooms she cleaned. The girl acted more like she was seven instead of seventeen.

Rose slung the mop across the floor and backed up a few more steps to the end of the hallway. She straightened, pushed her hand against the small of her back, and flexed her shoulders to work out the tightness. She was ready for this day to end. All that was left was to sweep the stairways. She lugged the bucket and mop down the stairs to rinse them at the pump station outside. The heavy bucket and awkward mop impeded her progress when she tried to push the door open. Water sloshed over the lip of the bucket and drenched half her apron with the filthy, gray water, and the mop handle tipped and hit her head.

An arm reached around her and she sucked in a sharp breath. Cullen Delany reached out and caught the door to prevent it from swinging back in her face.

"Allow me."

How did he manage to turn up everywhere she was? Surely he wasn't following her. Was he?

He pushed the door open and took the bucket from her. "Let me help you with this."

She stared at him as he carried the bucket over past a tall fence and dumped the water out over a gravel area. Aggravation battled with weariness. Should she be insulted that he apparently thought her incapable of doing her job? Or was she too tired to care?

He set the empty bucket down on the ground beside the pump, and before she could pump clean water to rinse her mop, Cullen worked the handle up and down.

A twinge of annoyance poked her, and she couldn't keep it from her tone. "Thank you, but I can manage."

He had the audacity to grin. Was he laughing at her? "I'm sure you can, but a gentleman should always help a lady when he can."

A lady? She was a servant, about as far from being a lady as she could get.

"It's just my way of saying thank you for the cookie today." That maddening grin on his face widened.

She finished rinsing the mop and hung it to dry. "You'll have to excuse me. I still have work—"

"Mr. Delaney, you must have something else to do besides delaying Miss Miller from getting her work done." For once, Rose was grateful for Miss Templeton's presence.

His countenance fell. "I was just helping her—"

Miss Templeton raised her eyebrows as if skeptical of his reply. "Yes, well, Miss Miller does not require your assistance. Move along, please."

He pressed his lips together and stepped back. "Yes, ma'am."

When he headed toward the tool shed, Miss Templeton turned and fixed her unblinking gaze on Rose. "Is that young man bothering you?"

Not wishing to get Cullen in trouble with Miss Templeton, she shook her head. "No, ma'am. He just saw me trying to open the door with the bucket and mop in my hands."

The housekeeper looked back in the direction Cullen had gone. "Don't encourage him."

Rose widened her eyes and placed a hand over her chest. "Oh, no, ma'am. I haven't."

Miss Templeton lifted her chin. "Carry on, then."

Rose hurried to fetch a broom to perform her final task of the day. As she swept the stairs, beginning at the top and working her way down, she thought again about Miss Templeton's question. She could not honestly say Cullen bothered her, at least not in the way Miss Templeton's question implied. He'd not crossed the line or been anything but a gentleman. She was more disturbed over what his possible motives might be. If he was simply being friendly, she'd have to discourage him. What bothered her more than his unwanted attempts at conversation was her fear of Cullen, or anyone else at the Mountain Park, figuring out who her brothers were. As long as everyone accepted that her name was Rose Miller, no connection would be made.

After finishing her sweeping, Rose returned the broom to the cleaning closet on the first floor and trudged up the stairs to the third floor room she shared with Cora. Her stomach growled, but her fatigue overruled her hunger for supper. All she wanted to do was rest.

As she approached her door, it opened, and Cora stepped out. Rose stopped in her tracks. Her roommate wore a bright blue dress of some kind of silky material, worn off the shoulders with a daring neckline adorned with an ornate trim. A lacy shawl hung loosely from Cora's elbows. Her hair was pinned up in an outlandish style, and rouge highlighted her cheeks and lips. Some kind of black substance darkened the edges of her eyelids, giving her an exotic look. A string of pearls drew attention to her throat, and a pair of matching pearl earrings dangled from her lobes.

Rose blinked, surprise rendering her lips speechless. The rules for female employees strictly forbade the use of makeup of any kind. Neither were any female employees permitted to wear jewelry, with the exception of a timepiece, which was functional. The guidelines for apparel, other than the work uniform, clearly stated modesty was to be observed when dressing for off-work hours. There was nothing modest about the way Cora was dressed.

Rose let her gaze skitter down to take in the satin slippers that peeked out from beneath the questionable dress. Surely Cora didn't intend to go down to the staff dining room in such attire.

Rose found her voice. "Wh-where are you going?"

Belligerence narrowed Cora's eyes. She sent Rose a scathing glare. "None of your business. And if you have any ideas about telling Miss Templeton,…well, just don't." She hiked the shawl up around her shoulders and brushed past Rose, leaving her standing in disbelief.

Her roommate was right about one thing—Cora's destination was none of her business. But why would she be so foolish to risk termination for an evening out with…who? Friends? After a moment of speculation over the kind of friends with whom Cora intended to keep company, Rose shook her head. That, too, was none of her business. If the girl was determined to break the rules, Rose didn't want to know about it.

She stepped into the room. Small glass jars, a hand mirror, and a soiled piece of rag lay across Cora's bed—no doubt those things she'd used to paint herself up. Rose turned away from the convicting evidence and crossed to sit on the side of her own bed. Tired to the bone, her aching muscles cried out for rest. She unlaced her shoes and pulled them off. Her stomach rumbled again, but her hunger wasn't enough to make her put her shoes back on and go downstairs for supper.

She glanced over at Cora's bed. Despite the girl admitting she'd been wrong about Rose lying to Miss Templeton about her, she'd remained aloof, resentful, and petulant. A weary sigh wafted through her as she lay back on the lumpy mattress and closed her eyes.

Cullen glanced up from his spot in the corner of the staff dining room every time the door opened. Rose had yet to make an appearance. He hoped he hadn't gotten her in trouble with Miss Templeton. He drained the last of his coffee cup and pushed the remains of his supper aside.

While he waited, the conversation he had with Sheriff Harper rolled through his mind. He owed it to the man to be honest with him, but there were some things he couldn't bring himself to speak—at least not yet. He'd found it hard enough to talk to God about it, and God already knew about it. Guilt still plagued him, and peace still evaded him.

Shame crawled up his throat and turned his stomach sour. He'd stopped short of telling Sheriff Harper the whole story, but the man deserved to hear it. Cullen respected the sheriff, just like he respected his pa. How disappointed Pa would be in him. Harper would be, too, once he knew about that awful day Cullen stood and watched evil happen in front of him and did nothing. The sheriff kept pestering Cullen about becoming his full-time deputy, but that would change once he knew the truth.

One by one, the other staff members finished their meal and carried their trays to the kitchen. Cullen was left alone in the dining room, and Rose had still not come. He hoped she was all right. Surely Miss Templeton wouldn't impose a punishment on her simply because he had opened the door for her.

He stood and picked up his tray. With one last lingering gaze toward the door, he made his way to the kitchen and handed his tray to one of the scullery maids. Mrs. Keegan greeted him with her usual cheerful smile.

"Good evenin', Cullen, me lad. I saved ye a piece o' the chocolate cake the rich folk are havin'. It's there on the sideboard." She winked at him, hung up her apron, and reached for her bonnet. Even after such a long, hard day, her cheerful disposition remained in place. He thanked her and scarfed down the delectable dessert, licking the chocolate frosting from his lips. The sweetness did little, however, to lift the dark cloud that hovered over him.

Instead of heading upstairs to his tiny room, he slipped out the rear door of the kitchen. Perhaps taking in the sunset from the rocks where he'd shared lunch with Rose would raise his spirits. The evening sky bore streaks of lavender, gold, and crimson. He detoured around the broad, flagstone patio where the hotel guests congregated, and walked through the gathering dusk where the junipers and hedgerow provided privacy. He sank down on the rocks and watched the lightning bugs dance through the grass and trees. The solitude allowed him to shut out the cacophony of noises and voices one could not escape within the confines of the hotel.

Was this why Rose sought out the seclusion of the rocks at midday? He couldn't blame her. The tranquility was enough of a reason to forfeit the relative comfort of the dining room. Quiet descended over him, interrupted only by an occasional tree frog, the whisper of the breeze stirring the trees, and the calling of a pair of whippoorwills. The harmony of mountain music.

If only it could drown out the cry of his soul.

# ℘ CHAPTER ELEVEN

Rose's eyelids fluttered open. Thin, gray light filtered in through the plain muslin curtain covering the single window. She pulled her arms up over her head, stiffened out her legs and arched her back slightly in a delicious, lazy stretch. She rubbed her eyes and blinked as she sat up.

The soiled apron and the black uniform she'd worn yesterday still bore evidence of the dirty mop water she'd splattered on herself. For pity's sake! She'd been tired last night, but how could she have slept in her uniform all night? She moved to swing her legs around to the side of the bed, and her stomach protested its emptiness. She remembered now—she'd been too tired to go to the dining room for supper last night.

She turned to see if Cora was awake yet, but even in the semi-darkness, the bed was empty. Not only empty, but the small paint pots, mirror, and torn bits of rag still lay scattered across Cora's bed. The covers hadn't been turned down, the pillow bore no indentation from cradling Cora's head.

More awake now, Rose shifted around and stared at her roommate's empty bed. She pressed her fingers against her temples. Last night's encounter with Cora arose in her memory. The sultry dress, the jewelry, her painted face. True enough, Cora's plans last evening were none of her business. Rose closed her eyes and tried to push away the what ifs, but her roommate hadn't come back to the room all night. Where was that foolish girl?

She pushed away from the bed and shook off the rest of the cobwebs of sleep. Not bothering to light the lamp, she reached out for the clean uniform and apron hanging from a peg close to her bed before she remembered.

"It's Sunday." She had the entire morning off. Her first Sunday morning off since she'd begun working at the Mountain Park. When the schedule was posted last Monday and Rose saw she'd been scheduled off, the anticipation of attending church like she and Mama used to do was her motivation all week.

She dropped back down onto the bed and frowned again at the face paint jars on Cora's bed. Whatever trouble her roommate may have brought down onto herself was her own doing. Would she have listened last night if Rose had tried to talk her into changing her plans? Not likely. The girl made it abundantly clear Rose should mind her own business. She wasn't Cora's keeper. She squeezed her eyes shut and told herself to heed Cora's warning, but it was no use.

There was no denying the desire rising up in her chest to go and search for the younger girl, to make sure she was all right. Why? Why should she change *her* plans? She knew the answer before she finished the thought. Because if Mama were here, she'd tell Rose to go and find Cora. Then Mama would quote the story in the gospels of the shepherd leaving the entire flock to go and search for the one lost sheep. Only Cora was no sheep, and Rose was no shepherd.

It wasn't as if she and Cora were friends. Her roommate had remained downright unfriendly. They shared a room because this was where Miss Templeton had assigned her.

Huffing out a breath of annoyance, Rose poured water into the basin and splashed water on her face. She set aside yesterday's dirty uniform and apron, and donned a clean, but slightly faded calico dress. It was the best thing she had to wear to church. She pushed the window curtain aside and peered through the glass. In place of the rays of the sun that usually gilded the edges of the eastern horizon, an ash gray sky gradually lightened. Maybe she could find Cora and still have time to get to church before the service began. She dragged her brush through her hair, and hastily pinned it up. Taking a minute to straighten her own bed, she then snatched up her reticule and headed out the door.

Nellie might have an idea where to look for Cora. Rose wasn't sure if Nellie was scheduled to work today or not, but even if she was, Nellie didn't live here at the hotel like some of the staff did, and it was still too early for the chambermaids to report to work. Rose didn't know the other maids who worked elsewhere in the hotel well enough to ask them. She hurried down the back stairs. Maybe Mrs. Keegan? But the woman in the kitchen wasn't Mrs. Keegan. The unfamiliar cook grunted a greeting and tipped her head toward a tray of ham biscuits set on the sideboard. Rose grabbed two, wrapped them in a napkin, and stuffed them into her reticule. The only two people she felt safe asking questions or directions weren't here, so Rose set out toward town, a short walk away.

Dull gray clouds hung low around the tops of the pines and hemlocks. The church service started at nine, so she had a couple of hours.

She hesitated at the edge of town. Since arriving three weeks ago, this was the first she'd ventured into the quaint little town. How was she to know where to look? Did a town this size have entertainment places? For surely Cora had been dressed up for some kind of amusement. Even in a larger city like Raleigh, however, those kinds of places didn't stay open all night. A thread of uneasiness spiraled through her. Might Cora have met a friend?

Surely she wouldn't have gone to one of those places where men... No, she refused to allow the thought to take hold. A shudder waffled through her, and a sour taste turned her stomach. She lifted a brief prayer for Cora's safety, if not her wisdom in making choices.

She pushed her reluctant feet into motion, walking up one street and down the next. Unwilling to draw attention, she refrained from calling out Cora's name this close to places of residence. She considered knocking on doors and asking the people within if they'd seen the girl, but balked. Not only did she not want to draw attention to herself, but if Cora had gotten herself into trouble, the girl wouldn't thank her for informing the entire town.

She cut through alleys and back yards, paid attention to sheds and other outbuildings, and climbed up a steep slope toward the opposite end of town from where she started. In the distance, the church bell rang, and Rose halted, panting in exertion. Had she really been searching that long? She'd so looked forward to going to church today. She wanted to hear preaching and sing the songs Mama used to sing. She wanted to close her eyes and pretend, if only for a few moments, that Mama was still here and everything was as it should be. But she knew without a doubt what Mama would tell her—to keep her mind on her mission. Her friend could be in danger.

Friend? Cora wasn't her friend, not really.

Perhaps not, but the dread in the pit of Rose's stomach grew into a lump at the knowledge that she'd covered almost the entire town, with no sign of Cora. "Lord, what has happened to her? Where is she? If she's in danger, if she's in trouble, please help me find her."

She continued searching, knowing if she didn't find Cora soon, she'd have to go to the sheriff, and the sheriff was the last person in town she wished to meet. She kept on, going up and down every little side street, and checking places the girl might hide. Was she hiding? Did she not want to be found?

The consideration gave Rose pause. Reality was she herself was hiding in this little town, tucked out of the way in the mountains. She didn't want to be found. Her plan was to earn enough money to continue moving farther away where nobody knew who her brothers were. She knew very well what it was to wish not to be discovered.

All the way to the far end of town, where towering spruce trees hung thick and heavy over a creek, she was far enough away from houses and other buildings, that nobody might hear her. She began calling out for Cora. Over and over, until her throat grew dry and raspy, she called Cora's name. Where could that girl be?

With fear reaching up to choke her, she knew she had no choice. She had to go to the sheriff. She turned and began retracing her steps over the moss-covered rocks along the shaded creek. Were there snakes around here? Maybe she should put some distance between herself and the creek. But as she stepped away from some large, damp boulders, she saw it—there, caught on a thorny vine. A scrap of blue cloth. The same shade of blue as the dress Cora wore last night.

Fear of snakes aside, she clutched the blue scrap in her hand and returned to the rocky creek bank, nearly slipping on the moss. Again and again, she called Cora's name. She climbed down the embankment, pushed through the thick underbrush, stumbled over the wet rocks, soaking her shoes and stockings in the process, but she continued to search and call out.

When she thought she'd exhausted all hope, finally, she caught a glimpse of a sliver of blue nearly hidden from view between clumps of juniper.

Her voice hoarse and strained, she called as loudly as she could. "Cora! Cora, are you there?"

Cora sat up and pushed a thick spruce bough away from her. The blue dress was torn and filthy, and her hair was all askew. Even from several feet away, tracks of tears through the dirt on her face were visible. A large bruise on her right cheekbone that caused her eye to swell partially closed and dried blood on her swollen bottom lip told Rose all she needed to know.

Cora didn't speak, but only choked back a sob. Rose made her way across the creek and rocks, and pulled herself up to where Cora sat in the middle of prickly juniper bushes. The moment Rose reached her, Cora burst into tears and clung to Rose as if her very life depended on the connection.

Rose let her cry for a minute, patting her back the way her mother used to do. "There now, let's get you up there where you can sit on a rock, and we'll have a look at you." Rose pulled Cora to her feet and put her arm around the girl's waist. "Easy. These rocks are slippery. Grab that exposed root there and pull yourself up."

One of Cora's shoes was missing, as well as the pearls that had adorned her neck and ears last night. Red marks on her throat and shoulder, along with the injuries to her face, suggested somebody had gotten rough with the girl. Scratches on her arms proved she'd crawled through the thorny vines—the same ones that had snagged her dress and helped Rose find her.

*Thank You, Father, for guiding my footsteps and helping me find Cora.*

Cora sobbed all the way up the creek bank. Rose grabbed her hands, pulled her the rest of the way up, and led her to sit under an ancient hemlock. Rose dug in her reticule and pulled out the napkin-wrapped ham biscuits. Crumbles of biscuit fell away from the napkin, but she pulled up the edges of the napkin and laid it on Cora's lap. "Eat this while I go down and get my handkerchief wet."

Cora's sobs slowed to hiccups as she devoured the food. Rose navigated her way back down to the creek and soaked her handkerchief. Once back up with Cora, she began dabbing at the dirt and blood on her face. Cora winced, but didn't complain, merely following Rose's movements with her eyes. Her expression a tangle of pain, fear, and suspicion, the girl kept silent except for a hiccup or two as her tears subsided.

"That's the best I can do for now." She helped Cora to her feet. "Let's get you back to the hotel. I'll bring some hot water upstairs and you can get cleaned up. Then I'll bring you some soup from the kitchen and you can lie down for a while."

Clearly, they couldn't walk up the street in plain sight of the town, not with Cora dressed the way she was. Rose looked out over the town to figure the best route to travel back to the hotel without being seen. She pointed. "Straight through town is the shortest way, but if we climb that slope, and then keep to the alleys and backyards, and cut through that patch of woods between the town and the hotel, we'll stand a better chance of getting back without anyone seeing us." She took Cora's arm, mindful of the bloody scratches. "Let's hurry before the church service lets out."

They took the route Rose pointed out, ducking behind houses, and dodging areas where they might be seen from the street. Every now and then, Cora cast sideways looks at Rose, her poor bruised face a mask of uncertainty.

They stopped to rest a minute behind what appeared to be some shops, and Cora held the damp handkerchief to her swollen lip. "Aren't you going to ask me what happened?"

Rose shifted her gaze from their surroundings to Cora for a fleeting second. "No."

Surprise flickered over Cora's features. "Aren't you going to demand to know where I went or who I was with"—she gestured to her face and torn dress—"or how this happened?"

Given Cora's belligerence, Rose wasn't sure she wanted to know. "No. You told me last night it was none of my business, and you were right. It's not."

Cora's scowl deepened, and defensiveness filled her eyes. "I suppose you're going to tell Miss Templeton the minute we get back to the hotel."

Rose gave a slight shake of her head. "That's not up to me." She tilted her head and looked at her roommate. "Besides, when she sees you, she's going to ask you yourself. It's going to take a while for those bruises to fade."

Cora hung her head, her silence an admission that Rose's statement was correct. "Why are you doing this? Why are you helping me?" She raised her head and looked Rose in the eye. "Why did you come looking for me?"

If she answered that her mother would have wanted her to do so, she feared Cora wouldn't understand. "Because you needed help." She stood. "Come on. It's not far now."

# ᥦ CHAPTER TWELVE

Josephine propped her feet on the low footstool in front of her green upholstered chair in the corner of her private room at the end of the staff hall. Her copy of *Northanger Abbey* lay across her lap. Was this the fourth read or the fifth? No matter. She'd read all her Jane Austen novels multiple times. The rest of them snuggled in the bottom of the trunk that sat beside her chair—the trunk she kept under lock and key. She had a bookcase, but the romantic novels were kept locked away from prying eyes. While she'd long ago abandoned all hope of romance for herself, she secretly escaped to Jane Austen's romantic world when she had a free hour or two. No one needed to know.

She lifted the porcelain teacup to her lips and savored her Darjeeling tea. Sundays were supposed to be a day to relax, so here she sat with Jane Austen and her favorite tea. But she never truly took a day off. Even on Sundays, she dressed in her normal housekeeper's garb, the white high-collared shirtwaist with tiny pleats down the front, her black brilliantine skirt, with her watch hanging from her neck and her set of keys attached to her waistband. One never knew when she might be called upon to see to the needs of a guest, and she'd not give Mr. Fairchild anything to criticize.

The church bell had rung well over an hour ago. She took her watch in her hand and calculated how much longer until the church service ended. She'd never attended the church here in Hot Springs, but the local preacher got long-winded at times. She pondered over the years of her adult life. How long had it been since she'd been inside a church? Thirty years, at least. The realization should make her sad or ashamed. Or embarrassed. Instead, she felt nothing.

The hollowness within her that some people filled with their religious beliefs remained cold, dark, and empty. If religion made one *feel*, she had no need of it. Feelings complicated her life many years ago, and she did not wish to repeat the experience.

She marked her place in her book with a piece of ribbon and closed it. Her head leaned back against the upholstery fabric, and she let her mind travel back to the days when she attended Ephrata Christian Church every Sunday. Her aunt and uncle made her go as a girl. Church attendance was expected of fine, upstanding citizens, and especially businessmen. Her uncle never let her forget how important it was for their family to be seen in church. His clients always smiled their approval at him every Sunday. As a child, she didn't understand how hypocritical her uncle was, but she understood it now, and the thought spread bitterness across her mouth. One more reason she shunned church.

Back all those years ago, she hadn't minded going to church. The reminiscing brought a shadow of a smile. Truth be told, she liked going to church when she was young, because it was the only time she was allowed to leave the house for anything other than school. For two hours each week, she left the prison walls of her aunt and uncle's house and sat without any work to do. The first minister she could remember was a pompous, red-faced man with bulging dark eyes and a bulbous nose. He frightened her as a little girl of six or seven years old. He bellowed from the pulpit about hell and how everyone was going there who didn't measure up to God's rules. Even now, the image made her shudder. But then he retired when she was about ten, and a new minister came. She'd loved listening to him talk about the God who loved everybody.

Over the years, she'd thought about attending church too many times to count. But that's as far as she'd ever gotten—thinking about it. She straightened the ribbon bookmark in her novel, reflection accusing her. God likely wasn't interested in her anymore. But for a while, during the years of her childhood, she had a friend. God was someone she could talk to while she performed the impossible list of tasks her aunt and uncle demanded of her. The preacher had said anyone could talk to God anytime, anywhere. So she did.

When she talked silently to God, she didn't even have to move her lips, so her aunt never knew she talked to God. She relished the secret friendship she'd had with Him.

She shook off the memory. The foolishness of childhood. When she'd prayed asking God to help her escape her life of drudgery, she thought Spencer Lombard was the answer to her prayers. All Spencer's promises and all her plans evaporated when Spencer jilted her. That was when she quit praying and only attended church because her aunt and uncle required it. She missed having a friend.

She leaned down to return *Northanger Abbey* back to its hiding place in the trunk. Beside her treasured Jane Austen novels lay her journal. She picked it up and opened it to the last entry just a few days prior.

*Sometimes I despise my position. I can demand those under my supervision comply with my instructions, but I cannot demand their respect. Respect and admiration go hand in hand, and I fear those around me do not, and will not ever, admire me, wish to emulate me, or desire friendship with me. It is the price one pays for being in a position of authority. But it is so lonely.*

She turned back several pages, written over the past year, and realized her journal had taken God's place. The entries written here were the private, personal secrets and thoughts of her heart that she used to tell

God as a young girl. Things she would tell a friend, if she had one.

She clamped her lips together with such force, her teeth bit into the tender flesh of her mouth. The word she'd written emerged again. She despised what she was. At one time, she despised being robbed of her childhood, because she was forced to work herself into exhaustion every day. She despised Spencer for breaking his promise to her, and she equally despised the bitterness that gripped her in his aftermath.

Here she was, in charge of a multitude of employees—the kitchen staff, laundry staff, the chambermaids, and others who worked maintaining the hotel. The clamor and busyness that defined the daily activity at the Mountain Park required a great many people to perform the necessary tasks. Sometimes the commotion was enough to drive her to distraction. How was it possible to be surrounded by so many people, and yet still be so alone?

Not for the first time she considered how she was now in the same position as her aunt and uncle all those years ago. Her job demanded that she set exacting standards and require compliance, but her rigid strictness didn't endear her to anyone. Perhaps that was for the best.

Friendship meant vulnerability, and that she could not allow.

She rose from her chair and moved to the window, pushing aside the curtain of plain, white muslin. There were no shadows visible this day, as the sun remained hidden behind the thick clouds. Was she peculiar in that she was more drawn to shadows than to the sunlight? She preferred for her personal life to be enshrouded, like her journal and her Jane Austen novels. Nobody knew of their existence, and she liked it that way.

She drained the last few drops of cold tea from her cup and tucked her journal back into the trunk. She stooped to insert her key in the lock and turn it securely. She checked her timepiece. She still had a few minutes, but folks would be returning from church shortly, necessitating her presence downstairs.

Rose tugged on Cora's arm, pulling her along as they passed among the trees behind the church. The strains of "O, For a Closer Walk with God" carried from the open windows of the house of worship. The sounds of the voices lifting up the hymn made her feet slow momentarily. Mama's voice echoed through her memory, and she could still see her mother scrubbing clothes in the big washtub, even before the sun had cleared the eastern horizon, singing while she worked—

*So shall my walk be close with God, calm and serene my frame;*
*So purer like shall mark the road that leads me to the Lamb.*

If she couldn't attend the worship service today, at least God bathed her heart with one of the hymns her mother had loved. But they couldn't linger too long. The congregation would step out the door in a manner of minutes.

"Come on." She seized Cora's hand and pulled the girl along.

"Slow down. I only have one shoe." A slight whimper threaded Cora's tone. Each step over the rocky ground was undoubtedly painful.

"Sorry. I forgot." She bent and tore a wide strip from the bottom of her petticoat and wrapped it around Cora's foot. "There, that should help." She gestured toward the church. "But people will be coming out any second, and that bright blue dress of yours will surely attract attention if we don't get away from here."

Cora glanced down at the once-beautiful, though unlady-like dress, now soiled and tattered. She picked up a handful of the skirt and hoisted it above her ankles. "Let's go." She limped alongside Rose without any further complaint.

Ducking past the low-hanging boughs of a copse of hemlock trees, they finally slowed their pace. Rose swiped her forearm across her face and paused to catch her breath. The trees hid them well in this spot. They could take a few moments to rest.

Cora craned her neck left and right, and pointed. "I can't see the hotel through all these trees, but I think the bathhouses are right through there."

Rose considered Cora's statement. The girl had been here longer than she and likely knew the lay of the land better. She tried to peer through shadows. "How far do these woods go? Where will we come out?"

With a slight lift of her shoulders, Cora frowned. "If these are the same woods that are alongside the bathhouses, they go all the way past them, almost to the back door."

Rose hoped she was right. "All right, then. Let's stay in the woods all the way around to the back of the hotel. It will take longer, but if we can get to the back door that way, it'll be the safest way to go."

"I don't understand... Why—" Cora shook her head. "Never mind. Let's go."

They set out again, picking their way through the thick underbrush. Tree branches swaying in the wind slapped against their heads, and vines reached out and snagged their clothing. Cora squealed as a spider skittered down her arm, but Rose brushed it away and nudged her forward. From what Rose could see, the thickly wooded area stretched from behind the church to the beginning of the hotel property. She could also see why they left it untouched. The dense screen lent privacy to the bathhouse area, but it also provided appreciated cover for her and Cora as they moved closer to their destination. Rose whispered prayers of thanksgiving for God's protection, as well as petitions to help them return safely to their room.

Several minutes of pushing their way past the dense woods, stumbling over downed limbs and exposed roots, they finally made their way around the back of the bathhouses. The staff doorway just ahead was a most welcome sight.

Rose motioned for Cora to wait outside the door as she poked her head inside and glanced back and forth from the door to the kitchen entrance. "It's all clear." She beckoned to Cora. "Everyone in the kitchen is busy, and there doesn't appear to be anyone on the stairway."

Before they could set foot inside, however, the voice of the Sunday cook rang out as she directed the servers to carry the trays of fruit and canapés to the dining room. Rose and Cora flattened themselves against the wall around the corner and waited for the servers to pass by.

Whooshing out a breath, she glanced over at Cora, whose face was pale as a ghost. "That was close."

Cora leaned forward to peer up the stairway. "Can you just go up and bring me some clothes so I can change?"

Rose shook Cora's arm. "Don't be silly. Where would you change? Here under the stairs?" She stepped out and ascended partway up the stairs before she realized Cora wasn't following. She hissed down to her roommate. "Come on!"

They tiptoed up the stairs, past the second floor. Rose again held up her hand, halting Cora on the landing. "Wait here. Let me check the hallway." She crept up the last few remaining steps and peeked through the crack of the doorway at the top of the stairs. Seeing nobody in the narrow slice between the door and frame, she motioned once again for Cora to come ahead.

"There's nobody in the hall that I can see. Come on."

Cora joined her at the top step and opened the door. But instead of an empty hall, Miss Templeton walked straight toward them with a teacup in her hand.

Rose's feet froze and her heart seized. They'd come this far only to be caught twenty feet away from their room by the one person they dreaded meeting. Cora sucked in a sharp breath and gripped Rose's hand.

Miss Templeton halted, her eyebrows lowered and pinched together. She sent her razor focus from Cora to Rose and back to Cora. "Girls? What is the meaning of this?"

# CHAPTER THIRTEEN

The preacher's long-winded sermon came to a close, and he directed everyone to bow their heads and close their eyes. Cullen complied, at least with the bowed head part. He'd stopped listening a half hour ago, when the reverend had left off preaching and gone to meddling. Leaning forward with his elbows propped on his knees and his hands embracing his head, he stared at the toes of his boots while the preacher's words rang in his ears.

With the congregation in a posture of prayer, the preacher summed up the points he'd stated over the past hour. Cullen agreed with most of what Reverend Bradbury had spoken, especially since the preacher's message was built on a foundation of God's word. While everyone else's eyes were closed and Cullen sat scrutinizing his feet, a question speared him. Was he disagreeing with the preacher or with God?

His pa had led him to faith in Christ from the time he was a young boy, and he'd been taught to believe all of God's word was true and trustworthy. This morning, however, scripture backed him into a corner and there was no way to escape it or slip past it. Everything the preacher said, he'd backed up with scripture after scripture, so Cullen had no choice but to admit his disagreement wasn't with the preacher. How was he supposed to tell God he disagreed with Him?

*God, the preacher said everything I need is found in trusting You. I agree—I believe—that You give me eternal life, everlasting love, shelter in the time of life's storms, wisdom, strength. I believe all of that. But God, Your Son said He gives peace to me. Peace...God, I haven't known peace in five years.*

He longed for it, but his thirst for peace went unquenched. He'd gone over all the "if onlys" in his mind so many times, he'd debated with himself, chasing a hundred excuses down dead-end trails. His practice of sitting up to watch lightning bugs or the moonrise or gaze at the stars was designed to delay going to bed. If he could resist falling asleep, the dreams wouldn't plague him. He knew slumber meant reliving that awful day when the peace he had was stolen from him. And he didn't know how, or if, he could ever reclaim it.

The preacher began praying his closing prayer, but Cullen only half listened as the man lifted up petitions for the people sitting in the pews around him. For everything the preacher prayed for the worshipers, Cullen added a "what if?"Reverend Bradbury's voice lifted to the heavens. "Lord God, I ask You to help us to trust You as we ought."

He did trust God, he did have faith. Or, he thought he did.

"We thank You, Father, for Your abundant promises to pour out Your love and mercy, Your grace and faithfulness. We thank You that we can seek Your wisdom and strength and You do not refuse us."

But what if all those things the preacher listed were conditional, based on one's performance as a believer?

"Father, we are grateful for Your blessings."

Cullen winced as if pierced with a needle. What if God found him wanting and took away blessings accordingly? What if he was undeserving of those gifts God gave His children? No matter how many times he wished he could turn back the calendar and change the events of that day, his wish would never be fulfilled. He'd had one chance and he failed. He couldn't turn back time, he couldn't change it. There was no second chance to make it right.

And people had died.

People in the pews behind him and in front of him began to move and speak. Apparently, the preacher had finished praying for those things Cullen believed were beyond his reach, and the service was dismissed.

Cullen stood and glanced around him, hoping folks didn't think he'd fallen asleep during the prayer. Several members of the congregation shook his hand or nodded their greetings. As if God had His hands on Cullen's shoulders and turned him around, he looked toward the back of the church. Sure enough, there was Sheriff Harper in his usual place near the door. Everyone at church knew that seat was reserved for the sheriff, so he could slip out quietly without disturbing the service if the need arose.

The sheriff's gaze made contact with Cullen's for a long moment. Then he shook hands with the preacher and a few others before making his way down the aisle against the flow of those headed for the door. Cullen drew in a breath, knowing what the sheriff was going to ask.

*Have you given any more thought to bein' my full-time deputy?*

"Mornin', Cullen." Harper shook Cullen's hand and clapped him on the shoulder.

"Morning." Here it came. With the sheriff blocking the entrance of the pew, he had no choice but to tell the man that he couldn't be his deputy. Not full-time, not part-time. Not at all. Unless he could get the man to step aside. "I suppose I should get moving. If you'll excuse—"

Harper tipped his head toward the pew. "Have a seat." The man's piercing stare nailed him in place. It was one of those looks a man didn't argue with, even if he wanted to. His pa used to look at him that way when he'd gotten into trouble at school.

Sheriff Harper, like his pa, wasn't in the habit of giving him an option when he made up his mind to speak. Cullen sat. The sheriff nudged him to slide down the pew and sat alongside him, crossing one leg over the other and hooking his hands around his knee.

Harper's stare softened. "You look like you need someone to talk to. I'm here."

Confound it, how did this man read his mind? It was downright un-nerving. Hoping he could speak without his voice croaking like an ad-olescent, Cullen forced a smile. "Nothing I need to talk about. I'm fine. How about you?"

The sheriff sent a narrow-eyed, unblinking squint at Cullen, and the creases across his brow deepened. "You're a terrible liar. Good thing you ain't a gambler."

Cullen held out his hands, palms up, and hiked up his shoulders. "I was just thinking about poor Mr. Greeley and how his rheumatism is act-ing up." It wasn't a lie. Mr. Greeley's rheumatism was always acting up. But judging by the look on Sheriff Harper's face, he wasn't buying the ploy.

The last of the congregants shook hands with the preacher and left, and the building was empty except for the two of them. Harper crossed his arms and appeared to settle in, willing to wait him out. "I'm a patient man."

Reverend Bradbury came back inside. "Oh, I thought everyone had left." He came and stood beside the pew where the sheriff had Cullen bottled in. The preacher glanced back and forth between the two of them. "Anything I can do?"

Harper lifted his fingers in half-wave gesture that suggested this was a private discussion. "No, thanks, Preacher. Me and Cullen are just havin' a chat."

Cullen hoped the reverend wasn't offended at being dismissed. His gut stirred. *Just a chat, my foot.* The lawman was holding him hostage, but it didn't seem wise to voice such an opinion. Cullen gave the preacher a slight nod and a smile. "Thanks, anyway, Preacher."

Reverend Bradbury hesitated a moment, but then he bid them a good afternoon and told the sheriff to lock up when they were done.

The man who had played the role of Cullen's mentor for the past cou-ple of years leaned back in the pew and laced his fingers behind his head. "I ain't in a hurry. Most folks in town behave themselves on Sunday, like they figure steppin' out of line on the Lord's day might put them in bad standin' with the Almighty." He stretched his legs out and crossed them at the ankles. "I reckon I'll have all afternoon for you to make up your mind to talk."

Cullen didn't know what to say, how to start. He'd tried to tell the sheriff last week, but he stopped short and carried a weight of guilt over it for days. The man had a right to know. He tried adopting a posture of indignation, pretending the sheriff's supposition was unfounded. That worked about as well as arguing with the man's steely-eyed stare.

Harper sat forward again. "Son, somethin's been eatin' at you for as long as I've known you. How long is that? Two years? All this time, I've been waitin' for you to spill whatever it is that's puttin' that bitterness in your eyes." He returned back to his previous posture and folded his arms, but for an unguarded moment, Cullen thought he saw hurt blink across the sheriff's countenance.

"Y'know, I kinda hoped by now you'd trust me enough to tell me what it is that's eatin' at your insides. I'm thinkin' it will make you feel better to get it off your chest."

It was time. Time to tell the sheriff the whole truth. He should have been honest a long time ago, but admitting his failures and short-comings to someone he admired and respected sure wasn't easy. For the same reason he hated disappointing Pa. He hadn't feared the anger or repercussions as much as he dreaded seeing that look on Pa's face—the look that said he'd let Pa down. That same dread crawled up from his belly now.

Cullen took a deep breath and began. "You aren't going to want me for your deputy, not after I tell you...what I have to tell you."

"Why don't you let me decide that, son."

Cullen wanted to look away. He didn't want to see the disapproval or rejection in the eyes of the man he'd come to admire almost as much as he did his pa. But even as ashamed as he was, Cullen had to look the sheriff in the eye.

"It was about five years ago. One of my younger sisters was going to spend the summer with our mother's brother and his wife to help with the children while our aunt gave birth to their fifth child. I accompanied her on the train to Lexington, Kentucky, and then secured passage on the stagecoach line to come back home. We were living in Waynesville at that time." He paused and pulled in a fortifying breath.

"The fourth day on the stage, we were only about thirty miles from Waynesville. There were three other passengers on the stage with me—a middle-aged man, I think he was a salesman of some kind. Then there was an older couple. I'd say they were probably in their seventies." Cullen's throat tightened, but he swallowed back the repugnance of the memory that haunted him and kept his focus on Sheriff Harper.

"We heard gunshots and yelling. I knew immediately the stage was being held up. There were three of them. One of the bandits pulled the door open and ordered everyone to get out. He held a gun on the old woman while one of his partners searched the men for weapons." A wince of pain pinched his brow. "I think the driver reached for a gun, and one of the outlaws shot him. He slumped over and fell from the driver's seat to the ground, but he wasn't dead. He was groaning. When that happened, the old man rushed at the bandit who was holding the gun on his wife. They struggled, but the old man was no match for the bandit. The gun went off, the old man dropped, his wife screamed. The driver was bleeding bad. He didn't last long." Bile rose in his throat. "The old woman was screaming, 'He's dead, he's dead, you killed him. You killed my husband.'"

Cullen closed his eyes. How many times would he beg God to forgive him? How long would he be choked by self-loathing?

He forced his eyes open again. Sheriff Harper sat quietly, listening without interrupting. After several silent minutes, the sheriff shifted around and leaned his elbow on the pew in front of him, never taking his eyes off Cullen. His voice was even and calm. "Then what happened?"

Cullen stared at the floor. Did he have to spell it out? "The outlaws grabbed some valuables, jumped on their horses, and left as fast as they arrived." He pulled his gaze back up to meet the sheriff's eyes. "And I did nothing to stop them. Two people were shot, two people died, and I stood there and did nothing." He slumped against the back of the pew, heartsore. "I'm not the man you need to be your deputy. I don't have what it takes to be a sheriff or a deputy."

Harper straightened and pulled his head back. "Is that what you think?"

Couldn't he understand? Wasn't he listening? "It takes courage to be a lawman, like my pa, and like you."

A tiny smirk pulled the sheriff's mouth up at one corner. "You think I've never been scared?"

"You've never been so scared you froze in your boots!" Cullen practically spat the words. "You've never been so scared you couldn't move. You've always done your job and acted—"

Harper held up his hand.

"Son, listen to me. Don't let that one day—how long did that robbery last? Five minutes? Don't let those five minutes deceive you into believin' you don't got what it takes to be a lawman."

Five minutes? For Cullen, it had lasted over five years.

Sheriff Harper wasn't finished, and the flint in his eyes pulled Cullen to attention. "You've been eat up with guilt ever since that robbery happened. Cullen, you were a green kid with no trainin'." He nudged Cullen's arm with his knuckles. "Anyone who makes the choice to be a lawman needs to think long and hard about it because, I'll grant you, it can be a dangerous job. That's why you train with someone who's experienced. Your pa couldn't train you—you were too young." He folded his arms over his chest and tilted his head, as if he was sizing up a prize bull. "But you ain't too young now. What I see sittin' in front of me is a man who cares about people, cares about right and wrong, and who sees bein' a lawman as a callin', not just a job."

Cullen wanted Harper's description to be him, but the sheriff needed someone he could count on. "I'm going to have to think about it."

The sheriff reached over and clapped him on the shoulder. "And pray about it, son. You pray about it."

# CHAPTER FOURTEEN

After a quick wash and tidying of her hair, Rose went to the kitchen and fetched two buckets of steaming water. As she carried them up the steps to the third floor staff hall, she tried to make sense of Miss Templeton's orders to help Cora get cleaned up. Maybe she didn't want the other employees to see the two of them in their unkempt state when they packed their belongings and left, which would certainly set tongues to wagging.

She set the buckets down outside the door of the bathing room and tapped on the door before nudging it open with her shoulder. Cora hadn't moved from the place Rose left her, sitting on a small bench beside the hip bath. Tears flowed down the girl's face, leaving streaky tracks through the dirt. The blue dress, once finely designed in a sophisticated style, now hung in tatters.

Rose added the hot water to the cold that was already in the tub. "Cora, stop pouting and get out of that dress. I don't think it can be salvaged, but we might be able to save some of your undergarments."

Cora huffed out a breath and scowled, but began tugging at the torn, off-the-shoulder drape. "It's stuck."

Rose stifled a sigh. "Stand up and turn around. I'll help you." She released the fasteners at the back and untied the lacing. "My mama would have told me to stop pouting if I'd done something so foolish. But then I had learned not to pout by the time I was eight years old." She reached into a basket on a stand near the tub. "Here is a cake of soap. I'll come back as soon as I can and help you wash your hair, and I'll bring you clean clothing. Is the water warm enough?"

Cora dabbled her fingers in it and pronounced it fine. Rose pulled the privacy screen out and positioned it around the tub. "I'll be back after while."

"Rose, wait." Cora's tone was thin and tentative. "You and I don't really get along that well. I haven't liked you from the first day you arrived, and I think you know that."

It was true. Cora hadn't tried to hide her animosity toward Rose, and it wasn't a secret among the other staff members, either. But now didn't seem the best time to address it. "Yes, I know."

The sound of water splashing indicated Cora had climbed into the tub. "If you have known how I felt, then why are you doing all this?"

Why, indeed? Because nobody she ever knew had a harder life than her mother, but the example Mama lived in front of her every day was one of charity and graciousness. Mama couldn't give her a lot of things, but she taught her a wealth of Christian wisdom. "My mama used to say doing something nice for someone else helps get your mind off your own troubles."

"Huh?" Another splash punctuated Cora's question. "What troubles do you have? You walked into the Mountain Park three weeks ago and Miss Templeton hired you on the spot. You always do everything so perfect, she never criticizes you."

Cora couldn't see her shake her head, and she didn't intend to stand here and list all the troubles she'd experienced, beginning with her father being absent most of the time and being abusive when he was home before he left for good. Then her brothers followed in their father's footsteps down a path of crime. Then the court, the sheriff, her landlady, and all of Raleigh thought her as guilty as her brothers, so that she'd felt she had to get as far from there as she could. No, she didn't plan on telling Cora any of that.

"You're wrong, Cora. Miss Templeton has pointed out the faults in my work plenty of times in the three weeks I've been here. I still make mistakes, but I'm trying hard to correct them." She put her hand on the doorknob. "I hung the 'Occupied' sign on the door, and I'll bring your clean clothes as soon as I can. But right now, Miss Templeton is waiting for me and I better not keep her waiting any longer."

She hurried down the stairs to the first floor where Miss Templeton's office was located. Fully expecting the head housekeeper to terminate her and Cora immediately, she was rendered speechless when Miss Templeton directed Rose to help Cora get cleaned up before reporting to her office. Losing her job was still likely, but why didn't the woman toss both of them out the moment she laid eyes on them?

Since the staff was paid monthly and she hadn't worked a full pay period yet, she had no money, and the partial wage wouldn't be enough to get her very far. She arrived at Miss Templeton's office, and hesitated outside the door. Delaying the inevitable was useless. She took a deep breath and knocked.

Miss Templeton's muted voice from the other side of the door bid her to enter, and she stepped inside. Miss Templeton sat at her desk, her hands folded primly and resting on the desk.

"Close the door."

Rose complied and took a couple of steps forward, her eyes downcast and her hands clasped at her waist.

The head housekeeper cleared her throat. "Sit down, Rose."

Surprise jerked Rose's head up, but she took a seat, and sat ramrod straight, without blinking.

"Relax. I'm not going to bite your head off." She raised her eyebrows and lifted her chin. "But I would like an explanation. Cora was crying so hard I couldn't understand a word she said, except for 'Rose found me.' I suspect I will get a more complete and honest version of the story from you." She tapped the tips of her index fingers together.

Rose rolled her lips inward and clamped her teeth down. If she told Miss Templeton everything, would that not make her a talebearer? What did it matter at this point? Miss Templeton already had more than enough cause to fire both her and Cora. Her eyes began to burn, and she blinked back moisture. As soon as she left this room, she'd take Cora her clothes, and then go pack her belongings.

She drew in a shallow and shaky breath. "Last night, as I was returning to our room, Cora was just coming out. I could tell by the way she was dressed that she was going out somewhere. I asked her where she was going, but she didn't want to tell me."

"Hmm. I can imagine." Miss Templeton gave a single nod of her head. "Go on."

"I was more tired than I was hungry, so I just laid down on my bed and went to sleep." She left out the part about the makeup jars on the bed and jewelry. There was no point in casting Cora in a worse light and getting her into deeper trouble. "When I woke up, it was morning and Cora wasn't there. Her bed hadn't been slept in. I got worried."

Miss Templeton's brow dipped, and her eyes darkened. "You had no idea where she was?"

"No, ma'am." Rose shook her head emphatically. "I changed my clothes and went looking for her. Since I'm new here, I didn't know where to start, so I just went up one street and down the next. I walked all the back streets and alleys. After I'd been looking for about an hour and a half, the church bell rang."

"Nine o'clock."

"Yes, ma'am. I kept looking, even in some places I was afraid to look. I was about to give up and go to the sheriff when I found a small scrap of blue cloth, the same shade of blue as her dress. There was a creek and a lot of rocks. The rocks were slippery, and the creek bank was steep. I finally spotted something blue showing through the underbrush. It was

Cora." Rose drew her hand up and covered her mouth with her fingers, struggling for composure. "She…she was bruised and b-bloody, and she started to cry, and she clung to me like she'd never let go. She…she looked like—" Her chest heaved up and down at the memory of Cora looking like Mama did after her father had come home in a drunken rage.

"Rose, take your time." Miss Templeton's voice sounded like somebody else—a gentler somebody she'd never met.

After a few deep breaths, she continued. "I cleaned her up the best I could there at the creek. Then I helped her get back to the hotel. We went through alleys and woods and behind buildings so nobody would see us. I tried to get her up to our room so I could help her get cleaned up."

"Mm-hm. And that's when you ran into me in the hall."

Rose gave a short nod. "That's all I know. She didn't tell me where she went or how she got…the bruises, or who—" Her breath caught in her throat as another image of her mother filled her mind. "She didn't say who did that to her, and I didn't ask."

Miss Templeton's frown was different. Not her usual strict and demanding frown. This was a puzzled frown. "Rose, I am aware of the hard feelings Cora has harbored toward you, however unmerited. Why would you go out of your way to help her after she has treated you badly?"

This was a question she could answer without reservation. "My mother always taught me to be kind to others. She said doing something nice for someone helped her forget her troubles. It's something I've tried to do."

"But Cora is not your friend, is she?" The housekeeper's question held not a shred of accusation.

Rose grimaced. "Not really. We share a room, but that's all."

Quiet settled over the office, and Miss Templeton appeared unable to reconcile Rose's answer. "And yet, you went searching for her and did all you could to help her. But you don't claim her as a friend."

Already resigned to the reality of losing her job—and likely not given a reference—she didn't suppose she needed to guard her words. "People don't become friends because they work together or see one another every day or share a room. Friendship based on something so temporal is shaky at best. Real friendship is born when one person sees another as someone they can trust. I don't know if Cora and I will ever be real friends, especially after today, but at least I will have done my best to show her she can trust me."

The housekeeper narrowed her eyes. "What do you mean by 'especially after today'?"

Rose sighed. "I assume we will both be terminated and likely go our separate ways."

Miss Templeton fell silent and studied Rose so intently, she was certain she must have missed some dirt spots on her face. Letting her nerves get the best of her now was pointless.

Miss Templeton interlaced her fingers, swallowed, and finally spoke, her voice controlled and even. "Go and see if Cora is finished cleaning up. When she is dressed, tell her to report here to my office."

"Yes, ma'am." She pushed away from her chair and hurried out the door, praying for a miracle.

Josephine sat behind her desk, alone in the semi-darkness. Dusk was falling outside, but she didn't bother to light a lamp. In all her years working as a domestic, she had never seen anything quite like the stories Rose and Cora told her that afternoon. Her years in Newport showed her the cutthroat side of working alongside other servants, most of whom would have done anything for a promotion. When she accepted the assistant housekeeper position in Asheville, attitudes of jealousy and resentment abounded among those on the staff, because she'd been brought in for the position instead of promoting someone who'd already worked there for years. The Mountain Park job was different in that she was recruited and hired even before the hotel opened. She was already in place when the rest of the staff was hired. But this was unlike any scenario she ever witnessed.

Cora came as directed, and tearfully told her the whole story, how one of the hotel guests—a man—had invited her to join him for the evening. When she'd arrived at the place he'd told her to meet him, she discovered his plans were neither honorable, nor gentlemanly. Josephine cringed even now, remembering how Cora described the man backhanding her when she'd tried to get away from him.

Neither of the girls had begged her to give them another chance. Both expected they had already lost their jobs. Clearly, she was within her rights to terminate Cora, breaking the rules the way she'd done. Rose was guilty of aiding Cora and trying to conceal her act of defiance. But Josephine had responded in a way that even she didn't recognize or predict. She listened.

If Mr. Fairchild caught wind of this, he would demand to know why she hadn't fired both girls on the spot, and he might even fire her. She rose from behind her desk and paced the small office—seven steps to the file cabinet, seven steps back to the desk. The air in the cramped space sometimes became so suffocating, she left the door ajar. Is that the way the chambermaids felt—suffocated by the rules?

What compelled Rose to act as she did? Why would she put herself in jeopardy of losing her job to go searching for a girl who wasn't even her friend? How did one determine the trustworthiness of another?

And why was she obsessing over these questions?

She returned to her desk and weighed the conundrum presented before her. The quandary stirred emotions she thought she'd squashed years ago. Years of experience taught her to disallow empathy or mercy, even though she'd longed to be the recipient of those virtues herself when she was a girl. In her present position, she'd always communicated strict adherence to the standards and compliance to the hard and fast rules. If she showed leniency now, she risked destroying the discipline she'd established.

She knew what she should do, but she also knew what she wanted to do. As head housekeeper, part of her job was hiring and dismissing, but the resort manager had ultimate authority. If Mr. Fairchild learned of the incident, the outcome would be taken out of her hands. But for now, the decision was hers. Back in the days when she used to talk to God, she could have asked Him what she should do. This evening, however, as she sat alone in the now-dark room, she lifted a whisper to heaven, just in case God was listening.

# ≫ CHAPTER FIFTEEN

Rose pulled her nightdress over her head and fumbled with the buttons. Even though she'd only worked a half day today, the emotional strain of the morning pulled at her every fiber to fall into bed and let sleep claim her. She and Cora hadn't talked at great length about the ordeal, nor did she think Cora fully understood her motivation for going to search for her. Rose wasn't entirely sure she did either, other than knowing it was what her mother would have encouraged her to do. Everything Mama did was according to the example Jesus set.

She pulled back the bed covers and sat on the edge, fearing if she climbed in and laid her head on the pillow, she'd be asleep in seconds without taking time to pray. She had much to thank God for, not the least of which was the fact she still had a job. She spent several minutes silently pouring out her grateful heart to her heavenly Father. When she whispered, "Amen," she glanced up and found Cora watching her as she pulled the brush through her dark blonde hair.

Rose pulled her legs up and tucked them into her usual curl. The pillow cradled her head and beckoned her toward slumber. Even through her closed eyelids, she felt Cora's eyes on her, and she wished her roommate would hurry up and finish her bedtime preparations so they could put out the light.

Without opening her eyes, she followed Cora's movements by the sound the hairbrush returning to the small chest of drawers and the *shush* of the bed covers being pulled back. Bedsprings squeaked under Cora's weight, but the lamp wasn't extinguished. If she told Cora goodnight, would the girl take the hint?

"Rose, do you pray?"

Rose opened her eyes. Cora still sat on the side of her bed, her face a reflection of uncertainty. Rose didn't pray aloud when Cora was in the room, but the girl had seen her pray nearly every night. "Yes, I do." If Cora meant to ask questions about prayer, couldn't she ask them tomorrow? Immediately smitten in her heart over her uncharitable thought, Rose battled drowsiness and lifted a quick prayer for the right answers to Cora's questions.

Cora wound a lock of hair around her finger, not looking at Rose. Instead, her focus appeared to be the small woven rug on the floor, as if the answers to her questions were written there.

"Is that why you came looking for me? Is that why you helped me? Because you believe in God? Would God even care about someone like me?" Once started, Cora's questions tumbled out.

Rose tossed back the covers and sat up, facing Cora. If the girl was recognizing that Rose was someone she could trust, Rose didn't want to disappoint her. "One of my mama's favorite Bible stories was the parable Jesus told about the lost sheep. A shepherd had a hundred sheep, and one of them strayed away and got lost. He left the ninety-nine sheep to go out searching for the one that was lost. When he found it, he rejoiced."

A frown of confusion creased Cora's brow. "But he still had ninety-nine. Why would he leave them for just one?"

"Because the ninety-nine weren't more important than the one, and the one was every bit as important as the ninety-nine. He loved the one as much as he loved the ninety-nine." Surely Mama was smiling from heaven.

"I wasn't *lost*. I knew where I was. I was just afraid to come out from where I was hiding, because I thought that man might still be around." Confusion tangled with denial in Cora's tone.

The account Cora had told her, about the man from the hotel luring her to a remote spot and then trying to accost her, sent a shudder through Rose. "Don't you see, by your own admission, you were afraid, but your fear was keeping you in a place that wasn't safe." A fleeting doubt squirmed through her. Cora had used every excuse she could find, and invented some that didn't exist, to keep Rose at arm's length. She might still continue to push Rose away out of resentment, but Mama never gave up on others so neither would she.

"Even if you weren't lost and knew where you were, you needed help to get home, just like the sheep did. The shepherd acted out of compassion." Cora listened, but did she understand?

Rose waited a few moments, and then swung her legs back under the covers. "If you want to talk more, let me know." She returned to her pillow and nestled in, praying silently Cora would accept what she'd told her.

A few minutes later, Cora extinguished the lamp, and the squeaks from her cot indicated she'd climbed into bed.

As weary as Rose was, wakefulness lingered. She stared into the darkness, qualms of self-doubt accusing her. She couldn't make Cora understand or agree any more than she could make Cora like her. But even if Cora continued to dislike her, she prayed the girl would come to be friends with Jesus.

After several long minutes, Rose assumed Cora had fallen asleep. It *had* been a long day. Rose let her eyes slip closed.

"Thank you, Rose."

A smile pulled at her lips. Mama would approve. "You're welcome. Goodnight, Cora."

Cullen tramped down the boardwalk toward the sheriff's office, greeting folks he encountered and tipping his hat to a couple of older ladies. After working with Sheriff Harper every afternoon for the past week, he knew what the man would ask when Cullen entered the office—the same question he'd asked every time they were together.

The sheriff looked up from the papers on his desk when Cullen pushed the door open. Harper grunted a greeting, separated the papers into piles, filed a few in the file cabinet, and pushed the drawer closed. "What did you read yesterday?"

The lawman was certainly holding him accountable. Cullen didn't know whether to be amused or irritated. Harper was acting like a father to him, even though that might not be his intention. But Cullen had had a wonderful pa—taken from him far too early, but a good pa in every way. Would Pa have quizzed him every day like Sheriff Harper did?

"Gospel of John, chapter fourteen."

Harper nodded mutely and crossed to the small coal stove. He poured two cups of coffee and handed one to Cullen.

A smirk pulled at Cullen's lips. "You know this coffee is nearly undrinkable."

Harper snorted. "Drinkin' lawman's coffee is part of your trainin'. You gotta sift it through your teeth."

Cullen grinned and took a swallow, grimacing to get it down.

"You read the whole chapter?" The sheriff returned to his desk. "Ain't but thirty-one verses."

Cullen nodded. "Yeah, I read it all. It was one of my ma's favorites. 'Let not your heart be troubled,' she'd say whenever anything went wrong. When the bills piled up, 'Let not your heart be troubled.' When a hailstorm destroyed our garden one year, and the roof leaked, 'Let not your heart be troubled.' I remember her going without so she could buy new shoes for my younger sister, and when I said something to her about it, she just said, 'Let not your heart be troubled.' Even when—" Cullen swallowed.

"Even when your pa was killed?"

Cullen blew out a breath. Sheriff Harper sure didn't mince words or tiptoe around anything. He nodded. "Yeah, even then."

Harper took a slurp of coffee. "My favorite part of that chapter, besides the part when Jesus told His disciples straight out that folks who loved Him would keep His commandments, is when Jesus talked about peace. That's where the 'Let not your heart be troubled' part comes in."

The sheriff tilted back in his chair. "Lots of folks lookin' for peace, but they look in the wrong place. If they'd just open up the pages of God's word, they'd find what they're lookin' for."

Cullen surely understood and agreed with that. "Ever since that stage holdup I told you about, I can't seem to find peace. I know you told me it wasn't my fault, but I can't help blaming myself. If I'd just done something."

"Son, if you'd tried to do somethin', you an' me wouldn't be havin' this conversation, 'cause you'd be planted in a cemetery somewheres." His chair returned to all four legs with a *thud.* "When God points at you and tells you to do somethin' and you don't do it, that's when you don't have peace. But it's 'cause you didn't obey God. Peace don't happen 'cause of anything me an' you do. Peace is when everythin's right between you an' God. Don't have nothin' to do with you bein' a hero."

"Hm. I suppose." He didn't want anyone to think of him as a hero, but he wasn't sure he'd ever get to the place where he didn't blame himself for not reacting when the bandits threatened those innocent people. If there was nothing he could do to change it, how could everything be right between him and God ever again?

Sheriff Harper pointed his finger at him and narrowed his eyes. "Suppose nothin'. It's truth, and you need to stick your nose in the pages of your Bible and learn it for yourself. An' when you don't understand somethin', read it again and again, till you do."

He shifted in his chair. "Now, today we're gonna talk about the next steps in your trainin'—trackin' down a suspect. If you start out armed with as much information about the suspect as you can get, you're more likely to be successful. Find out if he's got kin, or if he's been spotted in a certain area more than once. That usually means he's got a place where he can hole up. Find out if he's right- or left-handed. That'll come in handy if you have to face him down. What kind of weapon does he use, and has he been known to carry more than one."

The sheriff continued, listing what information to dig up on a suspect, as well as how to prepare and what to pack in his saddle bags before heading out. Then he moved on to the legalities and laws connected to the limitations of sheriff's and deputy's authority—where they could go and what they could do to bring in a suspect—as well as how to work with lawmen in other jurisdictions. Cullen hung on every word, imagining his pa sharing his wisdom and experience with him.

These teaching sessions—training, Sheriff Harper called them— were to prepare him for the next situation where a bad guy was bent on hurting somebody. He was grateful for everything the sheriff taught him, but what if that situation came and the same thing happened? What if he didn't have the courage to act? If he truly was a coward, then all the training in the world wouldn't help.

Harper showed him some files he kept on suspects and prisoners who had come through the area over the years, pointing out similarities and differences. "There ain't any two alike. Sometimes you run across a youngster, thinks he's got somethin' to prove, or he's tryin' to live up to someone else's history—maybe thinks one o' the notorious criminals is his hero, and he'll try to do what he figures some other ne'er-do-well would do. But they usually ain't a patch on the criminals you read about in the headlines."

Cullen tapped his finger on one of the files. "Have you found those young bucks—the ones that think they've got something to prove—to be more dangerous? More reckless?"

"Sometimes." Harper thumbed through a few more files. "This here one. He was wanted for breakin' into a couple houses in town and stealin' money and a gold watch. Didn't think he was too dangerous, so there was only three of us in the posse. The whole time we tracked him, we kept sayin' how he wasn't too bright 'cause he left such a clear trail, my half-blind grandma could've tracked him. Didn't cover his tracks at all. I chalked it up to his youth and inexperience."

The thought flitted through Cullen's head—he was young and inexperienced, as well. But his advantage was having a man like Sheriff Harper training him.

Harper stuck a toothpick in his mouth and wobbled it around some until he found a comfortable spot for it. "We caught up to him when it was near dark. He was about a quarter mile ahead of us, and was makin' camp. So we decided to wait till it got dark and sneak on into his camp and take him.

"Then he did somethin' so stupid, it made me stop and question my own good sense. He made a campfire. Not just a small fire to cook his vittles, this was almost a bonfire. We could see it clear as day from where we were. It was like he wanted us to find him. Made the hair on the back of my neck stand up, and I realized he was layin' a trap for us."

"That's why he didn't cover his tracks." Cullen nodded with understanding.

"That's right." Harper sent him a sideways look.

Cullen's interest piqued. "What did you do?"

The sheriff drew lines in the dust on top of the file cabinet with his finger. "We closed in but didn't enter the camp where the firelight would've made us good targets. The three of us surrounded the camp the best we could, and then we waited. When the fire finally burned down to where he would've had to either let it burn itself out or add more wood, he figured we were bedded down all cozy in our own camp. He went and pulled the saddlebags out of his bedroll that were supposed to look like a man sleeping under there and climbed in." A smirk deepened the creases around the man's mouth. "When he saw three shotguns aimed at his head, he gave up pretty easy." He tucked the file back into the drawer.

"The point is, he about had me fooled into thinkin' he was just a dumb kid, and he was really lurin' us into a trap. Don't ever think you got an outlaw figured out." He shoved the file drawer closed. "Next week, we'll go out and do some trackin'."

Cullen drained the rest of his coffee. "I look forward to it. You're a good teacher."

"Ha!" Harper dragged his hand down his chin. "You're a good listener. Oh, before you go, I wanted to let you know I got a wire yesterday sayin' the Fellrath gang showed up in Morganton and tried to rob a mercantile one night. Deputy makin' his rounds heard them breakin' a window, fired off a blast from his shotgun. Didn't hit 'em, but got a good look at their faces."

"Morganton?" Cullen did some mental figuring. "Morganton's not that far away."

"Yeah. I'll keep you informed."

Cullen pursed his lips. "Sure wish we had a Wanted poster with their likeness so we'd know what they look like."

Harper grunted his agreement. "Might get one in next week's mail. Till then, we'll stay ready. If I get any more information about them coming closer, I'll let you know. I just hope they don't show up in Hot Springs."

Cullen didn't say so, but the idea of facing seasoned outlaws made him nauseous. He prayed he could do what the sheriff needed him to do. The man had become more than his teacher and mentor. Cullen believed God allowed his path to cross with Sheriff Grant Harper's to fill his pa's boots. He couldn't let the man down.

# CHAPTER SIXTEEN

Rose dipped her scrub brush into the bucket again. Looking at the hallway in front of her—the part she'd already finished—sent a wave of encouragement to her heart. The gleaming floor and baseboards reflected the way Mama had taught her to take pride in her work. But she didn't dare glance over her shoulder at the rest of the hallway floor she had yet to scrub, lest her encouragement evaporate.

Still amazed Miss Templeton didn't fire both her and Cora, Rose figured being assigned extra chores wasn't so bad. At least she didn't think so until she had to scrub all the first floor hall floors for a week. Her knees hurt, and the lye soap in the bucket made her hands raw, but stinging hands were a small price to pay for her part of the broken rules. Miss Templeton assigned Cora to the laundry for two weeks, plenty of time for her bruises to heal. Rose suspected she didn't want Mr. Fairchild to see Cora with visible bruises on her face and ask questions. The head housekeeper reminded her and Cora they were both on probation—Rose for a month, and Cora for six months. Any infraction of the rules during that time would result in immediate dismissal.

Determined to use the time spent on her knees in a positive way, she prayed and sang silently in her heart. She scoured and swabbed the brush in wide circles, keeping time with the music in her head and lifting her heart to God, asking Him for continued protection. She might not have been able to attend the church services a few days ago, but she worshipped on her knees all the way down the hall. Just two more days of floor scrubbing and she could return to her regular schedule. The other chambermaids who were assigned her rooms would be as glad as she.

"Here you are." Nellie approached from behind her.

Rose straightened, planted one hand on her lower back and bent backward, flexing the tight muscles. "You're over halfway finished, and it's not even 1:00 yet." Nellie's usual wispy hair was neatly tucked and pinned. She angled her head for Rose to see. "What do you think? I took your advice and used a bit of laundry starch, then rinsed it over my hair. I pinned it while it was still damp, and it's stayed in place all day. Miss Templeton hasn't scolded once about my hair slipping out of its pins."

Rose sat back on her heels and grinned. "It looks very nice."

Nellie reached into her apron pocket and pulled out a napkin-wrapped bundle. "Here. I brought you a sandwich."

Rose glanced up and down the hall and behind Nellie. The sandwich smelled wonderful, and her stomach rumbled in response. Ham, if her nose was correct. But she hesitated to take the bundle. "Thank you, but I don't want you to get into trouble with Miss Templeton."

A smile pulled Nellie's dimples into place. "Miss Templeton is the one who told me to bring you the sandwich." She shoved the packet toward Rose and lowered her voice to a whisper. "I know what you're thinking. I was surprised, too. I think she didn't realize you were skipping lunch to get the hallways done."

Rose accepted the food and her mouth watered, accompanied by more curious noises from her stomach. Breakfast had been a long time ago. "That was very kind of her. I'll thank her when I see her."

"Stop by the kitchen when you have a chance." Nellie took a few backward steps toward her assigned rooms. "Mrs. Keegan is saving you and

Cora some cookies." She fluttered her fingers in farewell and scurried down the hall.

*Bless Mrs. Keegan.* While she was asking for God to hand out blessings, she should include Miss Templeton, not only for the sandwich, but for the fact she was still employed. She returned to her knees and resumed her scrubbing.

*Father, forgive me for not praying sooner for Miss Templeton. Because of her, I still have a job. So if You would, please bless her as well.*

"Whoaahh!"

Rose jerked her head up just in time to see Cullen Delaney slip on the wet floor and grab the corner of a hall table to right himself. A fancy vase on the table wobbled and Rose held her breath. Cullen grabbed the vase before it toppled and set it to right.

"Oh my, I'm so sorry!" She dropped her scrub brush into the bucket and scrambled to her feet, wiping her hands on her apron. "I should have blocked off that hall. I'll do that right now."

Having regained his balance, he waved her away. "No harm done, except to your clean floor." He surveyed his skid marks. "Sorry. If you'll hand me your mop, I'll—"

Cullen's offer made her gasp. "Oh, heavens no! I can't let you do that." She leaned to one side and peered in dismay at the footprints he'd left on her still-wet floor. Cullen chuckled. "All right." He held up both hands. "But allow me to set the rope barricade in place." Without waiting for her reply, he fetched the two polished brass stanchions, set them at either corner of the hallway entrance, and attached the fat velvet rope to them. "We can't have hotel guests skating across the floor like I just did. They are more dignified than I am and would likely frown on an unplanned adventure."

His good-natured humor placated her unsettled nerves. She placed her hand over her chest where her heart still pounded. "Thank you. Please accept my apology. I let my mind wander when I should have set up those stanchions myself." His smile and deep brown eyes nearly unraveled her composure.

"Like I said, no harm done."

She grabbed the mop and hurried past him, swabbing the mop over Cullen's footprints and hoping her warm face wasn't glowing red.

Cullen leaned one shoulder against the wall. "I've been looking for you at noon for the past few days. Where have you been?"

She finished wiping out the trail he'd left and set the mop aside. She could sidestep the question, but instead, she chose to be honest with him. "I broke a rule, so I was assigned extra work." His expression softened into a look of sympathy that sent another shot of warmth through her, but she managed a shy smile. "I've used the time wisely. Since I'm on my knees anyway, I've spent the time praying."

"Which is a good reason why your mind wandered." He tipped his head. "When do you think you'll be finished? I thought maybe we could meet in the staff dining room and have supper together."

Her defenses immediately stood at attention, and her hands halted for a moment. Why was he so persistent in trying to pursue a friendship with her? There was nothing special or noteworthy about her. She wasn't attractive, not like some of the other girls, and she couldn't really tell him why she was being standoffish.

"Thank you for your kind invitation, but I'm sure I won't be finished with my work yet. Mrs. Keegan has been setting aside a plate for me. When I get my work done, I go to the kitchen and fetch it." Would he take her refusal gracefully?

Disappointment defined his eyes, but he gave her a faint smile. "Maybe some other time, then." He lifted his hand as he departed.

She watched his retreating back until he turned the corner. Secretly, she was flattered that a man as good-looking and gentlemanly as Cullen Delaney paid attention to her, but she couldn't afford to encourage him. She'd had to be candid with Miss Templeton and Cora regarding Cora's escapade and the role she'd played in it. But becoming friendly with anyone else was too risky. She reluctantly hoped he'd give up and leave her alone, but the thought made her a little sad.

Josephine walked down the hall, her heels clicking on the polished terrazzo floor. Every inch, from one baseboard to the other, fairly sparkled. Rose had done an excellent job. Even the baseboards gleamed. If the girl resented being assigned floor-scrubbing duty, her work didn't reflect it.

She reached her office and unlocked the door. The muted early evening light fell softly across the desk, illuminating the two files she still needed to finish. Technically, she was required to enter a report regarding any action she took with an employee. Cora broke several rules, and the resulting disciplinary measures Josephine took were written in Cora's file, including Josephine's explanation of the reasons why she chose not to terminate the chambermaid. But in order to record the assigning of the extra duties to Rose, she'd have to include the role Rose played in Cora's rule violations. She hesitated to do that. Documenting Cora's infractions in Rose's employee record implied she'd taken a more active part in helping Cora plan what she'd done, and that wasn't the case. True, Rose helped conceal Cora while accompanying her back to the hotel, but the alternative would have been to abandon Cora to make it on her own. If the man who'd tried to coerce Cora had still been in the area, the outcome could have ended very badly.

Try as she might, Josephine hadn't been able to get Rose's words out of her mind.

*"People don't become friends because they work together or share a room. Friendship based on something so temporal is shaky at best. Real friendship is born when one person sees another as someone they can trust."*

Real friendship. Josephine leaned back in her desk chair. Had she ever had a real friend? Rose apparently did. She knew what it meant to have a friend and be a friend. A tiny twinge pinched Josephine's middle. How did this young girl less than half her age have the wisdom to understand something so deep? The twinge tightened. Josephine laid her hand over her stomach and frowned. Was she…jealous? Of a chambermaid? A girl who was barely an adult?

A girl who didn't truly deserve disciplinary action at all.

She opened Rose's file to the page she'd added, but on which was written only the date. She stared at the blank space below the date. What could she write to justify the punishment but not implicate Rose in Cora's wrongdoing? Truth be told, Rose was only guilty of being a friend, being a person who demonstrated compassion.

Guilt skewered Josephine's chest. Compassion wasn't something she knew much about, but she recalled the pastor talking about it when she was a girl. One Sunday, the pastor told a story about a man who was traveling and found another man who'd been beaten and robbed. She'd been mesmerized by the story, especially when the man the preacher called a Samaritan showed such kindness and cared for the man as if he was his friend. But the one who'd been hurt wasn't his friend. He was a perfect stranger. Yet the Samaritan man went out of his way to take care of him. Everything Josephine knew about compassion was told in that Bible story so long ago. Is that what Rose had done? Cora wasn't a stranger, but the two of them certainly were not friends. Yet Rose acted in a way that demonstrated Cora could trust her if she chose to do so.

If what Rose said was true, and trust is what it took to establish real friendship, then Josephine couldn't imagine ever having a real friend. The only person she'd ever trusted was Spencer, and for well over thirty years she regretted putting her trust in the man. Once burned, she wasn't inclined to give her trust so easily again.

Her feet itched to move, to do something besides sit. She rose and went to the window, wishing she'd thought to bring a cup of tea with her. The sunset over the mountain was magnificent. Gold, orange, peach, pink, and purple swaths glowed and mingled one into the other. She watched, fascinated by the colorful waltz as the hues entwined and finally began to dim, flatten, and fade. Just as all her hopes, dreams, and plans shriveled and died all those years ago. The choreography of how her life might have turned out grew further and further out of reach.

When Spencer promised he'd come for her, she believed him, she trusted him. She entertained fantasies of how he would come by night and sneak her out through the window. She visualized the two of them running away and getting married. Dreams of having babies, raising a family, and being truly happy had occupied her mind. But he didn't come. For days, she lied to herself, thinking he'd only been delayed and would come as soon as he could. But when weeks turned into months, and he still didn't come, her trust began to waver and crumble. How long had she held onto hope?

The sultry days of her eighteenth summer had dragged by. Autumn had come and gone, and the first flurries of winter flew outside the window the day she'd taken an old newspaper to wrap the kitchen garbage. There in a month-old newspaper was Spencer's name along with a woman's name she didn't recognize. The article announced their engagement and upcoming wedding. That was the day she'd stopped trusting. Stopped trusting people, stopped trusting God.

If people like Rose and Cora chose to trust others, that was all right for them. If Rose elected to put herself out for someone who didn't even like her, she could, if that's what she wanted to do. She could be friendly with anyone she wanted. It was her choice.

Josephine shook her head. Dread of betrayal froze in her veins. She'd hidden behind her gruff exterior for so long, she didn't know how to do or be anything else. She'd spent over half her life building an imaginary brick wall around herself and not caring what others thought. Doing her job became her singular focus until she was married to it. Recently, however, the mortar securing the bricks in her defensive wall showed signs of crumbling, and the very thought of such an occurrence should have scared her witless. In truth, she feared letting her guard down. She feared letting the people with whom she worked see her as a real person with emotions and feelings. What if they saw that she was human? What if they lost respect for her?

She blew air past her lips. Who did she think she was fooling? The people who worked under her didn't respect her. They feared her and, for the first time, she realized the two weren't the same thing.

The last rays of light dulled and darkened, and she turned away from the window. This was her life, and there was nothing she could do to change it now. As much as she feared lowering her defenses and letting the other employees see the person beneath the hard shell she exhibited, she realized there was something she feared more—being friendless for the rest of her life.

# ✒ CHAPTER SEVENTEEN

C ullen stretched his arms over his head and blinked in the inky darkness. He wasn't sure how long he'd lain here awake, nor did he know what time it was. He'd tossed and turned until he fig- ured he'd gotten more exercise lying here in the bed than he usually did working with Mr. Greeley.

Finally giving up all attempts to sleep, he swung his legs over the side of the cot and felt around on the small table for the oil lamp. He struck a match and touched it to the wick. Having a room the size of a broom closet wasn't so bad. He had the place to himself, and the flame from his lamp had no trouble illuminating every corner of the tiny space.

Cullen rubbed his gritty eyes. "What time is it?" He fumbled in the pocket of his good pair of trousers hanging from the peg—the trou- sers he saved to wear to church—and found Pa's watch. He pressed his thumbnail against the release latch and the cover opened. Cullen squint- ed at the face. "Two-forty." He groaned and stuffed the watch back into the trouser pocket. Looked like sleep wasn't going to be his friend to- night.

He adjusted the lamp's flame and pulled it closer to the bed. He punched his pillow so it would cushion his back as he leaned against the wall. Then he opened his Bible to the same place he'd read for the past three nights. Sheriff Harper told him to read it over and over again until he understood what the Lord was telling him.

"God, what is it I'm not seeing? What do You want me to learn?" The simple prayer would make Sheriff Harper smile, but how was he to figure anything out in his groggy, sleepless state?

*Let not your heart be troubled.* He stopped and began thinking of questions to which he could find the answers within the context. His finger tracked across the page, stopping frequently to allow him to stare at the words he'd read. He examined his heart to determine whether or not he believed what God's word said. He knew enough to realize if there was something written on these pages he disagreed with, he needed to change his thinking.

The verses about Jesus preparing a place for him always put him in mind of Pa. Both of his parents believed, trusted, and practiced God's word, and he believed with all his heart that Pa resided in heaven.

His eyes moved on down the page, taking every verse as a personal challenge and letting God's light of introspection shine in all the corners of his heart, much like his single lamp lit up all four corners of his room. He liked the parts about asking in Jesus' name and Jesus not leaving him. He took time to consider why Jesus sent the Spirit, the Comforter, and how God would send the Holy Ghost, as it said in John 14:26, in Jesus' name to teach him all things. He held on to the promise of that verse.

No longer sleepy, he leaned forward and hunched over the Bible in his lap. "Yes, Lord, this is what I want. This is what I'm asking. God, teach me."

He turned the page. Verse twenty-seven loomed before him. That part about Jesus giving peace again. This was where he always got stuck. With the Bible on his lap, Cullen laid his hand over the words, as if covering them would take away the mocking he felt in his heart. Sheriff Harper said peace didn't come from anything a man did for himself. He'd wished a thousand times for a peaceful night, one that wasn't interrupted by nightmares or waves of guilt crashing over him.

"Lord, You said here that we would have peace, but I don't have peace, and I'm beginning to think I never will have peace again. The only thing I can think is that I forfeited my peace that day of the stage hold-up." The familiar sick feeling that accompanied every thought of that awful day gripped his belly once again. But Sheriff Harper told him to read it over until he understood what God wanted to teach him.

He moved his hand and read the words that taunted him. ""Peace I leave with you; My peace I give unto you; not as the world giveth—""

His eyes came to a dead stop. "Wait. What did He say?" He read the verse again. He rubbed his eyes and blinked. One word—one short word—shook him to his toes.

How had he overlooked that word having read this verse so many times? Jesus said He would give peace, but then He specified. "'*My* peace I give'— not as the world gives..."

Cullen gulped for breath and his pulse began to pound. Unable to remain sitting propped up in the bed any longer, he leapt to his feet. Why had he never noticed this before?

"God, the peace I've been trying to chase isn't real peace. If I'm reading this verse right, Jesus said His peace is different from the world's peace." He laid the Bible on the bed and clapped both hands over his face. "Oh, God, how could I have missed that? It's just like Sheriff Harper said. Peace doesn't come from anything I can do. Real peace comes from You!"

For five years the guilt had haunted him, no matter how hard he tried to smother it or snuff it out. He lifted his hands. Regret spilled through him for the time he'd wasted and the pride he'd exhibited trying to accomplish something only God could do.

"Oh, God, I can't erase this guilt. Nothing I do will cancel it out. Father, forgive me. Forgive my foolish pride." He fell to his knees beside the bed and held his head in his hands. "It's Your peace I need, Lord. Any crumbs of peace I try to scrape together are worthless, because it won't last. It shatters like glass."

He buried his face in the twisted bedcovers. "That's why Ma could say 'Let not your heart be troubled' with so much assurance. She didn't just have temporary peace. She knew *Your* peace. Oh God, I want to know Your peace."

Rose scurried in the direction of the employee dining room Monday morning for breakfast ten minutes later than usual. Cora had asked Rose to show her how to pin up her hair in the same style Rose wore, and she couldn't say no. In the two weeks since Cora's foolish exploits, the girl had been Rose's shadow. Cora snatched every opportunity to be with Rose, talk to Rose, and do whatever Rose was doing. If Cora could have managed it, she would have accompanied Rose to the bathing room. The girl asked more questions than a five-year-old. Rose had never had a little sister, but this must be what it was like to have a younger sibling trailing after her. Last night, Rose had to feign sleep so Cora would stop talking.

Stealing time alone to sit on the large rock out back and eat her lunch in solitude was nearly impossible, and she missed that quiet time. Cora begged to meet her for lunch nearly every day. Rose doubted the girl would understand her need for privacy, even if just for a half hour each day. She'd come to depend on that brief respite to commune with God, think about all the things her mother had taught her, and to settle herself. Guilt needled her when she recalled how she'd taken a late lunch break last Friday. There were no sandwiches left, but she'd grabbed an apple and a cookie, and for the first time in days, sat alone out on the rock. She didn't resent Cora's plea for friendship, not really. She simply mourned the loss of her quiet time.

Nellie sent Rose a wink as she entered the dining room. "I've noticed Cora has changed her tune about you, and about her job. What magic did you work?"

Rose returned Nellie's greeting with a smile. "No magic. She just needed some help, and I was available."

Nellie's smile broadened, plumping her double chin. "You've been a good friend to her. I think that's what she needed."

What Cora needed was Jesus, and Rose hoped by opening the door of friendship with her, she'd be able to tell Cora about her own relationship with God. Perhaps if she discovered how much God loved her, she wouldn't feel the need to seek love or attention from the wrong places and people.

Rose threaded her way around the tables and chairs to the buffet table where she grabbed a cup. Three coffee pots lined up like sentinels over the bowls of eggs and trays of bacon and sausage. She picked up the first one. Empty. Likewise, the second one was dry. When she picked up the third pot and shook it, a slight sloshing noise encouraged her. But when she tipped the pot over her waiting cup, about eight drops slid out.

*No coffee!*

Rose sighed. Tea would have to do. Pinning Cora's hair had taken longer than she thought. She scraped a scant spoonful of eggs onto an empty plate and took the last piece of toast. Both were cold, but they were better than going hungry.

She carried her plate to an empty spot at one of the long tables, but before she could sit, a steaming cup of fragrant coffee was set before her. She blinked and turned.

Cullen Delaney stood at her elbow, a cup in his hand as well. He gave her a mischievous smile. "I noticed you were running a little late today. I've also noticed you like your coffee in the morning." He tilted his head toward the kitchen and lowered his voice to a conspiratorial whisper. "Mrs. Keegan always saves me some coffee in the kitchen, although she did look at me as if pouring two cups might be illegal."

The crashing sound she heard in her mind must have been her guard coming down. How many times had she harbored irritation at Cullen's attempts at friendship? She couldn't be annoyed with him this morning, not if he brought her coffee. Her gaze slid from his face back to the curls of steam rising from the cup. She didn't turn her face away from him as she usually did, so if the warmth filling her cheeks was a pink blush, he'd see it, but for once she didn't care. She looked him in the eye. "Thank you. That was very thoughtful."

Cullen grinned, and a dimple she'd never noticed before appeared in his left cheek. Her gaze lingered on the indentation for the space of a heartbeat before she lowered her eyes again. Before she could take hold of the chair, Cullen pulled it out and held it for her. She couldn't remember any man—her brothers, her pa, her boss, not anyone—ever performing such a gentlemanly act. She felt like a princess lowering herself to the seat.

She bowed her head and asked a blessing on her food, such as it was. Then she wrapped her fingers around the mug and slowly breathed in the bracing aroma of the coffee.

"Do you mind if I sit here?" He tugged the chair beside her out a few inches from the table. The last time he'd asked her that, she'd been forced to share her midday quiet time with him. Resentment and fear had tangled together in her stomach so tightly, she could barely stand to take a bite. This time, however, she heard someone reply, "No, I don't mind," and she realized she'd said it.

"Thank you." He slid into the chair. "I could probably get Mrs. Keegan to give you some fresh, hot eggs if you'd like."

She poked her fork into the cold eggs. "Oh, no, this is fine." They weren't fine, but she swallowed them anyway rather than accept his offer. Sinking her teeth into the cold toast produced a shower of crumbs falling like sleet. She brushed off her chin and the front of her shirtwaist.

Cullen took a noisy slurp of his coffee. "It looks as though you and that other chambermaid, Cora, have become good friends. The two of you share your lunchtime almost every day now."

The same thought that accompanied his observation of how she took her lunch outside and sat alone recurred in her mind. He could have only known that if he'd been watching her. If he had, then he knew how Cora had trailed around after her like a puppy for the past two weeks.

"She's young, and I suspect she's lonely."

A deep chuckle rumbled from his chest. "You aren't exactly old."

If he was waiting for her to tell him her age, she didn't plan on taking the bait. "I'm older than she is." That wasn't saying much. Nearly every employee at the Mountain Park was older than Cora. She reached for her coffee cup.

He didn't appear deterred. "Do you have family around here?"

The simple question paralyzed her for the space of a few seconds and robbed her of her breath. The coffee in her mouth went down hard and turned to lead in her stomach. She shook her head as nonchalantly as she could muster. "No."

A change of topic was safer that tiptoeing around his subtle inquiries. "What are you and Mr. Greeley planting today?"

"Nothing today." He drained his mug and set it aside. "All the planting is done for now. There will be the usual maintenance on the flower beds, roses, and shrubbery of course. There are always weeds to pull or overgrown stalks to trim. But Mr. Greeley said we won't plant anything else until fall. He has ordered several hundred bulbs—daffodils, tulips, irises—and those will be planted in October and November." He folded his hands and leaned back in his chair. "So, I have some extra time on my hands."

Curiosity niggled at her, wondering what he did in his spare time, but she didn't ask. If she expressed interest, he might get the wrong impression and think she was flirting, which she most certainly was not.

"One of my favorite things to do in the summer is go outside at dusk and watch the fireflies. Listening to the whippoorwills and crickets is almost like a concert." He turned in his chair to face her more fully. "Maybe you'd like to join me some evening. It's very relaxing after a hard day."

She hated to admit his invitation sounded most appealing, but she ducked her head. "Male and female employees are not permitted to fraternize after dark." But that wasn't the only reason. She couldn't deny she found Cullen charming, but she couldn't risk letting him get too friendly. Even dealing with Cora was becoming a challenge. She wanted to be a friend to Cora without getting too friendly. How was she supposed to manage that?

The questions Cullen had asked her ever since she'd arrived unnerved her. She shuddered remembering her brothers' trial when the prosecuting attorney fired question after question at her, trying to make it appear as though she were guilty. Cullen wasn't a prosecuting attorney, but his questions fired fear in her gut.

# ✏ CHAPTER EIGHTEEN

Sitting in Mr. Fairchild's office always made Josephine's nerves twitch. Moisture popped out on her forehead, but she wouldn't allow the hotel manager to observe her blotting sweat from her brow. She schooled her features to appear completely poised and composed...and professional. Mr. Fairchild tolerated nothing less. With practiced stoicism, she kept her expression, demeanor, and tone even and detached, without a hint of the underlying passion that motivated her request.

It wouldn't do for Mr. Fairchild to detect intimidation or apprehension in her. Neither did she want to appear as if she revered him. The man already thought highly enough of himself without her feeding his arrogance, and she'd come to recognize the man's ego as her biggest challenge.

He silently skimmed over the proposal she'd handed him moments ago, and she forced herself to ease out the breath she was holding. He lifted his gaze from the paper and looked down his nose at Josephine. For the first time, she realized the chair in which she sat, facing his desk, was lower than where he sat behind his desk—as if he'd had the legs of the chair shortened so he could look down on whomever sat there.

Mr. Fairchild cleared his throat and drew himself up, as if she might not notice he was two inches shorter than she. Disdain stained his tone. "The Mountain Park has never before done what you are suggesting. In the four years this establishment has been in operation, all of the domestic, kitchen, and laundry staff have worked six and a half days a week, which is standard for service staff. I don't see the need to change their hours now." He dropped the paper on which she had carefully written up a proposed schedule change for her staff onto the desk and pushed it toward her with one finger. His action suggested the very paper containing the proposal smelled as if a skunk had perfumed it.

The hotel manager might be short in stature, but he was long on pomposity. He was neither an easy man to work for, nor to convince. She reached out and placed her fingertips on the paper, but did not pick it up—her way of communicating to him that she wasn't finished presenting her case and wasn't willing to take no for an answer.

She stiffened her spine "I feel giving the chambermaids a full day off each week, instead of just a half day, and letting them take turns having Sunday as their day off, will make them more productive. If they can enjoy a diversion or some restful time, they will have a better attitude and more energy."

A scowl darkened Mr. Fairchild's face and his hooded eyes turned accusatory. "Do any of them have a poor attitude? If so, dismiss them immediately. Every employee should be grateful to have a position. The Mountain Park Hotel and Resort will not tolerate petulance or churlishness in the staff." Never mind that he was the very picture of churlishness.

Josephine couldn't escape the skewer he aimed in her direction that insinuated she, too, had better step cautiously or she could find herself unemployed. She removed her hand from the paper that still lay on the desk. "No, sir. I did not mean to imply that any of my maids had a poor attitude. I only—"

"Well, what then?" His tone took on an intensity and a layer of impatience. "You've not stated an adequate reason for making a change in the scheduling. I cannot see what purpose it would serve, other than creating laziness in the servants who were hired to do a job. The hours were presented to them at the time of their interviews, and they knew when they were hired the job was six and a half days per week." The volume of his voice rose. "I do not see the problem here, Miss Templeton."

Was he not listening? She'd clearly explained that an employee who was allowed a full day to rest or enjoy being with friends and family was a more productive worker. She shouldn't be surprised that he'd dismissed that part of her proposal. She didn't dare point out that Mr. Fairchild himself always took a full day off, and frequently took two days off in a row. He most certainly would not appreciate the observation.

Her real reason for proposing the change had more to do with the weariness she'd witnessed in her girls, the sincere effort she'd seen them put forth, and her desire to reward them for their diligence and hard work. There was an underlying personal desire as well, but Mr. Fairchild would not understand, nor would he accept regret as a reason. Examining her stony heart over the past month and seeing things in a new light, she regretted being the harsh, critical, and demanding taskmaster that everyone who served under her had come to recognize. She didn't know how to express that regret to her girls any other way. Perhaps, if they could catch a glimpse of another side of her, a side she'd kept buried for years, then she might become someone they could grow to trust, like Rose said.

She lifted her chin. "All my girls work hard. They are diligent and dedicated to the standards we strive to uphold here at the Mountain Park." She interlaced her fingers, more to prevent them from trembling than anything else. "I have read in a recent issue of the *Elite Innkeepers Journal* that a number of upscale resorts, up and down the seacoast, have begun a similar practice of a six-day work week with alternating Sundays off. Some have even raised the wages of their staff based on the quality of their work and the length of time they've been employed. The point of the article was in order to keep the best employees, they had to be well compensated. Why, the renowned Royal Majestic on Long Island has done this for over two years."

She gave a slight sniff and a blasé lift of one shoulder. "The Mountain Park Hotel certainly ranks as high or higher than those mentioned in the *Elite Innkeepers Journal*."

If Horace Fairchild had been a dog, Josephine decided he would have perked up his ears and let his tongue loll out. He might not care a whit about her regrets or the maids' weariness, but status and prestige meant everything to him. He drummed his fingers on the desk and narrowed his eyes.

She let him digest what she'd told him, her heart pounding as she waited for his reaction. In Horace Fairchild's opinion, his ideas were the only ones that held merit. He stared, unblinking, at her for a long silent minute. Perhaps she'd overestimated his hunger for such distinction. A knot in her throat hampered her breath, and she could barely keep her feet still. Unable to bear the tension and unwilling to listen to his further rejection, she slowly reached for the proposed schedule that still lay on his desk. Before she could grasp it, however, his hand shot toward it. He snatched it up and pulled it to him.

A muted snarl growled in his throat. "I'll look this over again and give you my answer in a couple days." He flapped his fingers as one would do to shoo away an unwanted intruder. She took that to mean she was dismissed.

She closed the ornate door to Mr. Fairchild's opulent office behind her until she heard the quiet catch of the latch. She stood there a moment and drew in a deep breath. It *whooshed* out in a rather uncouth manner, but a quick glance from side to side showed her nobody witnessed her relief at finally standing on the outside of Mr. Fairchild's door. A tiny smile tipped the corners of her mouth. She didn't know what delighted her more—the possibility of him approving her proposal, or the way he nearly salivated at the thought of besting the Royal Majestic. As she started down the hall, every word she'd spoken to him paraded through her mind, and a question startled her. Her footsteps halted and her smile faded. When had she started thinking of the chambermaids as *her* girls?

Cullen fetched himself a cup of coffee and glanced toward the door of the employee dining room. Should he save a cup for Rose again? For the second time in as many days she didn't show up for breakfast. Perhaps she was getting an early start and had already come and gone. Or maybe Cora wanted Rose to style her hair for her again.

A bit of a smirk tugged at his mouth. Cora had latched onto Rose like a flea on a dog. A chuckle bubbled up from his middle when he remembered all the ways he'd tried to dodge his younger sisters when they were growing up. He doubted if Rose would attempt to avoid Cora's company. She was too kind-hearted to tell Cora no. Besides, she'd mentioned she and Cora were roommates, so avoiding her wouldn't be possible.

Not wishing to get Rose in trouble with Miss Templeton, he'd tried not to talk to her while she was on duty. If he happened to see her in passing, he merely gave her a smile, said hello, and kept moving. But every time he saw her when she wasn't on duty, Cora was tagging after her. He heaved a sigh as the humor evaporated and irritation nipped at him. After they'd shared coffee together the other day, he'd hoped she might accept an invitation to have dinner with him. He wanted to take her to the café in town, if he could get permission, of course. But with the way Cora stayed in her shadow, he might never get the chance to ask.

Laughter reached his ears, and his heart lifted as he turned to see if Rose had finally arrived. But it was only a couple of women with the kitchen staff who'd come to clear away the serving dishes. He fiddled with his empty cup for a moment and then pushed his chair back. Rose wasn't coming.

He stopped by the tool shed to check with Mr. Greeley. Other than keeping the flower beds free of weeds and the lawns mowed, there wasn't a great deal to do—certainly not enough to keep both him and Mr. Greeley busy every day. But he didn't want to leave the old gentleman in a pinch if he needed help.

Cullen poked his head in the door of the tool shed. "Morning, Mr. Greeley. Do you have work for me to do today?"

Mr. Greeley waved him away with a ruddy-faced grin. "No, the roses are pruned, the grass looks like velvet, and there's not a weed to be found anywhere. G'on with you, now. You're supposed to be learnin' to become a sheriff."

It was true, Cullen spent more and more time at the sheriff's office. As he strode down the drive and turned toward town, he rolled over in his mind all that Sheriff Harper had taught the past two weeks. Saying they needed to start with the basics, Harper had instructed him on the laws of the state and the county, the regulations for making arrests, under what circumstances could they hold a person in the local jail, and the details they had to follow for transporting a prisoner to another jurisdiction. Cullen loved every minute of it, found it not only fascinating but also a bit frightening. Some days when he left the office, his head nearly burst with the load of information he needed to digest.

Today, Sheriff Harper spelled out the differences between the authority of a local sheriff versus a federal marshal. After an hour, Harper closed the manual and set it aside. "You got any questions?"

Cullen blew out a stiff breath. "Not now, but I probably will. I just hope a question doesn't pop into my head while we're facing down a bad guy. It's a lot to take in."

Harper clapped him on the shoulder. "You're a good student. Shows you have a heart for this business." He pulled out one of the desk drawers and deposited the manual. "Tomorrow I'd like to ride out of town a ways and do some practice shootin'. You need to be comfortable with your weapon and able to use it under pressure."

Cullen nodded. He'd known for a long time Sheriff Harper had a lot of experience, but he'd underestimated the wealth of knowledge the man had to share. If Cullen was going to be effective in his role as deputy, he needed to learn all that Harper could teach him so he'd be competent and capable. Most importantly, the sheriff had to be able to depend on him.

"Yes, sir. I keep my gun clean, but I could sure use some practice."

Harper's blue eyes narrowed and nailed Cullen. "You've changed. You ain't so hesitant as you once were." He gestured to Cullen. "Your whole attitude, your mood, has changed. What happened?"

The same peace he'd asked God to give him during his middle-of-the-night prayer time a few nights ago washed over him again. Cullen couldn't keep the smile from his face. "You know how you said if there's something in the Bible I couldn't grasp, I should read it over and over until I do?"

Harper thumped his booted feet up on top of the desk and interlaced his fingers over his middle like he was settling in to listen. He smiled like a cream-fed cat. "Well? You gonna tell me about it?"

No dread formed in the pit of his stomach. No guilt lay heavy on his shoulders. Freedom in the form of real peace loosened his tongue, and he gladly testified to his mentor what God had done for him in the wee hours of the morning a few days earlier. He described how a portion of scripture that had filled him with self-loathing for so long, finally became the source of what he'd sought for five years.

Cullen shook his head. "I'm not sure how many dozen times I read it, but I kept missing that one word. *My* peace. I kept trying to find peace, or do something to create peace, when all the time, Jesus wanted to give me *His* peace." Even breathing in and out was easier. "It made all the difference."

The sheriff pulled a much-used toothpick from his shirt pocket and stuck it in his mouth. "Figured you'd get it sooner or later." He rolled the toothpick to the other side of his mouth. "It ain't somethin' I could explain to you. It's one o' those things you have to stumble over. When it hits you in the face and God speaks to you, that's when you finally get it." The toothpick waggled when he smiled. "It takes longer with hard-headed people."

# CHAPTER NINETEEN

Josephine drew in a deep breath. Something as simple and mundane as sitting down for a meal shouldn't stir such anxiety. Nevertheless, she stood halfway down the hallway that led to the employees dining room, watching staff members enter as they chatted amongst themselves. In the four years she'd worked at the Mountain Park Hotel and Resort, she could count on one hand the number of times she'd sat in the employee dining room for lunch. Her usual order included someone from the kitchen carrying a tray to her office.

Today, however, she stood twisting the timepiece that hung from her neck, trying to convince herself this was a necessary step if she was to move beyond the bonds that held her aloof from the rest of the staff. She ran her hand over the tightly pulled strands of her hair to ensure each was in place. In truth, she didn't feel much like eating, but this wasn't about quelling her hunger.

She straightened her shoulders and forced her feet forward. Hesitating only a moment at the open doorway, she walked straight to the serving line, painfully aware of the sudden decrease in conversation occurring around the room. Without glancing around, she felt rather than saw the stares that followed her as she scooped up a helping of shepherd's pie, chose a roll, and poured a cup of tea. At the end of the line, she realized this was the hardest part—finding a place to sit.

Halfway across the room, she spied Rose, Cora, and Nellie sitting together and engaged in conversation. Were they talking about her and her unusual appearance in the dining room? Josephine threaded her way through the crowded space. As she drew near the three chambermaids, she heard Nellie relating a story about something one of her children had done. Rose and Cora laughed at the anecdote, but the moment Josephine set down her tray across from them, the laughter ceased and all three of them stiffened.

Undoubtedly, they braced themselves for criticism of their work or a new change in assignments. She tried to pull a smile into her countenance, but her nerves hardened her face into granite. She sat across from the trio and gave them a brief nod of greeting. "Girls."

A foreboding quiet settled over the room. Josephine attempted to send an inconspicuous glance around. Staff members stared, but jerked their focus back to their food when they saw her look around. Some spoke in low tones with their heads leaned toward each other. She could only imagine the whispers flying back and forth.

She picked up her fork and looked at the girls. Cora kept her eyes downcast, and Nellie gave Josephine a blinking glance before blotting her mouth with her napkin. Only Rose looked straight at her, holding her gaze for a long moment before finding something on her tray to capture her attention. All three appeared to be holding their collective breaths.

She poked her fork into the mound of lamb, vegetables, and mashed potatoes on her plate. "I'm especially fond of shepherd's pie." She took a bite and could only assume it tasted as good as Mrs. Keegan's usual cooking. Today, the swallow went down like sawdust.

The dark cloud of uncomfortable silence hovered over the room. Josephine took a sip of tea. "It's a lovely day outside, is it not?" The day was unusually hot and muggy, but it was the first thing that came to mind. Talking about the weather was supposed to be a non-threatening way to generate conversation, wasn't it?

Cora still didn't look up at her. Nellie murmured a concurring reply, but didn't sound very convincing. A flicker of understanding softened Rose's features.

"It's a warm day." Rose's non-committal response gave her enough encouragement to continue her attempt at conversation.

"Have you seen the new rugs in the lobby and common areas?" The question didn't require more than a yes or no answer, but perhaps it would stir the girls to offer their opinions.

Nellie nodded. "They're quite beautiful."

Cora stuck another bite of food into her mouth with an almost imperceivable shake of her head. Clearly, the girl had no inclination to exchange small talk with her.

Rose laid her fork aside. "They *are* lovely. Nellie told me they are made locally."

"Yes." Another sip of tea bolstered her confidence. "A young woman from the area creates them and sells them to the hotel."

Another stretch of silence lapsed. She could hardly blame them. They didn't know what to think of this turn of events—their dictatorial supervisor eating lunch with them, something that had never before occurred. Josephine herself couldn't remember the last time she'd had a casual conversation, or any conversation that wasn't connected to work. This was harder than she anticipated. Perhaps a different direction.

"I believe I will inquire of Mrs. Keegan if she would like the hotel to obtain some fresh peaches, strawberries, or rhubarb from some of the area farmers. Don't you think they would make splendid pies?"

"Mm. I like making peach pie for my family." Nellie appeared to be making an effort, but her words still came out stilted and distant.

She glanced at Rose, willing the girl to respond with the same honesty with which she'd spoken the day of Cora's escapade.

A small, if hesitant, smile pulled a glimmer of light to Rose's eyes. "I haven't had rhubarb pie since my mother died, and peach pie would taste heavenly."

Droplets of relief trickled through Josephine's middle at Rose's observation. "Then I shall ask Mrs. Keegan this afternoon."

Cora deposited her fork on her tray with a clatter and stood, excusing herself and mumbling something about being needed in the laundry. She snatched up her tray and fairly pushed her way past the other seated staff members.

Rose looked in Cora's direction, dismay fixed in her expression. She returned her focus to Josephine. "I apologize for Cora's bad manners—"

Josephine lifted her fingers in a gesture meant to halt Rose's words. "I don't imagine any of you expected to share your lunch table with me. I apologize for intruding on your free time." She started to pick up her own tray, but Rose reached out and put her hand on Josephine's arm.

"Cora doesn't bear any ill will toward you, not really. She's still struggling with her feelings. I think shame over what happened a couple of weeks ago is showing in her behavior. She isn't sure how to act around you." Rose removed her hand, but maintained her gaze. "You are welcome to share our lunch table any time."

Nellie said nothing, but her eyes widened at Rose's statement.

Josephine forced a semblance of a smile. "That's very kind of you." She sent her glance back and forth to include Nellie. "Both of you."

Nellie pushed back her chair. "I have three more rooms on the second floor to attend to. I'd best get to them." She picked up her tray. Almost as an afterthought, she added, "As soon as I'm finished on the second floor, I'll take all the linens to the laundry."

Josephine nodded, not knowing if she should say thank you to the woman for doing her job. Perhaps this wasn't such a good idea. After all, she would frown on any of her girls over-stepping their bounds. Had she over-stepped hers?

The dining room began clearing out as the staff returned to their tasks. Josephine checked her watch. Twelve fifty-five.

Rose took her own tray. "I also need to get back to work." She slid her chair back.

"Rose." Josephine's gaze connected with the young woman. "I've noticed the diligence with which you have done your job, and I'm pleased with your work."

Rose's mouth didn't drop open, nor did her expression change into one of shock. A faint smile graced her face. "Thank you. I hope you have a good afternoon."

Rose and Cora climbed the stairs to their room at the end of the long day. Cora lifted her fingers and touched the place where the bruises had appeared on her face. "Miss Templeton came and talked to me when I was leaving the laundry this evening. She told me I can come back to my chambermaid duties, now that the bruises have faded. She said she didn't want Mr. Fairchild to see them."

They reached the top of the stairs and Rose looked sideways at Cora. "Did you apologize for behaving so rudely to her at lunch?"

"No." Cora shuffled her feet. "I guess I should. I just didn't know what to say when she kept trying to make small talk. She said I was still on probation, but I don't mind that as long as I don't have to go back to work in the laundry."

Given Cora's improvement in her attitude, maybe there was hope for the girl. "You know if Mr. Fairchild had seen your bruises, Miss Templeton would've had no choice but to tell him what happened. I know working in the laundry isn't fun, but I think she did it to protect you."

"I know." Cora's reply was so soft, Rose almost missed it.

As they walked together down the hallway toward their room, Rose noticed pieces of paper stuck into the doorframe of every room. She and Cora exchanged puzzled glances. Sure enough, when they reached their room, Cora pulled a folded note from their doorframe as well. Rose pushed the door open as Cora unfolded the note and read it aloud.

"It's from Miss Templeton. 'All domestic staff, kitchen staff, and laundry staff will meet in the employee dining room tomorrow morning immediately following breakfast for a staff meeting.'" Cora looked up and held the paper out to Rose. "What do you think this is about?"

"I'm sure I don't know." Rose pulled her apron off and unbuttoned her cuffs.

Cora plopped down on her bed. "I bet they're going to let people go. That's it. Some people are going to lose their jobs, and I'm probably one of them." Distress threaded her voice.

"You don't know that." Rose sat beside Cora and held the note in front of her. "It doesn't say what the meeting is about. It could be anything—a change in hotel policy or some new rule." The bedsprings squeaked when she stood up. "At any rate, why don't we wait to hear what Miss Templeton has to say?"

Cora gave a disgruntled huff and began unpinning her hair. "I'm still afraid."

"'What time I am afraid, I will trust in Thee.'"

Cora paused in brushing her hair. "Is that from the Bible?"

Rose unfastened her skirt and deposited it with the rest of her soiled clothing bound for the laundry. "It's from the Psalms. It was one of my mother's favorites."

There had been too many times over the past couple of months that she'd been afraid. Had she trusted in God all those times?

After a restless night, Rose and Cora dressed and hastened downstairs. While Rose nibbled on a biscuit and sipped her coffee, Cora pushed her plate away and leaned close to Rose. "I can't eat a thing."

Miss Templeton stepped into the room holding a paper. "May I have your attention, please." Every eye in the room fixed on the head housekeeper.

Cora mumbled, "Here it comes." Rose elbowed her.

Miss Templeton cleared her throat and looked over the room. "I am pleased to inform you that beginning immediately, new scheduling will take effect. Instead of a half day, everyone will now get a full day off per week, resulting in a six-day work week instead of six and a half days. Sundays off will be on a rotation basis."

A few gasps and mutterings intermingled in the stuffy room, and amid exclamations of wonder, several people voiced concerns.

"A whole day off?"

"Our hours are being cut?"

"We will receive shortened pay?"

Miss Templeton held up her hand for quiet. "Let me finish. I assure you that you will still be paid your full wage. In fact, some of you who have worked a certain length of time will receive raises. Some will receive more than others—as long as you have a clean work record and your work is acceptable."

Her words were met with everything from shock and skepticism to delight. "Those of you who are candidates for a raise will be notified privately. If you have any questions, please address them to me and do not speculate amongst yourselves. The new schedule will be posted later this morning." She dismissed the meeting and stepped back so the employees could be on their way to their jobs. Miss Templeton caught Rose's eye. "Miss Miller, will you please remain for a few moments?"

For once, Rose's first thought wasn't one of Miss Templeton or anyone else finding out her real name and identity. She wasn't sure what the housekeeper wanted, but she felt confident that by now her brothers were far away.

As soon as the rest of the staff had departed, Rose stepped over to her supervisor. "You wanted to speak to me?"

"Yes, Rose." She let the paper slip from her fingers onto a table. "I want to thank you for being so honest with me the day you went searching for Cora. I am chagrined that it took someone thirty years my junior to make me understand what being a real friend truly means."

Heat filled Rose's face. "I was afraid I was speaking out of turn. But then, I was also fairly certain I was about to lose my job."

A shadow of a smile mellowed Miss Templeton's expression. "I wish I could tell you that you are one of the staff who will be receiving a raise, but not only have you not been here long enough, you are officially still on probation."

"Yes, ma'am." Rose lifted her chin and looked Miss Templeton in the eye. "I don't regret being on probation, because I don't regret going to help Cora. It was the right thing to do."

Miss Templeton arched her eyebrows a moment. No doubt she found Rose's comment a bit impertinent. But this time, a smile—albeit a small one—cracked the housekeeper's face. "I don't condemn you for helping Cora. I'm just sorry I had to impose a penalty."

# ⁀ CHAPTER TWENTY

I t wasn't often Cullen opened up the tool shed before Mr. Greeley arrived in the morning. The old gentleman lived two miles out of town
and walked to the hotel every morning, and he still managed to get
there ahead of Cullen most days. But this morning, Cullen had risen earlier than normal, grabbed coffee and a biscuit, and was already busy at
the workbench, cleaning and sharpening tools when Mr. Greeley came
in.

"Hulloo, lad. Thought I was runnin' behind myself when I seen the
shed door standin' open." The old man's greeting fell gently on Cullen's
ears like a mountain breeze stirring the pines.

"Ah, there you are Mr. Greeley. I was about to send out the blood-
hounds to find you." Cullen's quip brought about the expected mischievous gleam to the gardener's eyes.

"Were ye now? You're not supposin' the hounds would tear me limb
from limb?" Mirth decorated the man's tone.

Cullen laughed out loud. "More likely they'd come looking for the
pieces of jerky you always keep in your pocket."

Mr. Greeley cackled. "Y'know me too well, lad. An' what's that you're
doin'?" He came and peered over Cullen's shoulder. He picked up a pair of

snips and ran his finger over the cutting edge. "Glory be, now that you're moving on to be a lawman, you finally learned how to put an edge on a blade."

A soft chuckle rose up from Cullen's belly. "We've trimmed the shrubs, pruned the roses, and every flower bed has been manicured. I don't think there is a single blade of grass that's taller than another, and the kitchen garden looks like one of the sketches in your horticulture book. Is there anything else you need me to do?"

Mr. Greeley's hand came to rest on Cullen's shoulder. "Not much here to keep you busy right now. I'm thinkin' it be time to come to an agreement on a shorter schedule for you, so you can be free to spend more time with the sheriff." He patted Cullen's shoulder before turning to pick up his worn leather gloves. "You've come to life in the past few weeks, trainin' to be his deputy, like an apprentice, as it were. Your fond memories of your ma and her garden are stirred when you have your hands in the soil. An' they're sweet memories for you, to be sure. But bein' a lawman is your callin', lad. Even I can see that."

Mr. Greeley's perception was uncanny. Not unlike Sheriff Harper's. Cullen gave a slight nod of agreement.

The older gentleman pulled off his hat and scratched his head. "For the time being, I'll need you two half days a week—let's say Mondays and Thursdays, and you'll need to check with Mrs. Keegan every mornin' to see if she needs anything from the kitchen garden. Fair enough?"

"Yes, sir, that's more than fair." Cullen hooked his thumb in the direction of the hotel. "What about my room? If I'm working shorter hours, will I still be allowed to stay in my room here, or will I need to find other accommodations?"

A small frown pulled Mr. Greeley's mustache toward his double chin. "That room is a closet! Stay. Once you're workin' full-time for the sheriff an' not workin' here no more, I suppose you'll need to move out, but I can't imagine anyone wantin' such a small space."

Cullen grinned. "I actually appreciate the privacy. The room is too small for two people." That privacy had allowed him to do some serious praying. "What about the autumn months coming up? You said you wanted to plant a number of bulbs. And then there will be all the leaves that need to be raked up."

Mr. Greeley nodded. "Had a chat with Hollis Perdue's boy, Tad, from town. The boy's sixteen now and wants to get him a job. I figure he's about the right age to apprentice. Seems like a right nice lad. Come September will be a good time to start teachin' him about plantin' and prunin'."

He clapped Cullen on the back. "Boy, don't lose your love for growin' things, even when you're a lawman." The crinkles around Mr. Greeley's eyes deepened with passion as he spoke of what he loved. "Buryin' bulbs during the crisp autumn days and waitin' for them to poke their heads out of the soil in the spring stirs the soul. There's a certain peacefulness to be found in plantin' seeds and nurturin' them into bloom. Whenever the stress of chasin' lawbreakers gets to be too much, take some time to put your hands in the rich soil and plant somethin'." He gave Cullen a nod and turned away. "Good for the soul."

The advice warmed Cullen's heart. Like Grant Harper, Mr. Greeley had helped him work through his burdens without even knowing he was doing so. A sliver of sadness pinched him. He'd miss working with Mr. Greeley every day.

Rose finished fastening her shoes and stood to slip her apron over her head. Cora had already left for breakfast, claiming she was starving, and she'd promised to pour a cup of coffee for Rose. Rose still couldn't get over the change in the girl. Even her complaining had slacked off.

Rose took an extra minute to glance at her reflection in the small mirror hanging above the washstand. She patted an errant lock of hair into place and smoothed her collar. Was she making sure her appearance suited Miss Templeton, or was she more interested in Cullen Delaney's opinion? She bit her lip and made a face at her own reflection. Perhaps she wanted to impress both of them. She admitted, if only to herself, that she looked for Cullen in the dining room, and usually tried to sit where there was an extra chair, just in case he asked if he could join her. A flicker of embarrassment put a pink glow in her cheeks.

She'd seen him in church yesterday. He smiled and nodded at her, and the same warmth that filled her face at this moment had made her dip her head yesterday. Knowing he was seated straight across the aisle from her certainly had made it hard to pay attention to the preacher, but she could almost feel Mama's elbow nudging her to pay heed to the Bible teaching.

She was breaking her own rule. From the day she arrived at the Mountain Park Hotel, she'd told herself she wouldn't get close to anyone and would hold herself aloof. That worked for a couple of months, but Cullen's persistence had worn her down.

Satisfied with her appearance, she turned away from the mirror and scurried out the door.

The dining room was nearly full, but Cora waved to her from the far end of one table and held up a coffee cup. Rose smiled and sent her a nod, but headed first to the buffet where she scooped a spoonful of eggs onto her plate along with a piece of toast. As she threaded her way toward Cora, her gaze slid around the room, but she didn't see Cullen.

Cora pushed Rose's coffee cup toward the seat beside her. "It's still hot, but I'm glad I got here when I did. All three coffee pots are empty now."

Rose settled into her chair. "Ah, thank you. I hate going without my coffee."

Cora snickered. "Yes, I know. Everyone else hates it when you go without your coffee, too."

Rose feigned offense and sucked in a dramatic gasp. "Are you saying I'm grumpy without my coffee?"

An unladylike snort was Cora's response. Rose ducked her head and giggled, but when she looked up at Cora, the girl stared wide-eyed toward the dining room door. Rose looked in the same direction.

A hush fell over the dining room. Miss Templeton stood by the door with a man wearing a tin star. "Let me have your attention, please." The housekeeper swept the room with her gaze. "Sheriff Harper would like to ask you all a few questions. Please listen."

The sight of the lawman hit Rose like an invisible hammer. Her pulse picked up and her stomach clenched. An ache in her chest evidenced the breath she held. She eased the air out of her lungs, but couldn't do anything to conceal the sweat that popped out on her forehead.

The sheriff took a step forward. "Ladies and gentlemen, there was a number o' break-ins and robberies reported yesterday—four businesses and a few houses. Best I can figure, they all happened while folks was in church."

He paused a moment, and several staff members murmured comments to each other.

The sheriff pulled a paper from his shirt pocket and unfolded it. "Mr. Dempsey from the Emporium reported boots, slickers, canned goods, coffee, and several boxes of ammunition were taken, along with about forty-eight dollars from the cash box. The feed and seed was robbed of twenty-two dollars. The dressmaker an' the telegraph office also reported money stolen. Some folks claimed someone entered their homes while they was at worship service. The things taken was some jewelry, a rifle, a shotgun, three huntin' knives, and some cash." He stuffed the paper back into his pocket and sent a steely-eyed, scrutinizing stare around the room.

Rose's throat constricted when his unblinking gaze moved in her direction. Could he hear her heart pounding? She didn't dare lift her hand to wipe the moisture from her brow and upper lip.

"There anyone here who saw anything?"

He waited, but no one responded.

The sheriff harrumphed. "Y'all workin' here at the hotel see folks comin' and goin' all the time. If you see anyone who looks...out of place, not like the usual guests y'all have here, please don't take any action your-self, but let me know. In the meantime, be on your guard, be watchful, and keep your doors locked. I've already spoken with Mr. Fairchild, an' he's takin' extra measures around the hotel." He tugged on the ends of his vest. "Anyone have any questions?"

Cora timidly raised her hand and Rose wanted to jerk it back down. The last thing she wanted was the sheriff's attention in her direction.

"Yes, miss?"

Cora's voice trembled. "How do we know all they want to do is steal? Could they—" She shot a look to Rose and gripped her hand under the table. "What if they want to...to hurt us?"

Rose's heart rent in two as a shudder quivered through Cora's hand. Of course, she was thinking of the man who had accosted her. How could she not? She'd voiced her fear to Rose about the man coming back for her, and frightened tears had filled her eyes.

A scowl deepened the lines around the sheriff's eyes. "The truth is, we don't know. That's why Mr. Fairchild is takin' this seriously. He's addin' extra locks, and he's talkin' about havin' a guard here at the hotel, least until whoever committed the stealin' is caught."

Rose patted Cora's arm, and whispered. "It'll be all right, Cora."

Miss Templeton stepped forward then. "I am announcing that effec-tive immediately, all staff members, especially the women, will not be alone anywhere on the hotel property. The chambermaids will work in pairs, and anyone going to and from the laundry will take a partner with them. Is that understood?"

Murmured agreement wafted through the room. When there were no other questions, the sheriff took his leave. Rose's nerves eased with his exit, but guilt smote her. Poor Cora still quaked in her shoes. Her ex-perience with that awful man was so much worse than Rose's own secret fear. Rose slipped her arm around Cora.

Nellie joined them as they got their assignments. Instead of working individually in separate areas, Miss Templeton instructed them to work as a team, never more than one room apart, and work their way down the hall of the second floor.

Miss Templeton's eyes connected with Rose's. "Stay together, girls. The guests will be notified that the cleaning schedule is being changed. Do your best, work quickly and efficiently. I know I can depend on you."

The positive encouragement of Miss Templeton's words made both Cora and Nellie blink in disbelief, but for some reason she couldn't explain, Rose wasn't surprised. She'd seen hints of change in the head housekeeper since the day Rose had gone searching for Cora. She was still unsure why Miss Templeton didn't fire both of them, but the woman's demeanor in the ensuing weeks bore overtones of gentleness. What Rose couldn't figure out was why.

Cora and Nellie both responded with a demure, "Yes, ma'am," but Rose hesitated a long moment. "You can trust us. We *will* do our best."

Was that a trace of a smile on Miss Templeton's face? With a slight lift of her chin, the housekeeper turned and left the dining room.

Rose followed Nellie and Cora toward the cleaning supply room. The two women ahead of her talked while they picked up their supply boxes. Nellie handed Cora a mop. "Since we are all working together, let's take one mop and one carpet sweeper."

A tentative smile pulled a light into Cora's eyes. "Is that what Miss Templeton meant when she said 'efficient'?"

Nellie gave her a playful shove. "Come on. Let's get to work."

Rose toted her cleaning box in one hand and the carpet sweeper in the other as they hurried up the stairs, her thoughts still occupied with Miss Templeton's words. What had happened to provoke the flicker of compassion she witnessed in the housekeeper?

"I'm glad Miss Templeton said we could work together." Cora's voice reminded Rose of a frightened child. "I don't want to be alone..."

She let her words trail off before finishing her thought, but Rose came alongside and sent her what she hoped was a reassuring smile. "You aren't alone, Cora."

Nellie set her supplies down and tapped on the first guest room door. When no one responded from within, she used her pass key to open the door. "I can't believe a little town like Hot Springs up here in the mountains has to be concerned about crime." She shook her head and set to work.

Rose and Cora moved to the next room and knocked before entering. While Rose busied herself opening the windows to air the room, Cora began stripping the linens from the bed. "The sheriff said we're supposed to be watchful, but what, or who, are we watching for? Strangers come and go here all the time. Some come by train, others by carriage, and even a few on horseback. How are we supposed to know if a stranger is simply a new hotel guest or somebody who wants to do harm?" She rolled the bed linens in a ball and turned to Rose. "I didn't know that man who... who tried to... I didn't know he was a bad man." Her voice broke, and Rose's heart constricted for her.

She crossed the room and squeezed Cora's hand. "That's why Miss Templeton wants us to stay together. But even if we aren't together, you aren't alone, Cora. God says you'll never be alone. He promised."

# CHAPTER TWENTY-ONE

Aside from his own pa, the best mentor Cullen could hope for was Sheriff Grant Harper. The seasoned lawman's experience and wisdom was better than a whole library of books, and Cullen soaked up every bit of advice and knowledge the man shared with him.

They tramped through the woods on their way to a small, secluded clearing where the sheriff said they'd do some target shooting. But every few feet they stopped so the man could point out telltale signs along the way, teaching Cullen to read the trail like a map.

"Lookee here." Harper squatted down and pointed to some fan-like fungus growing on one side of a rotted stump. "Some animal's been through here and broke off a couple of these fungus layers. But if you ain't watchin' for 'em, you'll miss 'em." He stood and looked in a wide circle. "Uh-huh, look right here. See how these leaves are disturbed, but all the other leaves are packed down? You expect to see leaves layin' loose durin' the fall. But after winter's snow, an' come spring, all the leaves is wet and matted flat. So this time o' year, when you see leaves that's been stirred, it's a sign some animal or a man has come through there. My guess is either a bear or a big ole buck, but could be a feller hikin' up through here huntin' a big ole buck."

They went a ways farther and Harper stopped again at a small stream. "See these rocks along here, the way they're pushed down into the soft dirt? Now look at this." He gestured toward a couple of palm-sized rocks that appeared to be partially pried up from the moist, sandy soil. "This weren't done by no raccoon or possum. Takes a heavier varmit like a bear"—he straightened—"or maybe a horse. Maybe even a man stoopin' down to fill a canteen."

The sheriff stepped across the babbling water. "C'mon. That clearin' is just up the ridge a ways."

As Cullen followed Harper up the rise, he told the sheriff about the meeting he'd had with Mr. Fairchild. "After you came and told him about the break-ins, he said you'd advised him to put an extra guard in place."

" Hmph. Glad he was listenin'."

"He asked me to be the guard since I've been working with you." Cullen shooed away a mosquito. "I told him I'd be glad to do that, but it would have to be part time—whatever hours I was working at the hotel. He was agreeable with that, but I don't understand something."

The sheriff kept walking. "What's that?"

"The person or persons who broke into those places in town..." Cullen widened his stride to come abreast of Harper. "Why did he only hit the emporium, the feed and seed, and such? Why didn't he try to break into the bank?"

Harper paused and Cullen took the opportunity to catch his breath. The sheriff didn't appear the least bit winded. "Couple o' reasons. Could be he thought it would make too much noise, and them other places was easier pickin's. Or, could be he was scoutin' out the town to see what he could do, get the lay o' the land, an' come back later to hit the bank."

Cullen stared at him. "You really think he'll be back?"

The sheriff took off his hat and swiped his sleeve across his brow. "It's likely. Think about what he took, other than money. Food, boots, ammunition, weapons. Like he's bidin' his time, waitin' for an opportunity. I could be wrong, but we got to assume this guy might be plannin' on comin' back."

Cullen set his jaw. Sheriff Harper had to know he could depend on his deputy. So be it.

They made their way up and over the ridge, and there was the clearing in the midst of hawthorn, pines, and sweet gum trees, like the sheriff described.

Harper glanced around. "Pick up some o' them pine cones and set 'em up on that downed log over there. They'll make good targets."

Cullen began gathering up the pine cones. But something caught his eye behind the log. "Hey, Sheriff. Come take a look at this."

"What is it?" Harper strode across the clearing.

"It's like what you were saying about old leaves this time of year. These leaves beside this log look like they were piled up, while the leaves all around here are flattened down." The sheriff leaned to examine the spot Cullen indicated. "Think some animal did that?"

Harper frowned and pushed the leaves aside with his foot. The soil underneath them had been recently dug. "Weren't no bear."

Cullen snagged a nearby flat rock and used it to scrape away the loose dirt. A couple of inches down, the rock clanked against something. The sheriff plunged his fingers into the soil and pushed it away, revealing empty tin cans. A few more scrapes with the rock uncovered an empty cartridge box.

"Canned goods and ammunition." The proprietor of the Emporium reported canned food and several boxes of cartridges were missing from his shelves. Cullen studied the cans and the box. "Judging by the looks of these, they haven't been here very long. There's no rust on the cans, and the label is still intact on the box. A day or two at the most."

The sheriff sent him a nod of approval. "Good observation." He took the cartridge box from Cullen and turned it over. "Forty-five caliber, so that tells us he's probably usin' a six-shot revolver. Safe bet whoever tried to hide this by buryin' it was the same feller that robbed the Emporium."

Cullen scraped away more dirt and uncovered three more cans and an empty wrapping that smelled like jerky. "And he was here not long ago, maybe this morning."

Harper pushed his hat back. "Time to put what I've taught you the past few weeks into practice. You start on this side of the clearin', an' I'll start on the other. Go over every inch and see if we can turn up anything else."

Cullen's pulse increased. Instead of a teaching session and target practice, the outing had turned into an evidence-collecting mission. But thanks to Sheriff Grant Harper, he was much better prepared to come face to face with an outlaw. His eyes moved over the ground, searching for those signs the sheriff had taught him to look for.

"There was a campfire over here." Harper called to him from the opposite side of the clearing. "It's been trampled and covered with wet leaves." The sheriff stooped and poked around in the ashes. "It's cold, but the cinders ain't fell apart a'tall, so the feller was here last night."

Cullen watched as the sheriff picked up charred pieces of wood, and then he kept combing the area. At one point, he stopped and sniffed. He turned in a slow half circle, scrutinizing the ground as he went. Several feet back from the clearing, there was an area where the trees hemmed in a tight section. He tramped over to take a look. "Sheriff, there's fresh horse droppings over here."

Harper joined him and sent his gaze sweeping across the entire area. He pointed. "Look down that way past those two pines. See where it looks like an openin'?"

Sure enough, upon closer inspection, Cullen found horse tracks. "Looks like he came up the rise from this direction."

The sheriff bent and studied the tracks. "He left goin' this way, too. 'cept, I'm guessin' he ain't alone. There's at least two horses. See how these tracks is deeper than those? Means it's two different animals, and one is carryin' a heavier load than the other."

They followed the tracks a little farther down the rise, and Cullen watched and listened as the sheriff pointed and instructed. "This here patch o' ground don't have no leaves, so you can see the tracks plainer. Here's where the horses went up to the clearin', and over there is more tracks headed back down. Definitely two shod horses, but these tracks here"—he traced the curved indentations in the soft ground—"was made by an unshod animal. Either a horse or mule, can't tell. But there's three animals, which means a greater possibility of more than one man."

Cullen straightened. "You think the third set of tracks is a pack animal since it's not shod?"

"Could be." Sheriff Harper rubbed his chin. "Or could be ridden by someone lighter." He pointed his chin toward the tracks. "Let's see if we can follow these and figure out what direction he—or they—are headed."

A quarter mile down the slope, the sheriff halted. "I don't like this." He pointed to the telltale tracks. "These tracks are headed too close to town."

Sheriff Harper always said the hair stood up on the back of his neck. For Cullen, it was an uneasy stirring in his gut. Not only had the man or men who had stolen from the people of Hot Springs not gone far, they appeared to be going back.

Josephine marched down the hall on the second floor. Having the chambermaids work in teams of two or three appeared to be working well, and the new arrangement gave her peace of mind. Until the perpetrator was caught, she'd not rest easy, especially after that male hotel guest attempted to accost young Cora. Even now, a shudder traveled through her at the memory of Cora tearfully telling her what had happened.

The rooms she'd already inspected at the near end of the hall were flawlessly completed, equal to the Mountain Park's exacting standards. Her girls were doing a good job, and by all indications were making excellent progress. Relieved she could report to Mr. Fairchild that the change in the cleaning schedule did not decrease efficiency, but rather enhanced it, she continued to the corner where the hall turned toward the rear of the building, creating an L-shape.

Too late, the sound of hurried footsteps met her, and she collided with Cora as the girl scurried around the corner. "*OOF!*"

"O-oh! Miss T-Templeton! I'm so s-sorry." Cora clapped her trembling hands over her mouth and her eyes widened.

Josephine reached out to grasp Cora's shoulder and the girl flinched before she even touched her. She pulled her hand back. "It's all right, Cora. There's no harm done. But I must admonish you to slow down."

Cora's mouth slackened, and then opened and closed as if searching for words. Her huge, unblinking eyes stared at Josephine. "Slow down? But I thought—" She clamped her mouth closed and bit her lip, tucking her chin. Red climbed up her neck and into her face.

The symptoms Cora displayed were achingly familiar, and a flash of ugly memories smote Josephine. She purposely lowered her voice. "Cora, I may have directed you to not waste time or dawdle in the past, but I do not wish for you to be injured. Likewise, we must be aware of hotel guests who might be coming around the corner." She clasped her hands together in front of her. "Now, suppose you tell me what it is you need, and I will go fetch it for you. Remember, you are to stay with your partners and not go off by yourself."

The young chambermaid blinked several times. "N-no, I'm s-so sorry, it's just, that is, I—I—I n-needed...You sh-shouldn't—" She gulped back whatever it was she was trying to say as moisture filled her eyes and she twisted her fingers.

Cora stiffened as Josephine reached out again, but this time, Josephine placed her hand softly on Cora's arm. "Take a deep breath. Is whatever you need a matter of life or death?"

The girl shook her head and swallowed, as if trying not to choke. Her face drained of color. She gave a valiant attempt to do what Josephine had said, but the deep breaths she tried to suck in were ragged. "I, uh, forgot—I'm sorry, Miss Templeton, I was in a hurry this morning, and I know I should have— That is, I was planning to, but someone asked me to hand them something, and I forgot to put a bottle of ammonia in my supply box, because I was already carrying extras of everything else so I wouldn't have to— And I need it for the windows, but—"

Cora's nervous babbling, her apologies and excuses by turn, accompanied by her wide eyes and trembling hands, drew a picture Josephine deeply regretted. The girl was afraid of her. She held up her hand to halt Cora's blathering.

"Shh. What room are you working in?"

"T-two seventeen."

"All right." She patted Cora's arm. "You go on back to where you are working. Remember, I want you girls to stay together. I will go down and bring back a bottle of ammonia."

Distress filled Cora's eyes, and she bit her lip again.

"Now walk, don't run, back to room two seventeen, and I will be back directly."

Cora mumbled, "Yes, ma'am," and headed back down the hall where she'd left her two partners working. She cast a look of bewilderment over her shoulder at Josephine, but did as she was bidden.

Josephine watched her go to ensure she arrived safely, and then retraced her steps to descend the stairs to the cleaning supply room. She observed more than discomfiture in Cora. It was fear. Cora's fear reminded Josephine of herself as a young girl. The trepidation and intimidation Cora displayed buffeted Josephine, and she abhorred that she had created in Cora exactly what her aunt and uncle had created in her all those years ago.

The muscles in her neck tightened against the memory. She reached the supply room, found a bottle of ammonia, and hurried back to the second floor. When she reached room two seventeen, her footsteps muffled by the carpet runner, she glimpsed Cora with her back to the open door. The girl sniffed and swiped her sleeve across her eyes.

Josephine stepped back into the hall to give Cora a minute to collect herself, and then tapped on the door frame.

"Here you are, Cora." She paused after she handed the ammonia to the girl. "I've been meaning to tell you, since you have returned to the chambermaid duties, I am most pleased with your work."

Disbelief etched across the girl's face. "Th-thank you, ma'am."

Josephine could only hope the young chambermaid would regain the confidence she had stolen from her.

Cullen didn't know what time it was, but his empty stomach cramped, and he felt as if he'd been in the saddle for days. The town was dark, most folks asleep, when he and Sheriff Harper halted their horses at the hitching rail in front of the sheriff's office. He swung his stiff leg over the saddle and dismounted. Based on the items they'd uncovered up on the ridge, they had every reason to suspect the tracks they'd followed belonged to the thieves who robbed the Emporium. Likely the other robberies that took place that same day as well.

The sheriff muttered as he did the same. "I'm gettin' too old for this."

"How far do you think we followed those tracks before they separated and went different directions?" Cullen stretched his neck from side to side.

Harper rolled his shoulders. "'Bout fifteen miles." He dusted off his trouser legs with his hat. "Bein' that one set of tracks headed straight southwest, and the other along with the unshod animal headed east, I think we're safe for tonight. But my gut instinct says we ain't seen the last of 'em."

# CHAPTER TWENTY-TWO

Rose and Nellie put away their cleaning equipment while Cora set up their supply boxes for the next day. Working as a team with Nellie and Cora had proven an efficient way to accomplish the cleaning and preparing of the rooms. Rose glanced at the hall clock. "We finished all the rooms a half hour ahead of schedule today."

Nellie hung the mop on a hook to dry. "The main reason for us to work together was to not leave any of the female employees working alone, but I'm pretty proud of the plan we came up with for doing two rooms at once."

Rose bundled the rags and towels destined for the laundry. "Each of us performing specific tasks and leap-frogging each other so we wouldn't stumble over one another worked well, once we figured out how to divide up the work."

"Even Miss Templeton was impressed." Cora piped in. The girl's attitude was changing, and Rose was glad of it.

The savory aromas coming from the kitchen announced supper was nearly ready. Rose gestured toward the stairs. "I'd like to run upstairs and freshen up before supper, since we have bit of time."

Cora and Nellie exchanged glances, and Cora giggled. "I think she's hoping she'll run into that handsome groundskeeper."

Nellie gave Cora's shoulder a gentle shove. "Don't tease her." The woman turned a smile to Rose. "I'm going to head home and have supper with my family."

The mirth fell away from Cora's face. "You aren't walking alone, are you?" A sliver of panic threaded her voice.

"No. The woman who cleans the lobby and common areas, Lucy, lives one street over from me. We usually walk together anyway." Nellie fluttered her fingers. "I'll see you tomorrow."

Rose waved to Nellie and turned to Cora. "Come upstairs with me?"

The two made their way up the stairs to the staff wing, and Cora rambled on in a dreamy voice. "I don't blame you for wanting to fix yourself up after working hard all day. That Cullen Delaney is so handsome and tall and strong. That sandy brown hair…hmm. I wish he'd look at me the way he looks at you." She pretended to swoon.

Rose rolled her eyes. "You're being silly. I simply want to—"

"To look your best, just in case Cullen Delaney happens to come in to sweep you off your feet." Cora finished Rose's sentence with a disturbingly accurate description of the emotion stirring within her.

They reached their room, and Rose collected her towel and the small piece of soap she had left. She scurried to the washroom. A quick wash restored some of the freshness the day's work had worn away. Knowing she'd have to endure more of Cora's teasing, she returned to their shared room to re-pin her hair, but wonder of wonders, the girl helped her do a French braid and loaned her a pair of ivory combs to hold the side strands in place.

When they descended the stairs to the staff dining room, Cora caught Rose's arm. "I'm going to go and sit with the ladies from the laundry. I haven't visited with them for a while." She leaned closer and whispered, "You look nice."

Before Rose could blink, Cora skittered away, leaving her to approach the buffet line alone. She took a serving of roasted chicken, a scoop of potatoes, and a few carrots and turnips. When she reached the end of the line, Cullen stepped up and placed a cup of coffee on her tray with a grin.

"May I carry your tray for you, miss?"

A nervous giggle slipped out before she could clamp her lips down on it, and a warm flush filled her face. "Thank you, kind sir."

She followed him to a table where his own tray waited and took the seat beside his. They both bowed their heads and Cullen led in a short prayer of thanks for their meal. His gaze slid her direction and admiration filled his eyes.

"May I say you look as fresh this evening as you do first thing in the morning?" He took a sip from his coffee cup. "How does a lady work hard all day and still appear as becoming as a…well, as a rose?" He finished his question with a grin.

The compliment sent a new flood of warmth to her face and she ducked her head. "Thank you." He didn't need to know she'd performed a quick ablution before coming to the dining room. The former uneasiness that induced her desire to remain aloof and distant faded, replaced by a desire to become better acquainted with this man. She tried to warn herself to be cautious, but everything about Cullen Delaney dismissed her defensiveness—a state of mind she did not at all find disagreeable.

Cullen sprinkled salt and pepper on his food and lowered his voice to a conspiratorial whisper. "Don't tell Mrs. Keegan I seasoned the food. Don't want to hurt her feelings."

"Since she supplies you with cookies?" Rose chuckled at the mischievous look on his face.

"Shh." He held his finger to his lips. "I don't want anyone else to know I'm her favorite."

Rose laughed out loud. "It might interest you to know she gives cookies to everybody."

He feigned shock, followed by wounded feelings. "No!" But the impish smile playing around his lips revealed his teasing.

She took a sip of coffee and returned her cup to her tray. "I hardly ever see you at lunchtime anymore."

He shrugged. "I have another job I go to, so I'm often not here at the hotel at noon. Do you still go out to sit by yourself on the rocks at lunchtime?"

She paused with her fork part way to her mouth, then lowered it. No, she didn't. At least not lately. In fact, the question took her by surprise. She'd spent less time secluding herself from everyone since the incident with Cora. Even more surprising was the fact she'd not been aware of it until now. "Not recently."

They ate in silence for a few moments before Cullen turned to her. "I just heard many of the staff have gone to a six-day work week. Is that why you were able to attend church last Sunday?"

Rose swallowed a bite of potato and dabbed her lips with her napkin. "Yes. We now get a full day off every week, and we rotate getting Sundays off. It's been wonderful. Some of the girls were afraid it meant a shorter pay envelope, but there's been no reduction in pay." She poked at the carrots on her plate with her fork. "It's especially nice for people like Nellie who have a family."

"Well, that *is* nice." The arch of his eyebrows indicated he'd not known about this until now.

She tipped her head. "Don't you have the same scheduling?"

He shook his head. "I report to Mr. Greeley, the head groundskeeper, so he is the one who sets the schedule for those of us who do the outside maintenance." He polished off the last bite of his chicken. "I've been working for Mr. Greeley here at the hotel for about two years. Several months ago, I picked up the other job, so I've just been working here part time. I'll be quitting here soon, as soon as Mr. Greeley's new assistant starts working."

Cullen was leaving? The piece of carrot she swallowed went down hard. His news sent disappointment spiraling through her. Not seeing Cullen every day would leave an empty place in her days. Her reaction didn't surprise her. She'd known some time ago she was beginning to be attracted to Cullen, even if she did try to resist doing so. She set her fork aside and pulled a forced smile onto her face. "I'm sorry you're leaving. I'll miss you."

Perhaps she shouldn't have been so forward, but her words were honest. Where was he going and when was he planning to leave? Before she could school her features enough to hide her feelings so she could ask the questions, Miss Templeton approached their table.

The woman halted and cleared her throat. "I apologize for interrupting your meal, but may I speak with you a moment, Rose?"

"Of course." Rose started to rise from her chair, but Cullen touched her arm.

"Please stay. I'm finished with my supper." He stood and picked up his tray. "Excuse me, ladies."

Rose watched him go, wishing she'd had time to inquire how much longer he'd be at the Mountain Park. Perhaps it was for the best. The pang of regret that accosted her served her right. She never should have let her guard down and allowed feelings for Cullen Delaney to steal into her heart and mind. It went against everything she'd determined to do when she first arrived in Hot Springs.

"I'm sorry, I didn't mean to run him off." Miss Templeton took the seat Cullen had occupied moments ago. "I'd like to ask you to consider something."

She purposely closed her mind's door on Cullen and pulled her full attention to the woman sitting beside her. "Yes, ma'am?"

Miss Templeton sat primly, with a slight lift to her chin. "The hotel is hiring two new chambermaids next week." A flicker of triumph shone in her eyes, and Rose suspected the housekeeper had to wage a battle with Mr. Fairchild to hire additional help. "I would like Nellie to train one of them, and you to train the other. They both live nearby, so they won't need live-in accommodations on the staff wing."

The housekeeper's words couldn't have startled Rose more. "Me?" Her voice came out in a squeak. "I've only been here a little less than four months." She didn't add that technically, she was also still on probation.

"That is true." Miss Templeton nodded. "But in all the years I've been employed in service, you are the quickest learner I've ever had. You are already one of the most dependable chambermaids on staff. Judging by the system for working as a team that you devised the last couple days, you're also very clever."

Rose dipped her chin and lowered her eyes, pleasure at the housekeeper's praise warming her face. She swallowed and blinked back her astonishment. She raised her gaze to meet Miss Templeton's. "Thank you for your kind words. I'll do my best."

Miss Templeton's expression took on a moment of discomposure, as if she struggled to find a suitable response. Rose suspected nobody had ever told her she was kind before.

"Thank you, Rose. I will let you know when the new hires are expected to begin." She started to get up from the chair, but reversed her motion. "Rose, I've noticed that Mr. Delaney seems to be...interested."

The remark, while casual and spoken in a non-threatening way, took Rose aback. Only minutes ago, she'd determined to put Cullen out of her mind. Since she couldn't deny being attracted to the groundskeeper, she now had to work at putting him out of her mind. But Cullen was leaving, so nothing would come of any attraction.

Miss Templeton leaned toward Rose and lowered her voice, speaking as privately as possible in the crowded dining room. "It is all right for the two of you to enjoy each other's company here in the dining room, or elsewhere on the hotel property as long as you are in plain sight. But I know I don't need to remind you not to let him distract you during work hours."

A faint smile briefly lifted the corners of Miss Templeton's mouth. "If you and Mr. Delaney wish to spend off-duty hours seeing each other, you must come and ask me. Mr. Delaney seems to be quite a nice young man, but of course, I am responsible for the well-being and watch care of all the ladies under my supervision."

Rose didn't know how to respond. Her stomach twisted, and she knew her face must be flaming red. Cullen had not asked her, at least not recently, to spend off-duty hours with him. The couple of times he'd broached the subject in the past, she had essentially slammed the door in his face. Now, with him soon to leave, it was doubtful she needed to be concerned with asking Miss Templeton's permission.

Cullen exited the dining room praying Rose wasn't in trouble with Miss Templeton. The head housekeeper didn't wear her usual scowl of disapproval, and she *had* apologized for interrupting their meal. Still, he never knew what would ignite the woman's wrath. He stood in the hallway shadows just outside the dining room's open door, peering through the sliver between the door and the frame. The exchange between Rose and the housekeeper didn't appear to be one of admonishment. He squinted. Was he was seeing correctly? Was that a smile on Miss Templeton's face? He had never seen the woman smile before, especially at a staff member. He waited and watched a minute longer, debating whether or not he should go back in and talk with Rose after the housekeeper left. Their conversation was none of his business, but he had hoped to tentatively tiptoe around the possibility of asking Rose if she would accompany him out to dinner. Her earlier responses hadn't encouraged him, but lately she seemed more friendly. Maybe he should try again. Or maybe not.

Miss Templeton stood and pushed the chair in. Not wishing to be caught lingering by the door, Cullen turned and hurried out to the kitchen to ask Mrs. Keegan what she needed from the garden tomorrow morning. After he got her short list—English peas, asparagus, baby carrots and fresh dill—he slipped out the back door.

Hoping to catch another beautiful mountain sunset, he ventured out behind the tool shed to the rocks where Rose used to go to eat her solitary lunch. The colors swathed across the sky were once again breathtaking. God had painted another masterpiece. But a hollow void took up residence in his chest, and he longed to fill it by asking Rose to share the sunset with him.

A cheerful glimpse backward to the memory of their shared supper teased him. Rose seemed to relax with him more this evening than she ever had in the past. He'd even gotten the distinct impression she was disappointed when he told her would eventually leave his job at the Mountain Park. It wasn't like he was leaving Hot Springs, but he had not included that bit of information. In fact, he'd never told her that his second job was as a part-time deputy to Sheriff Harper.

Initially, he didn't want her to know, because he'd harbored unsettled feelings about her when she first arrived. But in the ensuing weeks and months, any suspicions he may have had disappeared. So why did he not tell her he was leaving the hotel to become a full-time deputy?

# CHAPTER TWENTY-THREE

This week, Rose's day off fell on Tuesday. She'd thoroughly enjoyed attending church last week when she'd had Sunday off. Remembering the worshipful singing and preaching brought a smile as she reminisced about Sundays with Mama. They nearly always made time for church, no matter how much work awaited at home. But even as a child, Rose pitched in and helped Mama do other people's laundry in the afternoon. They'd sing every hymn they could think of to make the entire day one of worship.

The small corner torn from the edge of the newspaper served as her short shopping list. Five items barely made a list. Nellie told her the Emporium in town would have everything she needed, so Rose donned her older dress—a faded gray calico with a much-mended collar—to wear to town. So accustomed to wearing the black chambermaid uniform with her pristine white apron, even the threadbare dress with the tiny yellow and blue flowers was a welcome change.

She tucked the scrap of paper into her reticule and set off for town. The Emporium wasn't hard to find. The long green and yellow sign that spanned the width of the establishment pointed the way while she was still several hundred yards up the street. She pushed the door open, and the combination of smells drew her back to when she was six years old. How she'd loved going to the mercantile with Mama and trying to identify all the different aromas. She stood for a moment and closed her eyes.

*Leather, lye soap, cheese, tobacco, pickles, new yard goods…*

"Help ye, missy?"

Rose's blinked. "Oh, y-yes, sir."

From behind the counter, a man with a shiny head fringed by gray and white hair around the sides, stared at her. "You all right, missy?"

Chagrin poked her. "Yes, thank you. I was just remembering how the store smelled when I was a child and went shopping with my mother."

He scratched his ear and gave her a peculiar look, as if he thought perhaps she'd taken leave of her senses. "Somethin' I can help ye find?"

She pulled out the scrap of paper and handed it to the man. He wiped his hands on his already-soiled apron and squinted at the list. "Don't rightly know how a body can write such tiny letters." He carried the paper closer to the window and held it up in the light. "Reckon mayhap a flea can read this, but I cain't. You best read it, missy." He handed it back to her.

"I'm sorry, Mr.…"

"Dempsey's the name. Luther Dempsey." The proprietor straightened his string tie. "This here is Dempsey's Emporium." The man's voice rang with pride.

"Mr. Dempsey." Rose gave a polite nod to the older man. "I'm sorry, but this scrap of paper is all I had." She held up the list. "I need some tooth powder and some castile soap."

Mr. Dempsey fetched the items as she read them. "We got that new Cashmere Bouquet soap. Smells real purty." He handed her a wrapped cake of the soap and she held it to her nose and sniffed.

"Oh my, it smells like a whole flower garden." She took one more sniff and then she noticed the price penciled on the bottom. Twenty cents! For a cake of soap! She handed it back to Mr. Dempsey. "I think I better stick with the castile soap."

She blew out a wistful sigh, but there was no point in wishing for things she couldn't afford. "I need a packet of sewing needles, some white dress buttons, and a spool of white thread."

The few items on her short list made a very small pile on the counter. She looked past Mr. Dempsey to the shelves behind him. "Do you have ladies' stockings?"

Mr. Dempsey bobbed his head. "We sure do, missy." He showed her several pairs of fine silk and lisle hosiery, but at more than thirty cents a pair, she opted for the cotton ones. "May I have one of those, and a spool of black thread so I can mend the ones I have, please."

While the storekeeper tallied up her purchases, she browsed over the hair combs. The graceful curves and ornate designs made of shell and ivory were truly lovely, but she couldn't justify such a lavish expense. She moved on to the spools of satiny ribbons. At four cents per yard, surely she could afford a new hair ribbon. She added it to the pile.

"All comes to eighty cents." Mr. Dempsey deposited the items in a small paper sack.

She counted out her coins and pushed them across the counter toward the merchant. "Thank you, Mr. Dempsey."

"You come on back and see me again, missy."

She clutched her package of purchases close to her as she stepped out the door. Pausing a moment to blink in the bright sunshine, she shaded her eyes to scan the street. She'd only visited the streets of Hot Springs a few times since she'd been here. The first time, she was too focused on searching for Cora to notice what a pretty little town it was. The other times, she walked directly to the church and then straight back to the hotel. Today, she allowed herself the luxury of dawdling, simply for the purpose of getting acquainted with this community.

Her original purpose in making Hot Springs her stopping place the day she'd boarded the train in Raleigh, was to put distance between herself and those who believed she was as guilty as her brothers. She'd only intended to sojourn here a while, work and earn enough money to move on. But this pleasant little town, and even the people she worked with at the hotel, were beginning to feel comfortable. Could this be the place where she'd find peace? Instead of stirring misgivings, the idea fostered feelings of sanctuary.

She ambled down the street, taking notice of the locations of the post office, dressmaker, livery, feed and seed... Her feet halted. Two doors past the feed and seed was a freight depot. Memories of the nightmare she'd experienced in Raleigh came flooding back. Anger toward her brothers and the anxiety they'd caused when they robbed the Griswold Freight Office speared her with scalding grief. Had it not been for Ned and Brock, she'd still be living in Raleigh.

Rose stepped into the shade of a wide elm tree and closed her eyes. "God, maybe I shouldn't have left there. When I ran away, it made me look as guilty as my brothers. But it's too late to change that now. I'm here in Hot Springs. Maybe this is the new life You have for me. Help me to know if I am to stay here or move on."

"Rose?"

Startled, she tightened her grip on her package and jerked around. Cullen stood nearby, his hat in his hands. Her breath caught in her throat. How long had he been standing there?

His easy smile made her forget why she'd determined to keep her guard up, even though she'd reminded herself to do so for the past two days. Every time the memory of their supper together arose in her mind, she pushed it away. But at this moment, the determination evaporated. "H-hi, Cullen."

His smile deepened. "This must be your day off."

She nodded. "It is. I had a little shopping to do, and I thought I would look around town a bit." A shrug lifted her shoulders. "I've been here almost four months and have barely ventured away from the hotel grounds."

He shifted his weight from one foot to the other and leaned against the hitching post, as if he were settling in to have a conversation with her. Despite her good intentions to shut him out of her thoughts and her life, she couldn't seem to stop herself from watching for him around the hotel since the evening they'd shared a table in the staff dining room. Each time she'd caught a glimpse of him, he was walking away from the hotel, and she couldn't help wondering if that was the last time she'd ever see him.

A breeze blew a lock of his sandy brown hair in his eyes and he brushed it away. "I was a little concerned the other evening when Miss Templeton wanted to speak with you. Did I get you in trouble by sitting with you at supper?"

"Oh, no. Not at all." A little swirl of excitement stirred in her middle. "She asked me if I would consider being a trainer for some new girls that are being hired later this week. She actually had some very kind things to say."

Cullen's eyebrows arched. "Well, that is certainly good news. She must think highly of you to ask you to train new girls." The grin returned to his face. "Congratulations. Miss Templeton isn't an easy person to impress."

Warmth stole into her cheeks and she ducked her head. "Thank you."

He pushed away from the hitching post. "I only have a minute. I have to get to my other job, but I—"

"Your other job?" Confusion clouded her thoughts. "But you said you were leaving for your other job."

"Well, yeah..." His brow wrinkled. "I'm leaving the Mountain Park. I'm not leaving Hot Springs."

Relief tickled her and she hushed the giggle that tried to bubble up in her throat. She covered her mouth with her fingertips until she yanked her self-control back into place. "Oh. I suppose I misunderstood, then." The dignified reply did not reflect in the least the giddy joy clamoring for release. Was this a nudge from God? Was He telling her to not be too hasty about moving on? Perhaps Hot Springs was her destination after all, rather than simply a stopping off point.

Cullen curled the brim of his hat in his fingers. "I wanted to ask you the other night before we were interrupted—would you consider accompanying me to the café for supper? Since today is your day off, maybe this evening?"

She watched him visibly swallow. His chest rose and fell with a deep breath. She'd never seen him nervous before.

"I will have to ask permission from Miss Templeton."

He nodded as if he'd known that already. "If it's all right with you, I'll ask Miss Templeton, and if she gives her permission, I can call for you by the door of the staff dining room at 5:30." His eyes danced with anticipation.

Rose didn't know if the flutters in her stomach were from the hopefulness in his voice and expression, or from the invitation itself. She gave him a shy nod. "That will be fine."

His broad grin stretched across his face, and he set his hat back on his head. "Then I hope to see you later." He tugged at the brim of his hat in a gesture of respect, then jogged down the street.

She turned back toward the hotel, whispering a prayer as she went. "Lord, please don't let me get too excited about this if it's not something You want me to do. Mama always said You will guide me if I ask, so Lord, I'm asking. Direct my steps and guard my heart."

Her spirit smiled within her as she walked. Talking with her heavenly Father always resulted in a unique tranquility pervading her being. If going to dinner with Cullen was not in God's will, He would give her the peace to accept whatever Miss Templeton decided.

But what if Miss Templeton said yes?

Her one good dress, the one she usually saved for church, hung in her room. It was a little faded from repeated washings, but it was the best she had. Perhaps she should take it over to the laundry building to press it. Just in case Miss Templeton gave her permission.

Oh, mercy, what should she do? She tipped her face upward and tried to look past the puffy clouds to the heaven of heavens. Whatever

God chose. But at the same time, she was certainly glad she'd bought that new blue hair ribbon.

Josephine's years of practice wearing a stern and unyielding expression paid off when Cullen Delaney asked to speak with her. She gave him her most authoritarian stare, but he didn't back down. He was respectful and mannerly when he asked permission to escort Miss Miller to the café in town for supper.

She arched her brows. It wasn't as though she hadn't seen this coming. There was no good reason to forbid Cullen and Rose from having a pleasant evening together.

Hope rang in his voice. "I promise to have her safely back to the hotel before eight o'clock."

"See that you do." She tried and failed to sound intimidating.

A small, reserved smile tweaked the corners of his mustache, but she suspected he wanted to grin wide and shout hallelujah.

"Yes, ma'am. Thank you." He gave her a courteous nod before taking his leave.

She watched him walk down the hall toward the back door. There was definitely a spring in his step, and she was tempted to watch out the window to see if he leapt up and punched his fist in the air in victorious celebration. She hoped she was doing the right thing by giving her permission for Rose to accompany Cullen to the café. All those weeks she'd tried to find fault with him, she honestly had to admit he'd never demonstrated any untoward motivations in the attention he paid to Rose. Still, she wished now she'd told him she would be standing at the door waiting for them to return.

Had it been one of the other girls, she might not have agreed so readily. But even in the short time she'd been employed at the Mountain Park, Rose Miller had proven herself trustworthy. Perhaps that was why Josephine felt so protective. Rose was a special young lady, and she surmised that was why Cullen Delaney was interested.

She returned to her office and sat behind her desk, working her neck back and forth to relieve the tension. She muttered to herself. "You foolish old woman. Just because Spencer Lombard proved to be a dishonorable man doesn't mean every man is like him."

Unexpected pleasure rained over her. Three months ago, she'd have felt nothing but resentment and bitterness. What had changed her? Becoming acquainted with Rose Miller had certainly opened her eyes to qualities and characteristics she'd long ago buried and forgotten. But she couldn't shake the feeling there was something she'd missed.

Rose had mentioned once that her mother had died, and by all appearances the girl had no other family. However, Josephine had become more and more aware that Rose wasn't alone, not truly. There was something different about her, a presence that she couldn't quite identify.

She knew Rose attended church when her hours permitted. Was that it? Was it her faith? Was it her upbringing? What made Rose Miller stand out? Perhaps one day soon, Josephine might ask her what made her different.

Meanwhile, she'd best go find Rose and tell her to get ready for young Cullen Delaney to call for her.

# CHAPTER TWENTY-FOUR

Cullen strode back toward town, his rhythmic gait keeping time with the pounding of his heart. Obtaining Miss Templeton's permission to escort Rose to the café made his feet feel as if he walked on clouds. But it was the memory of Rose's shy smile lingering in his mind that induced the light flutters in his belly.

Sheriff Harper would smirk and probably engage in some good-natured teasing when Cullen told him, but he didn't care. He was actually going to take Rose Miller out to dinner. This time, he determined he would tell her about his job as deputy. After all, it wasn't a secret, but a shaft of guilt skewered him that he'd withheld the information. He still wasn't sure why he was ever suspicious of her. Should he tell her that part? Maybe that was best left unspoken.

He stopped at the telegraph office on the way to the sheriff's office to see if any notifications from neighboring jurisdictions had come in. "Hey, Sam. Any telegrams for Sheriff Harper?"

The older man with the protruding belly and wispy gray hair peered at him over top of his spectacles. "Telegraph key's been quiet all day. Say, you fellers find out who done the thievin' around town yet?"

The same frustration he'd shared with the sheriff two nights ago

Connie Stevens

jabbed his chest. "Not yet, but we're working on it."

He stepped out the door and nearly collided with Sheriff Harper. "You decide to come to work yet?"

Cullen snorted. "I was just checking the telegraph, but Sam said nothing has come in."

Harper held up the mail. "Looks like we got some new Wanted posters." He tipped his head toward the office. "Let's go have a look."

Back at the office, Sheriff Harper spread the new posters out on the desk. The first was for one Oscar Meade, wanted for the theft of a pair of Belgian geldings from a freight company in Salisbury.

Cullen scowled at the second poster. He'd never heard of this man, Rooney Phelps. But he was wanted for the murder of his own grandparents, the theft of their money, and for setting fire to their house. "What kind of an animal does this to his own grandparents?"

Harper shook his head and sucked on his teeth. "Who knows what drives people to do what they do? Says here he headed northwest out of Yadkinville. That would take him toward Kentucky. If he gets lost in those mountains, they'll never find him. That feller needs an appointment with a rope."

The third poster described a man wanted for forgery and impersonating a government official in Fayetteville. Not likely the man who committed the robberies in Hot Springs.

The sketches portrayed on the last poster were of the Morgan gang. Sheriff Harper set it aside. "This is an old poster. Three of the Morgans were shot and killed almost six months ago, and the other two were caught, tried, convicted and hanged about four months ago."

Cullen picked up the first three posters. "It's not very likely any of these are the ones who came through here." He tacked the posters up on the board behind the desk. "I know we followed the trail for a good ways out of town, but you don't suppose it could be someone local who laid that trail on purpose, do you?"

"Ha. You're startin' to think like a lawman." Harper dropped the poster about the Morgan gang into the trash basket. "That ain't a bad thing, 'cept it tends to make you suspicious of everybody." He shrugged. "Nothin's impossible. But in this case, I don't think it's anyone local, because that trail weren't that easy to follow. You could tell they tried to cover their tracks. If it were someone from around here, they would've laid a trail so clear a blind man could've followed it, jus' so we'd think they was headin' out of town."

"Hm." Cullen mulled over what the sheriff said. "You know, after we were about three hours away from town following that trail, I got to thinking, what if they're trying to lure us away from town so they can circle back and rob the bank while the sheriff and deputy are on a wild goose chase?"

Harper let out a cackle. "You really *are* startin' to think like a lawman. Looks like I trained you pretty good." He settled behind his desk and handed Cullen his empty coffee cup. "There's been no more thefts since two Sundays ago. Findin' that campsite up on the ridge made me edgy, so we can't rule out them varmints comin' back. Even followin' the tracks as far as they went and then seein' where they parted company don't mean we can relax."

The sheriff's wisdom and experience once again offered valuable gold nuggets to tuck away for future reference. Cullen filled the sheriff's cup and one for himself. "Will you need me this evening?"

Sheriff Harper eyed him and accepted the cup Cullen handed him. "No. I plan to spend the night playin' Solitaire and guzzlin' coffee. Why?"

Cullen got the distinct impression the man could see straight through him. An act of nonchalance wouldn't fool Harper, but he could try. He shuffled his feet and a sheepish smile found its way to his face. "No reason."

"In a pig's eye!" The sheriff took a tentative sip of the steaming brew. "Are you finally courtin' that girl?"

Oh, for Pete's sake! How did he even—"What girl?"

"What girl!" Harper sent a narrow-eyed, eagle stare at him. "The girl from the hotel. The one you said made you suspicious and you wanted to check into her background. The one you couldn't figure out because she wouldn't talk to you. You really think I fell for that?"

Guess there was no point in pretending. "I'm not courting her." *Not yet.* "I just asked her to go to dinner with me, and I had to ask Josephine Templeton's permission."

The sheriff's expression sobered in an instant. "You asked Josephine Templeton's permission to take this girl to dinner?" Harper's bushy eyebrows arched so high they became hidden in his hairline. "Whoaaa. You must think a whole lot of this girl."

Cullen blew out a dismissive breath, but inside his thoughts raced. *Yes, I do think a lot of this girl.*

Rose left the laundry holding her freshly pressed dress across her arms. Even without having the dress with her to compare the color when she was in the Emporium, her new hair ribbon matched the dress perfectly. She hoped Cullen liked blue.

A thought rattled through her. She might be acting out of presumption, preparing for an evening with Cullen without knowing how or if God would work it out. But Mama used to set extra places at the supper table after she'd prayed and asked God to bring her sons home. More often than not, Ned and Brock came dragging in, looking for a place to lay low for a few days. Mama used that time to try to talk sense into them, to plead with them to change their ways, and beg them to come to church with her. They never accompanied her to church, but she never gave up praying.

Rose slipped through the rear door on her way upstairs to the staff hallway. When she reached the second floor, she heard the unmistakable sound of someone weeping. Immediately, every nerve went on alert as she stepped past the stair landing. One of the other chambermaids who generally worked at the opposite end of the building leaned against the doorway of the stairwell, tears flowing from her reddened eyes.

"Kathryn? What's wrong? Did somebody hurt you?"

The young woman shook her head and opened her hand to reveal a crumpled piece of paper. "It's my pa. He lives with us now that Mama passed. He helps out the best he can, but he's not strong. One of my young'uns brought this note a little while ago. One of the girls from the kitchen brought it upstairs to me." She held it out.

Rose draped her dress over the stair railing, took the crumpled paper, and flattened it out. *PaPaw sick he kant breth gud Me and Kassy iz skard pleez kum home*

The words, written in childish scrawls, chilled her. "Oh, Kathryn. You must go."

"I can't." Kathryn's wail intensified. "I need this job. My man left us. I'm afraid if I leave, I'll lose my job. Then what'll me and my young'uns do?"

"But it sounds like your father is in trouble and needs help. I can explain to Miss Templeton—"

"What is going on? Kathryn? What is the trouble?" Miss Templeton climbed the last two stairs and joined them on the landing.

Kathryn blanched and tried mightily to halt her tears, but to no avail.

Rose held out the note to Miss Templeton. "One of Kathryn's children delivered this note to the back door by the kitchen, and someone brought it up to her."

Miss Templeton frowned as she read the crude message.

Kathryn wrung her hands. "I can't go. I can't lose this job. I still got six more rooms to do. I'm behind schedule 'cause three of the guests who was stayin' in some of the rooms checked out late, and then one lady wanted me to carry up some bathwater for her, and she demanded I go to the kitchen and find out why her breakfast tray wasn't brought up. And then—"

The desperation in Kathryn's voice and eyes nearly shredded Rose's heart, and she looked to Miss Templeton, praying for compassion.

"Miss Templeton, please let her go. I can finish her rooms." She turned to Kathryn and gripped the young woman's shoulders. "I'll finish your rooms for you. You have my word." She wrapped her arms around Kathryn and patted her back while casting a pleading look at the head housekeeper. "Please, Miss Templeton. Let me finish her rooms. Her father and her children need her."

Miss Templeton hesitated a moment, then put her hand on Kathryn's shoulder. "Go to your family, Kathryn, and come back to work when you can. Your job will still be here."

Rose wanted to hug Miss Templeton for being understanding and compassionate. Instead, she picked up Kathryn's cleaning supply box. "Which rooms?"

Kathryn hiccuped. "Rooms 227 through 232. Th-thank you." She turned to the housekeeper. "Thank you, Miss T-Templeton."

"You're wasting time." Miss Templeton shooed her toward the stairs. "Go."

Kathryn dashed down the stairs. "Rose, wait." Miss Templeton picked up the blue dress from where Rose had left it hanging over the stair rail. "You need to go and get ready for your young man to call for you."

Rose stared at her, her thoughts muddled. "I beg your pardon?"

A minuscule smile tweaked Miss Templeton's face as she held out the dress. "Mr. Delaney came and spoke with me earlier, and I gave my permission for him to escort you to the café in town for supper. He will be here in a couple of hours." She nudged the dress toward Rose again.

God had worked it out? Miss Templeton said yes? She could go? But, no, she couldn't. The excitement that welled up within her a heartbeat ago withered like a tired flower. Rose shook her head. "I can't go. I promised Kathryn I'd finish her rooms. I gave my word."

Miss Templeton pulled back and studied her so intently, a shiver ran down her spine.

Rose sent her gaze down the hallway to where Kathryn's rooms still awaited cleaning. "I better get busy."

She entered room two twenty-seven and set to work, the routine so familiar to her, she could perform the tasks without thinking. As her hands moved through each detail, her thoughts went to Cullen. After this morning's conversation with him and after he'd so sweetly asked her to accompany him to supper, she'd thought perhaps Hot Springs could be her home. Especially if something more came of a relationship between her and Cullen. Now, she tried to not let herself dwell on the fact that he would come shortly to call for her. She'd have to tell him—or have someone else tell him—that she couldn't go, even after Miss Templeton had given her permission. It wasn't hard to imagine what he might think.

Within a matter of ten minutes, not a speck of dust could be found on any surface or piece of furniture. She took up the bottle of furniture polish and a rag. Footsteps behind her startled her, and she turned. The head housekeeper entered the room and walked straight to the cleaning supply box. Miss Templeton picked up the bottle of ammonia and a soft towel. Without a word, she went to work on the windows.

"What—" Rose gulped. "Miss Templeton, what are you doing? Please, I volunteered to finished Kathryn's rooms. You don't—"

The head housekeeper held up her hand and halted Rose's protest. "How do you think I got to be head housekeeper? I've certainly cleaned my share of rooms over the years. Besides, the rooms, as well as the chambermaids, are ultimately my responsibility."

Confusion tangled Rose's thoughts. There was no possible way to finish six rooms in time to prepare herself to meet Cullen, even with Miss Templeton's help. "But..." She shook her head. "I don't understand. You don't have to do this."

Miss Templeton lowered the cloth with which she'd just finished putting a shine on the first window. "Perhaps not. But I cannot demand my girls do a job I am not willing to do myself. I must also admit I have another reason for working side by side with you. There is something I'd like to talk with you about. Something that has been on my mind for a while."

What in the world? Rose stood there like a fencepost, holding the bottle of furniture polish. "Ma'am?"

Miss Templeton moved to the second window. "There is something different about you, Rose. I've watched the way you've worked, the way you've interacted with others, the way you helped Cora when she treated you spitefully. You've taken instruction and criticism with a positive attitude. I've never heard you complain, even when I felt I had to execute a penalty for doing what you did for Cora—a penalty that very well could have been construed as unfair. Now, you're giving up your evening with your young man to help someone in need. I want to know what makes you the kind of person who can do that. You have something that makes you different, and I think perhaps it's your faith. If you are willing, I'd like to ask you some questions."

Rose blinked. And blinked again. "Questions? About my faith?"

Miss Templeton finished the window and began stripping the bed linens off the bed. "Yes, that is, unless you find that offensive."

Offensive? "Goodness, no, it's not offensive. It would be a privilege to tell you about my faith."

Could there be more than one purpose for God bringing her here? Did God lead her to Hot Springs so she could tell Miss Templeton about the Savior?

# ❧ CHAPTER TWENTY-FIVE

Her room was shrouded in shadows. The coming of night and consuming darkness always left her lonely, but Josephine didn't bother lighting a lamp. Despite working together with Rose, they still didn't finish in time for Rose to accompany Cullen to dinner. Josephine experienced a pinch of guilt about that, but she'd told Rose to go down to meet Cullen and explain the untimely situation to him.

Josephine could have gone to inform Cullen of the change in plans, but coming from Rose herself meant she spoke with him face to face to explain why she couldn't go. Flickers of memories mocked her, remembering how she'd waited for Spencer to come. If only he'd come to tell her personally that he'd changed his mind. The least he could have done was send a note. But she'd been left to wonder why he didn't show up. She didn't want that for Rose and Cullen.

She watched the gloaming gather outside her window. Even the mountains were no longer visible. As she and Rose had worked side by side, Josephine listened to Rose praying for Kathryn and her family. Not a single word of regret that she'd forfeited her time with Cullen, even though Josephine knew she'd looked forward to it. Why else would the girl make sure she had a freshly laundered and pressed dress to wear?

Rose's kindness to Kathryn impressed her, as did many other things Rose did and said. However, the private conversation they had after they finished the work is what lingered in Josephine's thoughts now.

After they'd put away the supplies, Josephine invited Rose to her office for a cup of tea. Sipping tea always relaxed Josephine in the past, but then she usually sipped alone. Rose's company this evening took on a different tone. Instead of speaking as she normally did in the role of supervisor, she'd tried to find a more level ground with Rose. Unfamiliar with the concept of friendship, her confidence wavered as she asked questions about Rose's faith and how she came to believe the way she did. Even now, an hour later, Rose's answers and explanations stirred feelings Josephine thought she had buried years ago.

She doubted Rose intended to awaken conflict in her, but that is what pulled at her now. The faith Rose described might work for her, but Rose hadn't lived with adversity, condemnation, and rejection. She'd even said she learned about her faith from her mother. It must have been a sweet way for a child to grow up—nothing like her own childhood years.

When Rose said God loved her and sent His Son to die for her, Rose couldn't know the kind of person Josephine was, because she'd kept things of her past well-camouflaged. Surely the kind of relationship, with a holy God of which Rose spoke, could only be for people who lived spotless lives—people like Rose, and apparently Rose's mother. Not her. God wouldn't want someone like Josephine Eileen Templeton. She was a throw-back.

After her mother died giving birth to her, her own father didn't want her. He'd dropped her off at an orphanage and, apparently, never looked back. She had no memory of him, and the people at the orphanage didn't either. The only thing she had was a piece of paper with her parents' names.

Her aunt and uncle didn't want her, other than for the work she was made to perform. Looking back on those years, she was more of an employee than a niece, except that she was never paid a dime. They came to the orphanage one day when she was six, showed proof of their family relationship, and got custody. She was the child of her aunt's sister. Whatever was written on the paper they showed must have satisfied the people who ran the orphanage, because her aunt and uncle took her away. The next thirteen years were spent laboring and cowering in fear of the two people who were her only family.

Spencer didn't want her. He said he did, made her believe he did, but betrayed and rejected her for someone else. He didn't even think she was worth an apology.

Most of the people she worked with over the years never wanted anything to do with her. Those she supervised hated and feared her, and those for whom she worked either spurned her or lorded themselves over her.

Why would God want her?

Rose made it sound too simple—be sorry for her sins, ask God to forgive her, and trust the sacrifice Jesus made for her on the cross. Josephine shook her head. That was fine for people like Rose, but after a lifetime of rejection, she'd have to do something to earn a shred of worth. What could she do to be good enough? There had to be more to it than Rose's simplistic explanation. She remembered the preacher at the church they attended when she was a little girl saying God loved everybody. In her child-like mind, she thought that meant even her. As she grew, she'd come to realize how wrong she'd been.

Josephine rubbed the heel of her hand across her forehead, trying to erase the dull ache. She hoped Rose wasn't disappointed. It sounded as if she wanted Josephine to make some kind of decision. They'd talked until their tea got cold, but Rose was an intelligent young woman. She would understand why a choice of that nature wasn't possible.

Before she left the office, Rose asked if Josephine had a Bible, and offered to loan her the Bible that had belonged to her mother. Again, a very selfless thing to do. And again, guilt needled Josephine at the untruth she'd spoken. She waved away Rose's offer, saying she could get a Bible. The truth was, she did have one.

Down in the very bottom of her trunk, under the Jane Austen books, and under the shawl that Spencer had given her. The shawl she could never wear because her aunt and uncle would demand to know where it came from. Then it was the shawl she could never throw away, even after she learned of Spencer's faithlessness. Beneath the painful memories the shawl represented, there lay a Bible that had belonged to *her* mother. The mother she never knew, who had died in childbirth.

Josephine slid from the chair where she sat and opened the trunk beside the chair. Since she knew precisely where everything was, even in the dark, her fingers found the Jane Austen books and the shawl. Under the folded shawl...yes, there it was. She wrapped her fingers around it for the first time in many years and withdrew it. Groping her way back to her chair, she sat in the dark with the Bible in her lap.

She'd found it one day when she was about fourteen. She'd been cleaning her aunt's parlor and discovered it in a bookcase behind several other religious books—none of which she'd ever seen her aunt or uncle actually read. Apparently, they only kept them to impress visitors.

Josephine leaned her head back against the chair, her fingers tracing the stamped letters on the front of the Book. The day she'd found it, she opened it and discovered her mother's name. She couldn't ask how her aunt had acquired the Book. To do so would have brought her aunt's wrath down on her as well as having the Bible taken from her. She could only assume her aunt obtained it after her sister—Josephine's mother—died. Since it had been tucked behind several other books, she figured her aunt and uncle would never miss it, so she took it, and hid it in her cramped attic room. It was her mother's, after all, so it should have been handed down to her.

Just as her aunt and uncle never read the high-toned sounding books in the bookcase, she never read the Bible she hid away. At the time, it was enough to know she had something of her mother's. Perhaps it was time. Rose had told her to start in the Gospel of John.

She ran her hand across the side table, found the matches, and lit the lamp.

Cullen looked over his belongings scattered across his cot. He didn't have a lot, but it was more than would fit in the carpetbag under the bed. Maybe Sheriff Harper had a crate he could use to carry the rest of his things. He and Mr. Greeley had discussed it, and he agreed to stay for a few extra days until young Tad Perdue could finish a job he'd promised his father he'd do before he started at the hotel. The days were ticking away in the countdown to his last day at the Mountain Park. Only four more days until he was officially a full-time deputy.

The sheriff had told him he could stay in the small back room behind the jail, and he apologized for the size. Said he'd stayed back there for a couple of years, and finally he moved into the boardinghouse because the room was so tiny. Cullen laughed. Harper had never seen this room, or more accurately, this closet. His new accommodations over at the jail were almost twice the size of this cubby hole.

He turned a full circle, able to touch the walls on either side with his outstretched arms. "Ha. The room at the jail is going to feel like a palace after this." He'd poked his head in the room to look it over after Sheriff Harper offered it to him. There was a bunk, small chest of drawers, several pegs on the wall, two shelves, and even room to put a chair. Of course, he'd have to clean it before he moved in. The dust and cobwebs were thick, and he'd have to evict a few spiders. Then he'd need some things from the Emporium—sheets, a blanket and pillow, maybe a small rug, and a kerosene lamp. He rarely spent money on anything, so he had a tidy nest egg. Of course, he'd planned to spend money taking Rose to dinner tonight, but that hadn't worked out.

Disappointment climbed his frame once again as he remembered Rose coming to meet him downstairs. As soon as he saw her with a kerchief tied around her hair and an apron over the same dress she'd had on this morning, he knew what she was about to tell him. When she explained, however, he was glad Miss Templeton had urged her to meet him by the staff dining room and tell him, herself, why she was working. He wasn't surprised that she offered to fill in for Kathryn—she was that kind of person. She'd apologized profusely, saying there was no way to get word to him since she didn't know where his other job was. Despite his disappointment, he told her he understood, and that he hoped she'd go with him another time. Her eyes lit up and her smile brightened.

Cullen yawned, pulled off his boots and dropped his britches on the floor. There was time later to pack his belongings. He gathered up the items cluttering his cot and piled them in a corner. For now, he extinguished the lamp and climbed under the covers, all the while letting his mind linger on the image of Rose's smile.

There were no streaks of dawn painted across the sky when Cullen dragged himself out of bed. The staff dining room wasn't open for breakfast yet, but he could always depend on Mrs. Keegan. The woman fussed good-naturedly at him, and then took a fat biscuit, fresh from the oven, broke it open, and stuck a sausage patty inside.

She pointed toward the stove with her chin. "Y'know where the coffee is." She pushed the biscuit toward him. "Don't you go off with nothin' in your belly."

Cullen grinned and scooped up the biscuit. "Yes, ma'am, but I'll get coffee later. Thank you."

The sky to the east was barely beginning to lighten, but Cullen could see the light from the window of the sheriff's office halfway down the street. He stuffed the last bite of his biscuit into his mouth and brushed off his shirt front before entering the office. The aroma of the sheriff's strong coffee greeted him.

Harper turned and looked over his shoulder at him. "Hmph. Don't reckon you brought me one."

Cullen grabbed a mug. "One what?"

The sheriff smirked and jerked his thumb toward Cullen's face.

"Whatever them crumbs are on your chin."

He brought his hand up and swiped across the entire lower half of his face. "Don't they feed you at the boardinghouse?"

A hint of a suppressed smile wobbled across the sheriff's face, as if he enjoyed their banter.

"Yeah, but you always look so fat and satisfied when you come in here, I figured you were holdin' out on me."

Cullen lifted his steaming cup. "You know I just come here for the coffee."

"Hope you came for more than that, 'cause I got a telegram late last night." Harper opened a drawer on the desk and pulled out a piece of yellow paper. "See for yourself." He extended it toward Cullen.

Cullen scanned the missive and looked up at the sheriff. "I'd almost forgotten about these outlaws. If they've robbed a bank in Waynesville, and another in Marshall, that's mighty close to Hot Springs."

Harper nodded and slurped his coffee. "You know how I've been tellin' you to sharpen your instincts and then trust them? Well, my instincts are tellin' me—"

"That these outlaws are the same ones who broke into the homes and businesses here in Hot Springs?" Cullen didn't need to look at the sheriff to know the man agreed. "When we followed those tracks and found where they separated and went opposite directions, one set of tracks went southwest, but could've veered toward Waynesville. The other went straight east, but there's a lot of territory in that direction. If they know these mountains, detouring toward Marshall wouldn't have been hard." He dropped the telegram on the desk. "Since they separated, do you think they carried out the bank robberies individually?"

"No." Harper turned and pointed to the map on the wall. "They might've each gone to scout out the two towns and then met up to decide their next move." His finger slid from one point to the other on the map. "Right through here there is a draw. Near impassable in the winter 'cause of the ice and in spring because of the snow melt and run off. But summer and fall, it's a good way to get from here to there unnoticed."

The sheriff pursed his lips and narrowed his eyes, as if all his thoughts were coming together. "What's more, I'd be willin' to bet my last pair o' socks that Hot Springs is next on their list."

"That makes sense because if they've already been here, they're familiar with the town and the layout." Cullen frowned in concentration. "That telegram says they hit Marshall the day before yesterday. If they're coming in this direction, you think we can intercept them before they get here? We already have reason to believe they are the ones that committed the robberies here a couple weeks ago."

Years of experience deepened the lines that mapped the sheriff's face. Determination hardened his eyes, and his shoulders straightened like a man of thirty instead of fifty. "That is exactly what I intend to do. We're gonna protect our town, an' nobody is gonna come in here harmin' our folks, not if I can help it." His gaze went to the telegram on the desk, and he picked it up in his fist. "This Fellrath gang don't know what kind o' trouble they're stirrin' up if they aim to head this way."

# CHAPTER TWENTY-SIX

"Don't reckon we can make solid plans till we hear back from the federal marshal." Sheriff Harper's calm demeanor loaned Cullen a crumb of reassurance, although he suspected Harper's anticipation of tracking down the outlaws who robbed area banks set him on edge.

Cullen admired the man's ability to remain cool-headed, especially if his hunch was correct. "I hope the federal marshal can give us more information on the Fellraths, assuming they are the ones who committed the robberies here in Hot Springs."

Despite the sheriff's unruffled mannerisms, there was nothing nonchalant in the way he spoke. "It's always best to know as much as you can about the suspects you're trackin'. In the meantime, you study the area an' make yourself familiar with every gulley, draw, gorge, and cliff. They're all good places to hide. Or to execute an ambush. If you know more'n the outlaws do, that gives you an edge."

For the next half hour, the sheriff painstakingly pointed out areas on the map that hung behind the desk. Cullen latched onto every word, memorizing the topography as if it were a fingerprint of the land. Once again, Cullen thanked God for Harper's mentorship.

"While we're waiting on a wire from the federal marshal, I'd like to go back to the hotel and check with Mr. Greeley to make sure he knows I'll probably be gone for a couple of days."

Harper nodded. "Old man Greeley is pretty tight-lipped, but don't share no specifics, in case anyone overhears your conversation. If them outlaws have an accomplice in the area, we don't want 'em gettin' wind of our plans."

Mr. Greeley's pleasant features turned somber when Cullen quietly related that he and the sheriff planned to head out on the trail of outlaws. The old gentleman set his clippers down on the workbench and placed both hands on Cullen's shoulders. He whispered a brief prayer for Cullen's safety, then said, "God go with ye, boy."

Cullen trotted across the lawn and poked his head in the kitchen door to check in with Mrs. Keegan. The cook's list was short, so he grabbed two baskets and headed to the garden. He pinched off tender lettuce leaves and coaxed green onions from the soil. He added a few radishes, cucumbers, and English peas. Both baskets were soon heaped with garden produce. He carried them to the kitchen where Mrs. Keegan pushed a napkin-wrapped bundle across the work table at him. Her cheeky smile accompanied the offering that no doubt contained whatever variety of cookies she'd made that morning. She would, of course, declare them his favorites.

"Here an' I go an' bake molasses cookies, your favorites, an' you barely take time to eat." She shook her head so vehemently, the flaps on her mob cap waved in the wake of the motion. "You ain't took your lunch at the hotel for weeks. S'pose you're gettin' tired o' my cookin'."

Cullen leaned down and hugged the diminutive woman. "Nobody will ever cook as good as you, Mrs. Keegan."

She cackled. "Don't let your wife hear you say that."

A chuckle worked its way up. "I don't have a wife."

She sent him a mischievous look. "Someday. Someday." She began going through the baskets of produce. "So tell me, what you been doin' with yourself that you can't take your meals here no more?"

Without sharing any pertinent details, he began telling her about the practical training and instruction he'd been getting with Sheriff Harper. "He's taught me a lot, but there's still more to learn—most of it by experience. But he feels I'm ready to take on the job of full-time deputy. So that's what I'll be doing starting the end of this week."

Mrs. Keegan put her hand against the side of her face. "Deputy! Merciful heavens. Why can't you stay here and work with old man Greeley? Sure would be safer."

"I should say."

Cullen turned and found Nellie standing in the doorway.

The woman's eyes widened. "I knew you were helping the sheriff part time, but I had no idea you were going to be a full-time lawman. My goodness."

He took a bite of one of Mrs. Keegan's cookies. "It wasn't a secret. I suppose it just wasn't something I talked about much."

A speculative expression arched Nellie's brows. "What does Rose think about it?"

Before he could answer, Nellie leaned closer to him and lowered her voice. "I've seen the two of you sitting together at breakfast and supper, and even a few times on the rocks out yonder at lunchtime." Her gaze slid from side to side, as if she was checking to see if anyone was eavesdropping, and her voice dropped to a whisper. "I thought fraternizing among male and female staff members was against the rules. I don't want Rose to get in trouble."

Cullen smiled. "It's nice that you're concerned for Rose, but don't worry. Miss Templeton doesn't object." He didn't mention the head housekeeper had given her permission for Cullen to take Rose out to dinner before Kathryn's family emergency prevented it. "In fact, she's been rather nice about it."

Nellie cocked her head. "I've noticed Miss Templeton seems gentler than she used to be. I don't know what happened to change her, but I'm glad of it."

She paused for a moment and gave Mrs. Keegan a room service order. "It's for the lady in room 142 again. She thinks when I come to clean her room, I'm there to run all sorts of errands for her, too." She lifted her shoulders. "At least she tips well."

While Nellie waited for Mrs. Keegan to fill the order, she turned her attention back to Cullen. "I didn't mean to eavesdrop, but I couldn't help hearing what you told Mrs. Keegan about working as the full-time deputy. What is Mr. Greeley going to do?"

Cullen offered a cookie to Nellie and helped himself to another. "There is a young fellow from town, Tad Perdue, who is going to start at the end of the week as Mr. Greeley's apprentice."

"I know Tad. Comes from a nice family." She munched her cookie.

"I've already discussed it with Mr. Greeley, and he is all in favor of me going to work with Sheriff Harper."

A frown furrowed the space between Nellie's brows. "But isn't being a deputy dangerous?"

The memory pricked him of the day two men came to their door to inform his mother that Pa had been shot. He could still hear her groans of anguish, and even after all these years the pain of the memories hadn't dulled much. Still, he believed Pa would approve of the training Grant Harper had been giving him. Without it, he wouldn't be prepared for the dangerous aspects of the job.

"There is a certain amount of risk with any job." He tilted his head toward the door that led to the work shed. "One day earlier this summer, I killed a copperhead while I was planting flower beds. There are a number of sharp tools out there that Mr. Greeley and I work with all the time. I could've cut myself and gotten blood poisoning. What about right here in the hotel? You and the other maids carry bulky loads of cleaning supplies and linens up and down the stairs every day. You could trip and fall down the stairs." He dusted cookie crumbs from his hands. "There are things that can happen with every job if you stop to think about it. Being a deputy might put me in harm's way more often than pruning rose bushes, but it's the training and preparation that makes the difference. I have the benefit of learning from Sheriff Harper's wisdom and experience."

Nellie lifted her shoulders. "I suppose you're right. My husband, Joe, was part of the building crew for this hotel. One day he fell off a ladder. He hasn't been able to work since." She blinked and sniffed. "I hope you're careful."

Mrs. Keegan handed Nellie a tray covered with a fancy napkin with flowers sewn into it. But before Nellie could turn to leave, Cullen stopped her. "Nellie, do you know where I can find Rose?"

With a slight grimace, Nellie shook her head. "I really don't. She's still helping to fill in for Kathryn, and those rooms were divided between two other maids besides Rose. I'm not sure which floor she's working on, much less which wing."

He sure did want to talk with her before he and the sheriff headed out later today or first thing in the morning. It all depended on when the sheriff got the reply to his wire.

"Sorry I couldn't be of more help." She took a step toward the stairs and paused. "You might ask Miss Templeton."

She scurried away and Cullen mulled over her suggestion. Miss Templeton's rule was no distractions or interruptions during work hours. Even though she'd given her permission for him to spend time with Rose, he didn't want to take advantage, or get Rose in trouble with her supervisor.

Two nights ago, Rose couldn't get word to him about the necessity to cancel their date. He supposed this was similar in nature. He had something important to tell her, but didn't know where she was. Maybe he should have asked Nellie to let her know.

The clock in the kitchen told Cullen he'd already been gone from the sheriff's office longer than he'd planned. He considered writing a quick note, but rejected the idea in favor of a face-to-face conversation. With a searching look down the long first floor hallway, he released a sigh and hoped Rose would be understanding.

Rose took a half sandwich and a cookie and slipped them into her apron pocket. She exited the servants' entrance door by the kitchen, hopefully unnoticed, and made her way past the hedgerow to the far side of the tool shed and laundry building. The friendly rocks where she sat in her early weeks at the Mountain Park welcomed her again. She'd not sought the solitude of the rocks at the back of the hotel property for a while, but today seemed a good day to do so. She desired the peacefulness of staring out across the mountains, the breeze against her face, the sun on her shoulders, and nobody but a chipmunk or a bird for company.

Having these few moments to herself helped give her fresh energy for the afternoon's work ahead. The note Kathryn sent to Miss Templeton this morning stated her father had suffered a heart seizure, and Kathryn was caring for him as well as her two young children. The housekeeper had, in turn, shared the news with Rose and two other chambermaids. The rooms Kathryn normally cleaned were distributed between the three of them. Even though her workload had increased, her method of working alongside the other maids, and leap-frogging each other, kept them from falling behind. Miss Templeton was so pleased with their progress, she had the maids on the other floors learning to use Rose's system.

She leaned back on the rock, propping herself up with her arms. The ham sandwich didn't tempt her, but she broke off pieces of the bread and tossed them to the sparrows that hopped around on the ground. When she unwrapped the cookie, she was struck by the memory of the first time Cullen had joined her out here at her favorite spot. *Joined her* might be stretching the description of that day. At the time, his presence felt more like he was trespassing, especially when he kept trying to strike up a conversation with her. She'd given him her molasses cookie that day, thinking if he had something to keep his mouth occupied, he wouldn't talk to her. The memory pulled a smile onto her face.

Cullen's news about leaving the hotel for another job affected her in ways she didn't expect. Slivers of unexplained sadness intruded where she'd been embracing more positive attitudes of late. Why was that? She shouldn't mope. Cullen did tell her he wasn't leaving Hot Springs. But knowing she'd not see him every day, or have the opportunity to sit with him at mealtime, formed a dark cloud over her. She berated herself for the silly schoolgirl thoughts. Her eyes lifted to the puffy white clouds overhead.

"Lord, why am I feeling this way? Mama would have called it nonsense, and she'd be right. I wish she was here to give me advice. She always taught me Your word was filled with all the advice a body needed. I'm confused, God. I thought I knew exactly what my plans were, but now I'm not so sure. Please turn my thoughts in the way You want me to go."

How did this happen? When she first arrived in Hot Springs, she'd been so diligent to not allow herself to be vulnerable. She'd kept her guard up and reinforced her defensive wall. She'd told herself as soon as she had enough money saved for another train fare, she'd move on. That was her plan from the beginning, from the day she left Raleigh. Hot Springs was never where she planned to stay. It was simply as far as she could go on the money she had.

Since this job came with room and board, she had no expenses to speak of, other than a few personal items. She had saved more than enough for a train fare to carry her a good distance away. How much did it cost to go to Ohio or Pennsylvania? Maybe New York? Maybe she could even venture west if she was brave enough. Now that she had the money, she really didn't want to leave. She liked it here. She had friends and a decent job, and even Miss Templeton had eased up, so it wasn't unpleasant.

Mama would scold her and tell her to stop being sulky. There was no reason to brood. Cullen had sat with her a few times in the staff dining room, and their actual date hadn't worked out. They had no understanding, and they weren't officially courting. Besides, it wasn't as if he was moving to the other side of the moon.

She looked down at the molasses cookie in her hand. There was no one with whom she could share her cookie today. She needed to reconcile her thoughts that Cullen was no more than a friend she would see from time to time, if God led her to remain in Hot Springs. She wouldn't mind living here, hidden away in the mountains. Surely she was safe enough from her past catching up with her.

# CHAPTER TWENTY-SEVEN

Rose gathered the small mountain of bed linens and stuffed them in the rolling cart. Leaning with her forearms, she packed the layers of bedding down as tightly as possible to make room for a few more. Hauling the empty cart up the back stairway in the morning was awkward, but one girl could manage it. Taking a loaded cart down the stairs in the afternoon, however, required extra hands.

One of the new girls, Cassie, was using the carpet sweeper in the next room. Rose poked her head in to see how she was doing. "Are you almost done?"

Cassie glanced up. "I love the way this thing works. I've never used one before."

Rose gave her an indulgent smile. "If you're finished, I need some help taking the laundry cart down the stairs."

The new chambermaid gathered her supplies and equipment and stowed them away in the housekeeping closet. She hurried over to where Rose waited with the cart. "Whew! How did you manage to get so much in here?"

"There's no real trick to it." Rose pointed out the layers. "Instead of rolling the sheets and towels up in a ball, lay them as flat as possible. They take up less space that way and you can pack more in."

Cassie nodded. "I'll remember that. You've taught me so much—I hope I can remember it all. I'm sure glad Miss Templeton assigned me to you."

They got to the top of the stairs, and Rose showed Cassie how to grip the cart between them and use the weight to slide it from one stair to the next. Taking the loaded cart down three flights had both the girls panting by the time they reached the first floor. Rose pointed down the short hall, past the kitchen. "We take it out that door and there's a path that leads to the laundry."

One of the cart wheels was uncooperative and refused to roll smoothly. They managed to maneuver it down the hall to the door, but when Cassie pushed the door partway open, Rose held up one finger.

"Wait." She bent to wrangle the cantankerous wheel. "Let me see why this wheel isn't rolling right."

While Rose pulled a tangle of threads out of the wheel, Cassie waited with the door ajar. Men's voices filtered in from just beyond the door. Rose paused. She recognized Mr. Fairchild's voice, but couldn't place the other one. Not wishing to interrupt Mr. Fairchild and whomever the other man was, she motioned for Cassie to wait. Their muted voices didn't carry enough for her to hear their conversation—not that she was trying to eavesdrop—but the intensity in Mr. Fairchild's voice led her to believe he wasn't happy. She peeked through the crack in the door and her breath caught. The other man was the town sheriff.

Her pulse kicked up the same way it did the day the sheriff came to the staff dining room and told them about the robberies. What were they discussing that had Mr. Fairchild so tense? Ignoring Cassie's raised eyebrows, she leaned slightly closer to the door. What she had at first thought to be an argument was in fact the sheriff giving the hotel manager an update on the robbery suspects.

"The wire I received a while ago confirmed it was the Fellrath gang that robbed the banks in Waynesville and Morganton, and we have strong reason to believe they are the ones who robbed several homes and businesses here in Hot Springs."

"How do you plan to ensure the safety of my guests here at the hotel, Sheriff?"

"My deputy and I—"

Rose couldn't breathe. Her heart pounded in her ears so loudly, the rest of the sheriff's words were drowned out. *The Fellrath gang.* Her brothers were in this area? Did they know she was here? How could they— Where— Did the sheriff know what her real name was?

*Breathe. Think.* One thought broke through all the others and screamed over the cacophony of noise bombarding her mind.

*Run!*

"C-Cassie, take the cart to the l-laundry. I have to— I have to—"

"But I don't know where it is." The girl's lament grated on Rose's ears.

Rose called over her shoulder as she dashed up the stairs. "Follow the path."

Panic climbed up her throat and strangled her. She paused at the top of the stairs. The small window afforded a narrow view of the grounds. Cullen strode purposefully across the manicured grounds toward the sheriff. As they conversed, Cullen gestured toward the hotel. Rose's heart hammered against her ribs, and scorching heat swelled in her chest. The sheriff jerked his thumb to gesture over his shoulder, and the two of them headed together in the direction of town.

"There you are."

Rose startled and spun, her hand to her chest. "Nellie, y-you frightened me."

Nellie leaned to peer out the window at the scene Rose had stared at only a moment ago.

"I see the sheriff and Cullen found each other. He was here earlier today asking for you. I think he wanted to talk to you about something important, but he had to get back to the sheriff's office."

"The sheriff's office?"

"Mm-hm, that's where he works now."

Every muscle in Rose's body slammed to a halt and froze in place. "Cullen works at the sheriff's office?"

Nellie nodded. "Didn't you know? He's been Sheriff Harper's part time deputy for more than a year. Starting this week, the position is full time."

Cullen was a deputy? How could that be? He'd never mentioned... She knew he had another job but had no inkling where he worked. That was why she didn't know how to get a message to him the other night when she volunteered to fill in for Kathryn. Rose's head spun with the information. Her throat burned and nausea roiled in her stomach. All this time, she thought Cullen was her friend. More than her friend. She'd begun to wonder if they might share something special between them. How could she have been so stupid, so naive? Cullen must know her real identity.

The urge to run sent an alarm throbbing through her again.

"Rose?"

Rose jerked at Nellie's voice. "What?"

"Why are you so jumpy?"

She yanked her focus from Nellie back to the window. Her hand moved down over her skirt of its own accord and her gaze followed it. "I have to go change—" She snatched at her apron ties behind her. "Change my apron." She tugged it off and rolled it in a ball. "I got a stain on it."

She ran down the hall toward her room. Behind her, Nellie's voice called out something about seeing Cullen, but Cullen was the last person she wanted to see now.

Her key trembled in her hand, and she fumbled with the door lock. When it finally released, she entered the room and leaned against the closed door, her heart racing and her breath coming in short, shallow bursts.

There was no time to waste. She locked the door in the unlikely event Cora might come to their room. Then she fell to her knees by her bed, reaching underneath to find her shabby carpetbag. A thought flashed through her mind. Had it come from God, or was she remembering how she and Mama used to pray together? On her knees beside her bed was exactly where she needed to be. But panic pushed her fingers to latch onto the bag and pull it out. She shoved belongings into it without thinking, but her hand halted on the faded blue skirt, the one she'd worn when she first arrived. She pulled it back out of the bag and tossed it on the bed. Her fingers fumbling in haste, she unbuttoned and unhooked her chambermaid uniform dress and laid it carefully across the foot of the bed. It didn't belong to her—the hotel provided the uniforms. She'd not take anything with her that wasn't hers.

She scrambled into the blue skirt and pulled on a much-mended light blue shirtwaist. Before she yanked on the leather fastener to close the bag, she shoved her reticule in on top. Every bit of money she'd earned since she arrived, except for the few personal purchases she'd made, was in her reticule. She had toyed with the idea of opening an account at the Hot Springs Bank. Now she was glad she didn't.

Over the past almost five months, Cullen had teased her along and charmed her until he wore down her defenses, because somehow he must have known she was Margaret Rose Fellrath, sister to Ned and Brock Fellrath. Was he using her to lay a trap for her brothers? How could she not have seen him for what he was? Betrayal branded her with a red-hot iron, and she couldn't stop the tears from flowing as she fastened the latch on her carpetbag. Through her blur of tears, she saw one thing for certain—she'd never let Cullen or anyone else do this to her again.

Where should she go? Her mind blanked for a moment. She couldn't just walk away from the hotel to the Hot Springs train depot in broad daylight, carrying a bag. There were too many people who might see her, including Cullen. No, her best bet was to skirt around the back of the hotel property behind the hedgerow and head out of town on foot. During her two-day journey from Raleigh to Hot Springs, she remembered the train stopping at a number of towns a ways down the mountain. She could buy a ticket and board the train there, but a sense of urgency sliced through her. She was wasting time.

Instead of the stairway she normally took that led to the hallway by the kitchen, she headed for the one at the opposite end of the hall. She moved as stealthily as she could to avoid attracting attention. When she reached the bottom floor, she peered down the hallway where Miss Templeton's office was located. A couple of bellboys hurried back and forth, carrying luggage for new arrivals, but they paid her no mind. She scooted out the exterior door, darted around the back of a hedge of rose bushes, and ducked behind one of the bathhouses. She paused to assess the route she might take. There were rocks and shrubs up the slope, but the more direct route to the road was too wide open. Climbing the rocks and navigating uphill and around the back of the hotel property would take longer, but it was safer.

Thorny vines raked her arm and entrapped her skirt. Ignoring the bloody scratch on her arm, she freed her skirt and kept moving, hoping there were no snakes among these rocks. Her eyes darted from side to side as she went. By the time she reached the rocks behind the laundry and tool shed where she'd gone so many times to seek solitude, she was panting and sweating from her exertion. She couldn't stop, not now. When she was safely out of town, she'd find a place to sit and catch her breath. A thick stand of pines clustered at the edge of the hotel property offered cover.

Approaching voices reached her ears and she ran into the pines, grateful for the carpet of pine needles that muted her footsteps. She crouched down and squinted through the saplings. Two of the women she recognized from the laundry passed between the laundry building and the tool shed, then proceeded toward the hotel. Rose released a pent-up breath and pushed her way through the pines in the opposite direction.

The river posed another problem. Again, she was faced with two choices—she could take the bridge and be in plain sight, or cross through the water upstream where nobody would see her. Her clothing would dry soon enough if she waded across, but if someone saw her crossing the bridge, it wouldn't take long for word to get back to Cullen and the sheriff. She pushed aside scrub underbrush and vines, hoping none of them were poison ivy, and went a hundred yards upstream where the shallow river made a bend. She sat and pulled off her shoes and stockings, tied the laces together and hung them around her neck with her stockings stuffed inside them.

Gathering up as much of her skirt as she could in one hand, she held it and her carpetbag up and stepped into the water. The shock of the cold water sent a shudder through her, but she concentrated on the rocks and where she was putting her bare feet. Almost to the opposite bank, setting her feet carefully to avoid falling, she stepped on something sharp. Pain shot through her foot. She clamped her teeth together and hissed. She pulled her foot away and a twisted piece of metal tangled against her ankle. Blood discolored the water.

*Keep going. Don't stop.*

The hem of her skirt dragged through the knee-deep water, but she managed to keep her carpetbag dry. On the other side of the river, she found a downed log to sit on while she examined the wound on the bottom of her foot. Blood seeped from the torn skin, and a burning sting seized her foot. She looked around and spied some moss at the base of a tree. She pulled a handful of it, shook off the dirt and held it to the wound to try and stop the bleeding. She dried her feet and legs the best she could, pulled her stockings and shoes back on with the clump of moss in place, and climbed up the riverbank.

The road that led away from Hot Springs beckoned through the trees. She bent to avoid a low-hanging vine, but it snagged her hair. She lost a few hairpins, but she couldn't stop to search for them now.

Once on the road, walking was so much easier without dodging limbs and vines, or crossing thick underbrush that threatened to trip her. Easier, except for the pain in her foot. She limped as fast as she could, putting distance between her and Hot Springs.

And Cullen.

Anger coiled like a bedspring in her stomach, as much with herself as with Cullen. It didn't matter how charming he was, she never should have allowed herself to be so gullible and vulnerable. He must be feeling awfully smug, thinking he had her cornered. Well, his smugness would change to disappointment when he found out she'd slipped away. She wondered if he and the sheriff would capture her brothers. Glad Mama wasn't here to see her sons meet the consequences of their outlaw ways, her heart grieved for Ned and Brock. But deep inside she hoped they'd be apprehended and taken to prison. Maybe a few years behind bars would make them change the direction their lives were headed.

Where was *her* life headed? She thought she'd found a quiet place to live, away from those things that caused her so much anguish. She shifted her carpetbag from her right hand to her left, then flexed her right-hand fingers to stretch out the stiffness. Sharp pain pulsated from her foot all the way past her ankle, and the limping began to make her other leg ache. This wasn't in her plans when she hoped Hot Springs would be a refuge for her. She'd sought peace. Instead, fear invaded and turned her peace upside down.

# CHAPTER TWENTY-EIGHT

Sheriff Harper poked his finger on the map tacked up on the wall. "The Fellraths hit the Waynesville bank almost two weeks ago. Waynesville is about sixty miles or so from here. Then they robbed the bank in Marshall almost a week ago." He slid his finger across the map to the little town southeast of Hot Springs. "Marshall ain't but about sixteen miles away."

Cullen stuck his thumbs in his belt and calculated the timeline. "We found where they'd camped up on the ridge a week ago yesterday. That means they likely came here and broke into those homes and businesses in between bank robberies."

Harper gave a short nod. "This is gettin' personal for me. The sheriff in Marshall, Jude Kingsley, was shot. Hurt pretty bad, last I heard. Jude is a good friend o' mine. Report said Jude got off a couple o' shots, an' he thinks he might've hit one of 'em."

A chill of memory sliced through Cullen as the image arose in his mind for the thousandth time—those two men standing at their door, telling his mother that Pa had been shot. Pa would tell him to stay focused on the evidence and the facts, and stay alert. He forced his attention back to Harper. "If one of them is wounded, do you think they might chance coming back here?"

"Maybe." Harper scowled. "I already checked with Doc Pryor this mornin' and told him about this. He sent Miz Pryor to stay with her friend at the boardinghouse in case them outlaws do show up. I got Otis Hogan to set over at Doc's place."

"Can Otis handle a gun if he has to?" Cullen checked his revolver for the third time.

The sheriff shrugged. "He wins the turkey shoot every year."

Cullen looked over the supplies they had laid out on the desk. Rifles, ammunition, jerky and hardtack, extra canteens, a couple of blankets rolled up, and slickers. Didn't appear they'd forgotten anything.

"It's almost two o'clock. Mail should be in by now." The sheriff jerked his head toward the door. "Go on down to the post office an' see if there's anything for us from the federal marshal. Even if there ain't, we need to head out. Horses are out back. I'll start loadin' up."

Cullen set out for the building that housed the post office, his long legs closing the distance in a minute. As soon as he entered, the clerk greeted him. "This jus' came fer ye, Deputy." He handed Cullen a large envelope.

"Thanks." This was what they'd been waiting for. He jogged back to the office, broke the seal on the envelope, and pulled out a stack of new Wanted posters.

Harper entered by the back door. "Ah, good. They came." He joined Cullen at the desk. "Let's have a look."

Together, they leafed through the posters. "Here." Cullen laid one down where they could both study it. "Ned and Brock Fellrath, wanted for escaping jail, multiple thefts, and bank robbery. Five hundred dollar reward."

"This poster must've been printed before they hit the Marshall bank, 'cause there ain't no mention of shootin' a sheriff." Harper gave disgusted sniff. "Reward woulda been more."

The sketches of the two frowning faces on the poster, and the descriptions under them, would help when the time came. But it was the third sketch that made Cullen's blood run cold. The sketch of the sister, Margaret Fellrath, bore an uncanny resemblance to Rose.

He tried to recall every conversation he'd had with Rose over the past five months. He did remember asking about her family and where she was from, and if she had any kin. Now that he thought about it, Rose always sidestepped the questions. In fact, that's when she usually shied away and appeared nervous. Wasn't that why his suspicions were aroused originally? He looked again at the image on the poster. This Margaret Fellrath was only wanted for questioning in relation to her brothers.

The sheriff took the poster and folded it. "Lock the door. We'll go out through the back."

Cullen set the bar in the cleats on the office door and followed the sheriff to the back alley. He already had the supplies tucked into saddle bags and lashed down. He swung into the saddle, nudged his horse forward behind Sheriff Harper, and prayed he was wrong about Rose.

Rose hobbled along the road, although it wasn't much of a road. Barely wide enough for one wagon, there were sheer-face rocks on one side that towered over her, and a steep slope on the other side. Sweat dripped down her forehead and her throat was parched. She stopped at a stream a little ways back and took a drink, but she had nothing with which to carry water. The next town shouldn't be much farther. The best she could recall from several months ago, the distance between train depots wasn't terribly far. She did remember the conductor saying there wasn't time to disembark the train for a comfort stop, and they would be back underway in a few minutes. The train had arrived at Hot Springs less than an hour later, so she should certainly come to the next town any time now.

Perhaps this might be a good time to check her foot. It throbbed something fierce. She plunked her carpetbag down beside an old stump and unfastened her shoe. When she pulled it off, she gasped. The flesh around the wound was red and purple, with a blackish center. Blood had soaked the wad of moss and had seeped onto her stocking. She discarded the moss and searched through her bag for something better to use, but found no handkerchief, not even an extra pair of stockings. A quick search around her turned up nothing to serve as a makeshift bandage. The petticoat she wore—one of only two that she owned—was the better and newer one, but she had no choice. She tore a strip from the bottom edge, cringing as she did so. She couldn't afford to spend money for a new petticoat. She wrapped her foot and hoped there were enough layers to afford her some cushioning.

Pulling the shoe back on made her wince in pain, and she set her teeth to stop herself from crying out. Perhaps if she didn't lace the shoe as tightly—

Hoof beats sounded, and she grabbed her carpetbag and dove into the underbrush down the slope. With her free hand, she grabbed hold of a sapling to keep from sliding down the steep ravine. Were the horses coming from the road behind her or from up ahead? She couldn't tell, but as the hoof beats grew closer and louder, she knew it was more than one horse. Praying there were no unfriendly creatures where she hunkered down, she held her breath.

Through the slits between the weeds and thick underbrush, she caught sight of two horses rounding the bend where she'd walked a few minutes ago, coming from Hot Springs. She didn't dare raise her head enough to see if she recognized the riders. Her heart pounded as it had earlier when she first heard the sheriff speak the name of Fellrath. After what felt like an eternity, the horses passed without slowing. Although the sound of the hoof beats faded, still she waited several minutes.

Finally assured the horses and riders were well away from her, she sat up and brushed leaves, dirt, and debris from her clothing. A few new scratches added to the ones she'd gotten earlier, and a scraped elbow now joined the collection of injuries she'd acquired. But they wouldn't stop her.

What might stop her, however, was knowing the two riders who passed by were now ahead of her in the direction she was walking. She reclaimed her seat on the stump and finished lacing her shoe, trying to ignore the pulsating assault of pain that hampered her ability to think clearly.

Staying off the road and navigating her way through the trees and underbrush would slow her progress considerably, but she'd be surrounded by ready cover. She wasn't moving fast anyway because of her foot. "The next town can't be too much farther." Speaking the words didn't offer much of a boost in confidence.

If she tried detouring through the woods, she'd be hopelessly lost in no time. Besides, the hollows and deep gullies along the road were nearly impassible. No, she had to stick to the road. Anyone coming from either direction would make enough noise to give her time to duck for cover. She hoisted her bag and resumed limping along the road, alert for the sound of unwelcome company.

The sun hung just above the treetops and the shadows lengthened across the road. Dismay squeezed her middle. She'd been expecting to come to the next town for the past two hours. Then the realization struck. Instead of following the road, she should have followed the train tracks. A groan of regret rumbled through her. She'd panicked when she overheard the sheriff speaking to Mr. Fairchild, and anger blinded her when she found out about Cullen's job. All she could think of was running. Her foolish failure to plan could cost her.

Of course, the direction she was walking was longer. The train probably traveled a straighter course, what with trestle bridges spanning the deep gorges. No wonder it didn't take very long for the train to travel between these little towns. Journeying by the road and on foot was far different. She sent a prayer heavenward. "Lord, please let me come to that town soon. I can't even remember the name of it, but You know what it is and where it is. Please direct my steps." She pulled in a shallow breath. "And please take away this awful pain in my foot."

With no other recourse, she kept walking. The road had to lead somewhere. She could only pray that "somewhere" had a train station where she could buy a ticket.

Shadows grew thicker and the air grew cooler as the sun dropped lower, and her stomach complained of its emptiness. Once again, she berated her impulsive failure to plan—she'd not thought to bring anything to eat. A jumble of sensations mocked her. Hunger, regret, weariness, and the fast-approaching dusk, not to mention the sharp ache in her foot, drowned out every other thought.

Up ahead, the narrow road forked. She halted and stared first down one road and then the other. Both looked to be fairly well traveled, and one wasn't any wider than the other, so there was no clear direction which way—

Wait, what was that? Nearly concealed in the weeds at the side of the road, there was a piece of wood. She pushed the overgrown weeds aside. A small sign, the letters faded by age and weather, proclaimed one road led to the town of Spring Creek. The other, pointed out by a dingy, dirt-coated arrow, led to the town of Marshall.

"That's it!" A tiny pinpoint of encouragement kindled within her. "That's the town the train stopped at before it reached Hot Springs." She might not have anything to eat, and her foot still pained her, but she knew where she was going. Maybe if she could find Marshall before darkness enveloped her, she might be able to get a bite to eat and find a place to stay. Right now, spending a few coins for sustenance and shelter seemed more prudent than a train ticket that could take her one more depot farther.

She could no longer see the sun, but its glow still gave enough light to see where she was walking. Growing discouragement, however, underscored how quickly she was running out of daylight. Lightning bugs flickered through the trees along the slope. She raised her eyes to scan the sky, hoping for moonlight, but found none. Barely able to make out the terrain on one side of the road, trying to navigate an area that might hide a steep drop off where she could plunge down into the gorge was too risky.

On the opposite side, several large boulders crowded against each other, creating nooks and crevices. Overhead a shallow, rocky ledge protruded. It wasn't much of a shelter, but she could no longer see more than a few feet through the darkness to search for anything better.

Mama always said God would protect her wherever she was. "Please, God, maybe I don't have the right to ask for Your protection. I ran away without even stopping to ask You what I should do. I'm scared, God. Help me."

She stepped gingerly to the big rocks, groping her way through the dark to find a spot to rest for the night. She dropped her carpetbag and sat in front of it, using it as a pillow to lean against. A coyote howled, and something moved through the underbrush. A raccoon or rabbit, perhaps? She didn't want to consider other possibilities. What was the verse she'd told Cora?

*What time I am afraid, I will trust in Thee.*

Mama always told her being afraid and worrying were the same as telling God He wasn't able to protect her. She drew in a fortifying breath. "Thank You, God, for these rocks. You are my Rock and my Fortress, my Shelter and my Refuge." She pulled off her shoe to free her throbbing foot, her stomach growled, and...was that a rumble of thunder?

With her parched throat, she began to sing one of Mama's favorite hymns, timidly at first, but stronger as the words filled her spirit. "'Rock of ages, cleft for me. Let me hide myself in Thee.'"

At some point she must have dozed, because she awoke with a start at a loud clap of thunder. Cloistered in on two sides by wet rocks, she tried to blink and force her eyes to see through the inky blackness, but the effort was futile. She couldn't see her own hand. Damp clothing made her shiver. Was God demonstrating to her how foolish she'd been? She already knew that.

The sound of the rain picked up from a drizzle to a heavier shower. Tears of despair burned her eyes and combined with the raindrops running down her face. Soaked to the skin, hungry, cold, and alone, she raised her face toward heaven. "God, I know I made a wrong choice. I shouldn't have run away. I had nothing to do with my brothers' deeds, but running makes me look guilty. I did the same thing when I ran away from Raleigh. I paid more attention to what people thought—or what I was afraid they would think—than I did to You. Forgive me, God."

An elongated flash of lightning that forked across the sky illuminated the mountain and her lodging place for several seconds. Just over her head, a small rivulet of rainwater poured over the rocky ledge. She moved her face beneath it and let it wash over her. She opened her mouth and captured the refreshing water, swallowing gulp after gulp. Thunder rumbled, less intense this time, and she leaned back against her carpet bag again as the rain slackened.

What did Jesus say? *If anyone thirsts, let him come to Me and drink.* Joyous laughter spilled from her lips. "Thank You, God, for Your presence and provision."

The lightning less intense now, she was once more immersed in total darkness, but she wasn't alone. She was held within the protective hand of God.

# CHAPTER TWENTY-NINE

Cullen stood near the door of the doctor's office while Sheriff Harper had a brief visit with his old friend. Jude Kingsley's pallor was pale and grayish, nearly the same gray as his hair. This time when the memory of his pa being shot crashed over him, it bolstered his resolve to do his job and stop these outlaws from hurting anyone else.

Harper tossed his hat on the chair beside the bed. "Jude, how'd you go an' get yourself shot?"

Jude Kingsley managed a weak smile. "Grant Harper, what're you doin' here? I thought you were too old to be a sheriff."

Harper laughed. "In a pig's eye. You're older'n me." His grin faded. "Listen, Jude. I don't want to wear you out, so let's keep this short. What can you tell me about these Fellraths? Your deputy wasn't much help."

Kingsley gave a slight nod. "He's a green kid. Just started helpin' out a few weeks ago. All he knows about bein' a deputy is what he's read in those penny dreadful novels." He made a floppy gesture with his fingers toward the cup of water sitting by the bed.

Harper slid his arm under his friend's shoulders and supported him while he held the cup to his lips. Cullen watched the sheriff's eyes soften as he dabbed a dribble of water from the corner of Kingsley's mouth. "More?"

The act of tender compassion wasn't lost on Cullen. These men had been friends a long time, and it showed. It also afforded him a deeper glimpse into Sheriff Grant Harper's character. Friendship meant something to this man, something more than just the superficial.

Kingsley shook his head. "Fellraths went into the bank just as it was closin' for the day. Money was still in the drawer. They hadn't locked it in the safe yet. Knocked the teller over the head. Old man Newbold, the banker, ducked under his desk when they come in, so I s'pose they didn't see him." Kingsley paused for a breath. "While they was fillin' a sack, Newbold slipped out the back door, ran down the street to my office."

Sheriff Harper laid his hand on Kingsley's shoulder. "Take it easy, Jude. Catch your breath." He gave his friend another sip of water. Jude continued. "My deputy and me went runnin' down there just as they was comin' out the door. My deputy hollered at 'em to stop, dang fool kid. They shot at us, we shot at them."

"An' you forgot how to duck," Harper teased.

"Hey, I hit one of 'em. He slumped over in the saddle." Kingsley winced. "That's when the other one shot me. The one that shot me was left-handed, dark hair. Rode a sorrel. The one I shot weren't as tall as his brother, light brown hair, right-handed. Rode a dark bay with white socks. They headed out of town to the west."

Harper patted Kingsley's shoulder. "That's enough, Jude. You rest now. I promise you, we're gonna get those two. They ain't gonna get away with shootin' my friend." He picked up his hat. "I promise."

The sheriff gestured Cullen toward the front door with his hat, and they stepped out. As they mounted up and left the doctor's office behind them, Cullen looked over at Harper. "How long have you known Jude Kingsley?"

"A lifetime." The sheriff pursed his lips. "Since the day he arrested me and threw me in jail."

Cullen reined back on his horse. "What? He arrested you?"

Harper kept going, and Cullen nudged his horse forward to catch up. Judging by the look on the sheriff's face, there were more than a few memories rolling through his mind.

"I was about twenty. Driftin', couldn't keep a job because o' my temper. Came through this part of the state with a big chip on my shoulder. Got into a fight and busted up the café in town. Jude Kingsley came barrelin' in and grabbed me by the back o' my neck." A shadow of a smile flickered over the sheriff's face. "He leans in next to my ear and says in a real quiet voice, 'Boy, you can come along the easy way, or I can drag you. Your choice.'"

Silent laughter shook Sheriff Harper's shoulders, and Cullen could tell the memory was something special to him. "So...did you go along easy, or did he drag you?"

Harper released a chuckle. "I must've had at least a little kernel o' good sense, 'cause I went along easy. You might not have been able to tell with him layin' in the bed an' covered up, but he's a pretty big man." He nodded, more to himself than to Cullen. "A big man in a lot o' ways."

"How long were you in jail?" Cullen's desire to know more about Grant Harper spurred the question. Besides, he had a feeling this was a good story.

Harper smirked. "Long enough for him to tell me if I didn't turn my life over to Jesus, I was headin' for trouble I wouldn't be able to fight my way out of. Locked up in that cell, I didn't have no choice but to listen." That same tender look Cullen saw in Harper's eyes when he gently wiped the water from Kingsley's face came over the sheriff again. "Jude Kingsley is the reason I became a Christian. Also the reason I became a sheriff." He shifted in his saddle and looked squarely at Cullen. "And that's the reason we're gonna find the polecat that shot him."

Cullen recalled the training Harper had given him, trying to think of possible scenarios. "How do we know where to start looking? Kingsley said they headed west, but that was a week ago."

"That's where a little experience and a little familiarity with the area come together." A mile out of Marshall, Harper reined his horse down a trail grown over with weeds and a tangle of vines. Had the sheriff not gone that way, Cullen wouldn't have known it was there.

They slowed their horses to a walk, picking their way carefully. Cullen kept his eyes moving, searching for any of those things Harper had taught him to look for. He guided his horse alongside the sheriff's and kept his voice low. "What is it we're looking for?"

The sheriff answered just above a whisper. "Well, a ways back through these woods, there's a shack." Harper brushed a spider web away. "Ain't been lived in for years, but once in a while, somebody comes across it and stays there a short while. Usually it's a hunter or a drifter. But sometimes the hair on the back o' my neck says to go check it out."

"I see a few broken twigs and crushed vines, like someone's been through here recently." Cullen leaned and studied the path. "Like right there." He pointed to a place flattened by something heavy, like a horse.

Sheriff Harper held up his hand and stopped. He put his finger to his lips, then motioned for Cullen to swing around to the left, while he indicated he'd go to the right. He dismounted and led his horse over the damp ground. Last night's rain made it soft, but also erased any tracks that may have occurred several days ago. Cullen glanced right to make sure he knew where Harper was. The sheriff waved his hat forward. Simultaneously, they converged on a ramshackle cabin that appeared ready to collapse.

Harper approached cautiously while Cullen watched two sides of the shack with his gun drawn, but saw no signs of life. The sheriff kicked the door in and leapt to one side. When he determined it was clear, he holstered his gun and went inside. Cullen remained watchful until the sheriff stepped back out.

"Someone was here all right. I'd say no more'n a couple days ago. Fresh ashes in the stove, empty tin cans. And blood." Harper tied his horse to a tree next to Cullen's. "Start lookin' for tracks headin' away from the shack. They might be washed out after the rain, but look for somethin'."

Cullen began the sweep with his eyes the way Sheriff Harper had taught him. After a half hour, he spied some indentations in the soft dirt that could have been hoof prints. "Sheriff, over here." He squatted down to examine the impressions. He pointed. "You think this is horse tracks? The rain made it hard to determine what it was, but—"

"Sure looks like washed out horse tracks to me." Harper clapped Cullen on the back.

Cullen scanned ahead. "There's more tracks that way. Looks like two horses."

Harper nodded. "Let's go."

They strode back to the horses and mounted. Cullen followed Harper's lead, while the sheriff kept an eye on the direction of the tracks, Cullen kept watching ahead and side to side, his hand resting on the butt of his gun. They covered three or four miles, and the terrain became steeper. When they got to the top of a rise, Sheriff Harper halted and turned his horse in a circle. "They stopped here." He pointed out crushed undergrowth. "Looks like they dragged somethin' through there." He pointed across the ridge.

Cullen dismounted and handed his horse's reins to Harper. He tramped along beside the tracks to the edge, where the cliff dropped off into a deep ravine. "Whatever it was, it went over the edge here and down. It's pretty deep. I can't see anything, but there's a lot of underbrush and rocks. You want me to climb down there and see what I can find?"

"No, let's keep going." He handed the reins back to Cullen. "I see what they're doin'. The road ain't but a hundred yards that way. They're followin' the road, but keepin' to the woods thinkin' nobody'll find the tracks."

They pushed on. "Sheriff?" Cullen again kept his voice low so it wouldn't carry through the woods. "This trail is fresh. They must've gone through here this morning."

Harper nodded. "Yep, but it ain't 'they' anymore. It's just one set o' tracks."

"You think they split up or something?"

"Or somethin'."

Harper's ominous reply drew a picture, and Cullen suddenly realized what was dragged over the edge of the ravine.

A couple of miles farther, Cullen caught a glimpse of something moving up ahead, and waved to Harper and pointed. The sheriff nodded. He'd seen it, too. Once again, they split up and approached from different angles. Cullen's pulse kicked up.

*God, guide me.*

A man knelt at a stream, filling his canteen. His back was to them. Sheriff Harper moved in from the right. The man must have heard something, because he jerked up and reached for his gun. But Cullen was right behind him. He stuck the barrel of his gun at the back of the man's neck.

"Drop it."

The man froze.

"Mister, don't make me tell you again."

The gun fell from the man's hand, and Cullen kicked it away.

Sheriff Harper quickly had the man in handcuffs. "Mr. Fellrath." He pulled the Wanted poster out of his inside vest pocket and held it up beside the man's face. "Ned Fellrath. Where's your brother?"

The defiant starch seemed to ebb out of the man. "He's dead. Got shot a few days back. He died last night."

Cullen and Harper exchanged looks. The drag marks that led to the edge of the cliff must have been Fellrath's idea of a proper burial. But another pressing question demanded release.

Cullen swallowed hard, hoping he was wrong. "Where's your sister?"

Fellrath gave him a confused look. "Margaret? How should I know? I ain't seen her in months."

"When was the last time you saw her?"

Even the sheriff looked at him as if he'd lost his mind.

Fellrath shook his head and frowned. "Uh, it was back in Raleigh. Like I said, months ago. Why you askin' about Margaret?"

Cullen jerked his thumb at the Wanted poster. "She's on there."

Fellrath scowled. "I don't know why. She never had nothin' to do with what me an' Brock was doin'. Her and Ma both kept harpin' at us to come to church and turn into good boys." He held up his bound hands. "Maybe I shoulda listened."

Harper went through the man's pockets, belt, and boots, making sure he didn't have any hidden weapons. "Are you the one who shot the sheriff in Marshall?"

Fellrath shrugged. "They shot at us. We shot back."

With a fierceness Cullen had never seen in Grant Harper before, the sheriff seized Fellrath by the shirt and shoved him up against a tree. "I oughta—"

"Grant!" Cullen grabbed Harper's arm. "Don't. Let the court handle it."

Harper hissed out a hard breath and let go of Fellrath. Cullen shoved the outlaw toward his horse. "Mount up." He pushed the man into the saddle and then took the reins and tied them to his own saddle. He looked over at the sheriff. "You all right?"

Harper gave a clipped nod. "You head out first. I'll be right behind you."

After a wet, uncomfortable night, Rose breakfasted on blackberries she found only feet from last night's resting place. Her prayer last night lingered with her. God must be shaking His head over her foolishness. Why hadn't she learned, when she fled Raleigh, that running away wasn't the wise thing to do? She'd done nothing wrong, she had nothing to hide. She knew she wasn't guilty. Staying and proving herself innocent made more sense than running, if only she'd remembered. Even though she knew she no longer had a job, she was determined to go back and make sure Cullen, the people of Hot Springs, and the people at the Mountain

Park knew she had nothing to do with her brothers' activities.

Especially Cullen.

Leaving her shoe off all night helped her foot feel a little better for a while, but once she put her shoe back on a started walking again, the pain felt like a hammer beating out a rhythm on her foot.

A narrow creek near the road was a welcome sight. She knelt on the damp ground and scooped up handful after handful of water and drank until her thirst was quenched. Then she pulled her shoe off again and soaked her foot. The cold water wrapped her foot in soothing relief. She leaned back with her carpetbag behind her head. Drowsiness pulled a veil over her, and she relaxed in its comforting solace. Her eyes drifted closed.

Cullen stood before her and held out his hand. His fingers gently enclosed over hers and he drew her toward him, but she resisted. He called to her, "Come." Why was she afraid?

When she opened her eyes, strong westerly sun caused her to squint. How long had she slept? She extracted her foot from the water and examined it. Her toes were wrinkled, and the wound on the bottom of her foot was still red, purple, and dark blue. The bleeding had stopped, but the wound gaped open. She rewrapped the piece of petticoat cloth around it and pulled on her stocking and shoe. The position of the sun indicated it was mid-afternoon, and she still had far to go.

# ✎ CHAPTER THIRTY

The cell door clanged shut and Cullen turned the key. After rattling the door to ensure it was secure, he returned to the outer office where Harper sat in the desk chair, his elbows on his knees and his head in his hands. He didn't speak, didn't raise his eyes. The seasoned sheriff might have brought in hundreds of prisoners before today, but Cullen suspected bringing Fellrath in especially moved him. Something about a promise kept.

Without a word, Cullen set about starting a fire in the stove and making a fresh pot of coffee. As soon as he had the coffeepot sitting and waiting to boil, he turned around. Harper hadn't moved. Was he praying?

"Grant?" That was the second time today he'd called Sheriff Harper by his first name, but it felt right. Cullen wasn't addressing the man as his boss, but rather as his friend.

Harper straightened slowly, stiffly.

"I'm going to go get the prisoner some supper at the café. Will you keep an eye on the coffeepot?"

Harper nodded and rifled through a desk drawer.

Cullen headed toward the café, but made a detour. The telegraph office door was closed, but Cullen was willing to bet Sam was still in there. He put his nose on the window and cupped his hands around his eyes. Someone was moving around in there. Cullen knocked on the door. A muffled reply told him to come back tomorrow, but Cullen knocked again, harder this time.

"Sam, it's Cullen Delaney."

The wizened old man opened the door. "You fellers is back. You catch them outlaws?"

Cullen stepped inside. "One of them." He reached for a piece of paper and a stubby pencil on the counter. "I need this sent immediately." He scribbled out the message.

Sam grumbled. "Why does folks always think ever'thing's gotta be sent right now?" He read over the message, his mouth moving silently as he read. He looked up at Cullen. "Grant Harper and Jude Kingsley go way back."

Cullen nodded. "I'm going over to the café, but I'll stop by here on my way back to the office to see if there's a reply."

He crossed the street and headed for the café. Halfway down the block, he heard his name called out. He turned. Nellie from the hotel hurried toward him.

"Cullen—" Nellie panted as if she'd been running. "Do you know where she is?"

The peculiar question raised the hackles on his neck. "Sheriff Harper and I just rode in about a half hour ago. What are you talking about?"

"Rose." Nellie's wide eyes related her concern. "Rose is gone. Nobody knows where she is."

An invisible fist punched him in the stomach. "When? Was she taken? Was there a fight? Did she tell anyone she was leaving? Did she leave a note?" *Did Ned Fellrath know anything about this?*

Nellie wagged her head. "Two days ago. There didn't appear to be signs of a fight. Cora said most of her things are gone, including the satchel she kept under her bed, and her uniform was laid out on the bed.

Miss Templeton looked all over town and even checked at the depot. But if she stopped long enough to pack a bag and leave her uniform behind—"

Nellie didn't need to finish the thought. Rose left on her own. Nobody forced her.

Cullen took off his hat and ran his hand through his hair, his heart ripping in two. *Where is she, Lord? Why did she leave? Oh, God, please keep her safe.* "Thanks, Nellie." He hesitated. What could he tell her? He couldn't promise he'd find Rose, although everything in him longed to do just that. "I'll talk to the sheriff and we'll put a plan together to try to find her."

He had no choice but to share his suspicions with Harper. He walked the remainder of the way to the café, put in his order, and stepped out on the boardwalk to wait. After they'd captured Fellrath, he'd prayed all the way back to Hot Springs that Rose was innocent. Her own brother had said so, but he doubted the sheriff or the court would take the word of a convicted criminal.

He paid the woman who ran the café for his order and strode back to the telegraph office. Sam was at the key, scribbling down an incoming message. The tip of the old man's tongue stuck out as he wrote. Finally, the key stopped, and Sam tapped back the received code. He stood and held out the paper to Cullen.

Cullen's eyes scanned the words. "Thanks, Sam." He slid a couple of coins across the counter.

By the time he returned to the office, Harper was sipping on a cup of coffee. Cullen set the sack on the desk, opened it, and pulled out two paper-wrapped packages. He stepped back to the cell area and stuck the two bundles through the bars. "Here's your supper."

Fellrath took them with a scowl. "Cold sandwiches?"

Cullen gave him a withering look. "I can arrange for you to get hardtack and water while you're here."

Fellrath grumbled something under his breath that Cullen was glad he didn't hear. He went back to where Harper still sat with his coffee. He reached into the sack and plunked two sandwiches in front of the sheriff.

A small frown indented the space between Harper's brows. "Ain't hungry."

Cullen crossed the office and poured himself a cup of coffee. He took the remaining two sandwiches and nudged the other two toward Harper. "You need to eat something." When Harper didn't reach for a sandwich, Cullen dug in his pocket and handed the telegraph message to the sheriff.

Harper's scowl deepened. "What's that?"

"I stopped at the telegraph office on the way to the café and wired Marshall. Here's the reply."

Harper's eyes scanned across the paper, and he blew out a relieved breath. "Thanks for doin' that. Knowin' Jude is gonna be all right is a huge load off my mind. Maybe I'm a little hungry after all."

Cullen gave him a short nod, his chest achingly heavy with the knowledge that Rose left without a word. He had a hundred questions, but the one that demanded first place was *why*.

He took a sip of coffee. "Rose is gone."

"Rose Miller? The young lady you were seein'?"

Cullen nodded and heaved out a sigh. "But her name isn't Rose Miller. She's Fellrath's sister."

Darkness had fallen by the time Rose limped to the bridge that crossed the river at the edge of Hot Springs. Tonight, however, she thanked God for the minuscule moonlight, pale as it was. At least she could make out the outline of the bridge. In town, a few lanterns burned, their pinpoints of light anchoring the location of a handful of buildings. The hotel, closer to the edge of town, twinkled with lanterns lining the drive and illuminating the sprawling porch.

Strains of music reached her. The small orchestra that played nightly in the hotel ballroom serenaded the guests with a Strauss waltz. At one time, the music might have enticed her to dance. But the combination of a throbbing foot and exhaustion dulled any semblance of pleasure in listening to the music. Instead, she pushed her feet forward. In only a few more minutes, she could collapse on her bed...if she could convince Cora to let her in, at least for one night.

Rose sagged in relief when she pulled on the back door and found it unlocked. She stepped inside. The hallway was darkened. Nobody remained in the kitchen. The back stairs used by the hotel staff was empty as well, most having already retired to their rooms or their homes.

The multiple flights of stairs in front of her loomed bigger and steeper than any of the mountain ridges she'd navigated over the past two days. She trudged up the stairs, unsure what she looked forward to the most—removing her shoe, washing off two days of filth, wearing clean clothes, or sleeping in a bed. The promise of all of those things kept her putting one foot in front of the other. She never thought she'd be so grateful to see a sliver of light coming from under the door of the room she shared with Cora. She turned the knob.

"Who is it?" Cora's voice carried a thread of fear.

Rose pushed the door open. "It's me."

Cora gasped and launched herself off her bed. She flung her arms around Rose's neck and burst into tears. "Where were you? Did someone come and take you? Miss Templeton had us working in teams so we wouldn't be alone and it would be safer, but Nellie said you ran off to change your apron and you were alone, and...and...I was so scared." Cora tightened her hug on Rose and sobbed.

Rose dropped her bag and patted Cora's back. "Shh, it's all right. Shh."

Cora's tears slowed to a hiccup. She took a step backward and surveyed Rose's appearance. "Where have you been?"

"I promise I'll tell you everything tomorrow. But right now, I'm so tired I can hardly stay upright, and my foot..." She hobbled to her bed and sank down, so grateful to finally be in a safe place. She leaned to unlace her shoe, and Cora dropped to her knees.

"Let me help." Cora eased her shoe and stocking off, and another gasp, this one more dramatic than the first, released from her lips. "Oh, Rose! This looks so painful. I won't ask how it happened, at least not now. You helped me the day you found me and brought me back to the hotel, and you didn't demand that I tell you anything. Now it's my turn to help you."

Cora told her to stay put and get out of her soiled clothing. The girl scurried out the door in her nightclothes while Rose pulled off her other shoe and stocking. She wanted nothing more than to fall back on the bed and let herself become unconscious, but she dutifully did what Cora said. When Cora slipped back into the room carrying a basin, soap, and towel, Rose's dirty clothing lay in a pile on the floor, and she sat in her chemise.

"You can get a proper bath tomorrow, but for now, this will have to do." Cora set the basin on the stand between their beds. "The water is still a little bit warm." The girl held the towel to give Rose some semblance of privacy, and when she finished her ablution, Cora draped the towel around her.

While Rose dried off and slipped into the clean nightgown Cora had laid beside her, Cora wrapped herself in a dressing robe and picked up the basin. Assuring Rose she'd be back shortly, she again disappeared through the door. Knowing if she sat on the bed, she'd be asleep sitting up when Cora returned, Rose crossed the room to retrieve her carpetbag. She rummaged through the items inside, but didn't tuck them away in the bureau, nor did she return the bag to its storage place under the bed. She'd need to repack it tomorrow. First thing in the morning, she'd have to report to Miss Templeton.

Cora returned with fresh water in the basin and a clean towel over her shoulder. She directed Rose to sit, and then knelt at her feet with the basin. "Put your sore foot in here."

The water was too warm to have come from the bathing room down the hall. "Did you get this in the kitchen?"

A sly smile pulled at one corner of Cora's mouth. "No. From the bathhouse the hotel guests use. It's the hot mineral spring water." She began tearing the toweling into strips.

Tears welled in Rose's eyes. Even if she was terminated tomorrow, she'd cherish the friendships she'd made here.

Rose smoothed her hands over her one good dress, then touched her hair to make sure the pins were still in place. Most of the staff was in the dining room for breakfast when she approached Miss Templeton's office. Prepared to face the head housekeeper's disapproval, Rose prayed she hadn't destroyed Miss Templeton's growing regard for her. She knocked on the woman's office door.

The muted voice within told her to enter. Rose opened the door, unsure of what to expect. The one thing she didn't expect was Mr. Fairchild's presence. Miss Templeton, however, set aside her usual stiff formality.

"Rose!" The housekeeper came around the desk and closed the distance between them in a half dozen strides. The woman grasped Rose's arms and pulled her into the office. "Rose, what happened to you? Where were you?"

Mr. Fairchild drew himself up as tall as he could. "This is the chambermaid who abandoned her job?" Without waiting for a response, he narrowed his eyes at Rose. His voice growled out a haughty accusation. "And now you come crawling back as if nothing out of the ordinary has happened?"

Rose looked from him to Miss Templeton. "Please, I've come to explain why I left so abruptly."

Mr. Fairchild sputtered, "I don't care to hear your excuses. Your behavior is completely unacceptable, and—"

"Come and sit down, Rose, and tell me what happened." Miss Templeton gestured to an empty chair.

Mr. Fairchild's face reddened, and his hands curled into fists.

Rose limped over to the chair, and Miss Templeton frowned. "What is wrong? Are you hurt?"

She didn't come to talk about her foot. She came to confess her deception and be honest with her supervisor. In the face of Mr. Fairchild's arrogant hostility, she tried to focus on Miss Templeton.

She pulled in a shaky breath. "First, I must confess that I haven't been truthful with you. The day I first arrived here and spoke with you about a position, I told you my name was Rose Miller."

Miss Templeton's brows raised. "That's not your name?"

Rose swallowed. "Not exactly. My middle name is Rose, and Miller was my mother's maiden name."

Mr. Fairchild planted his hands on his hips and glared at Rose. "You mean to tell me that you lied—"

"Rose," Miss Templeton said as if the hotel manager hadn't begun a diatribe, "what is your real name?"

She clasped her trembling fingers together, but she willed herself not to stammer. "My name is Margaret Rose Fellrath."

"Fellrath!" Mr. Fairchild bellowed. "That's the name of the outlaws the sheriff went after—the ones who robbed the homes and businesses in Hot Springs. And now I'm told they robbed two banks not far from here." He pointed his finger in Rose's face. "She's nothing but a common thief."

"No!" Rose stood. Fiery pain shot through her foot and she winced. "My brothers did those things, but I had nothing to do with them. I changed my name because I didn't want people to associate me with my brothers." She turned back to Miss Templeton. "I thought if nobody knew my name was Fellrath, they wouldn't assume I was guilty. When I heard the sheriff say my brothers were the ones who committed those crimes and they were in this area, I got scared. I panicked. All I could think to do was run."

Miss Templeton pressed her fingers to her head, as if she was trying to sort out what Rose had said. But Mr. Fairchild shook his finger at her. "The mistake you made was coming back here." He reached out and seized her arm. "You're coming with me to the sheriff."

# ❦ CHAPTER THIRTY-ONE

J osephine opened her mouth to protest Mr. Fairchild's rough handling of Rose, but Mr. Fairchild had already jerked the door open and there were hotel guests in the hallway. The man strode as fast as his short legs would carry him, and poor Rose limped and struggled to keep up. She hadn't answered Josephine's question concerning her apparent injury.

She lengthened her own stride and came alongside the hotel manager. She ground out a muffled entreaty through gritted teeth, "Mr. Fairchild, please slow down. People are staring."

He instantly reduced his speed and pasted a phony smile on his face. Even with his slowed pace, Rose still favored her right foot. As soon as they exited the doors, Josephine maneuvered in front of Mr. Fairchild and held up her hands. She tugged Rose's arm away from him and ignored his widening eyes and purple flush of outrage at her audacity.

"Rose, answer me. Why are you limping?"

Rose blinked several times and lowered her eyes. "I hurt my foot a couple days ago. It will mend."

Mr. Fairchild reached out, trying to reclaim Rose's arm, but Josephine stepped between them. She locked her stare at the man. "We will go to the sheriff's office, because you demand it, but you will not abuse this girl, and I insist that she be allowed to present her full explanation."

"*You* insist?" The veins in Mr. Fairchild's neck distended and his eyes bulged.

"That's right." She replied in the same steady and unruffled voice she used when speaking with the chambermaids. "I also insist she be treated fairly. I know more about this girl than you do, and I suspect there is far more to her story than you gave her the chance to say."

Surprised at her own boldness, Josephine placed Rose's arm atop her own. Supporting her, she proceeded at a more sedate pace toward town. She couldn't speak what was on her heart to Rose, not with Mr. Fairchild hovering behind her. The moment her office door had opened and she'd seen Rose standing there, relief had surged through her and moisture welled in her eyes—a wave of emotion she'd not known for... Had she ever known such a feeling? The conversation with Rose about her faith from almost a week ago had lingered in her thoughts, as if the God in whom Rose trusted tugged at her, inviting her to trust as well. She didn't know all the details that motivated Rose to run away, but she was fairly sure the reason Rose came back was because of her faith.

When they reached the sheriff's office, Mr. Fairchild barged ahead and pushed the door open. "Sheriff, I have one of the Fellraths here. I demand you take her into custody."

Josephine wanted to kick the man in the shin, but the hotel manager's challenge was met by the sheriff's scowl.

Sheriff Harper stood from behind his desk. "Mr. Fairchild, you aren't the one who makes those decisions. I am." He glanced from Mr. Fairchild, to Josephine, and finally to Rose, whose hand trembled, sandwiched between both of Josephine's.

"Rose!"

They all turned in unison. Cullen stood in the doorway with a covered plate in his hands.

Rose's breath caught at the sight of Cullen. A maelstrom of emotions swirled through her, too tangled to identify. The feelings of betrayal she'd harbored for the past forty-eight hours lost their edge under his gaze that also bore a mixture of relief and agitation by turn.

She owed him an explanation as well. She prayed Cullen, and everyone else in the room, would listen without judging.

Sheriff Harper cleared his throat. "Cullen, take the prisoner's breakfast in to him, and then bring an extra chair so these ladies can sit down."

Cullen glanced down at the plate. "Yes, sir."

Him? They only caught one of them? Rose's heart pinched, despite her disapproval of her brothers' activities. Which one of them sat in the jail cell?

Cullen moved past the group and reached for the ring of keys the sheriff handed him from the desk drawer. He unlocked and opened a door that led to another area. "Fellrath, wake up. Your breakfast is here."

She noticed he didn't say, *Your sister is here.* Was that because he wanted to hear her side of the story first?

Mr. Fairchild continued to grumble and criticize, telling the sheriff what he ought to be doing. "I don't know what you think you're waiting for, Sheriff. I've told you who this girl is. She's a Fellrath. Arrest her."

Cullen reentered the room as Mr. Fairchild spoke. He carried a ladder back chair with chipped green paint, and he shot a glare at the hotel manager as he maneuvered past him. After pulling a second chair from the corner, he positioned them side by side. "Ladies." He leveled his gaze at Rose, a hint of tenderness softening his eyes.

As she and Miss Templeton sat, the housekeeper reached over and patted her hand. The small gesture nearly undid Rose's composure. Gratefulness filled her being for the woman's nearness. When she looked at Miss Templeton, the woman smiled at her. *Smiled!*

Sheriff Harper came around and leaned against the front of the desk. "First of all, Mr. Fairchild, the young lady is not wanted by the law for anything other than a few questions, so I can't arrest her."

Mr. Fairchild took a step in Rose's direction with his finger pointed at her. His badgering threatened to make her cower in the face of his intimidation, but her God was greater. She was innocent. She had nothing to fear. Before the man could utter another word, the sheriff intercepted him.

"Mr. Fairchild, you've said enough. Now you go stand back there and be quiet. I don't need you to tell me how to do my job."

Cullen took up a position behind the sheriff, leaning against the wall directly in her line of sight. He didn't bother giving Mr. Fairchild much notice, but instead settled his attention on her, giving her an almost imperceptible nod of encouragement. Her heart lifted.

"Now, young lady." The sheriff folded his arms. "Suppose you start at the beginning. Take your time."

Rose drew in a slow, deep breath, asking God for His peace and strength. "First of all, Mr. Fairchild is correct, I am a Fellrath. My name is Margaret Rose Fellrath. Since I was nine or ten years old, my mother and I prayed that my brothers wouldn't follow in my father's footsteps. But no matter how many times we begged them to stop, they continued to steal and cheat and bully people. By the time I was fifteen, they were going off for two or three weeks at a time. Mama and I didn't know where they were or if they were all right. Every time they came home, Mama cried and pleaded with them to stop their thieving ways and turn their lives over to the Lord."

She paused and glanced at Cullen to see if she could detect a shred of understanding, but his face was expressionless. The inkling of encouragement she'd glimpsed a few moments ago dissipated, but she pushed on. "For the past two years, I worked as a clerk at the Griswold Freight Office in Raleigh, and I lived at a local boardinghouse. I only saw my brothers a few times during those two years. One morning I went to work, and Mr. Griswold told me there had been an attempted robbery the night before. He was frowning at me, but I didn't know why. He told me that my brothers had been arrested for the break-in, and he thought I had something to do with it. But I didn't. I swear I didn't." Her throat tightened and tears threatened, but she blinked them back.

"I was served with a summons to appear in court for the trial. The district attorney made me get on the stand and tried to make me say I had helped my brothers with the robbery since I worked there." She shook her head. "I didn't even know anything about the robbery until after it happened, and I was sick when I learned it was my own brothers who were caught in the act."

Miss Templeton lifted her fingers in Cullen's direction. "May Miss Miller have a few sips of water, please."

"Her name's not Miller!" Mr. Fairchild blustered. "It's Fellrath, and she's—"

Sheriff Harper pushed away from the desk and stood with his hands on his hips. "Mr. Fairchild, one more outburst from you, and I'll throw *you* in jail." He punctuated the threat with a glare that made Rose glad it wasn't aimed at her.

Mr. Fairchild hiked up his trousers and pushed out his chest. "On what charge?"

The sheriff didn't blink. "Interfering with an investigation." His ominous tone brooked no argument.

Cullen bent to hand her a cup of water and he whispered, "You're doing fine. Just tell the truth."

Did he think she planned to do otherwise? Her hand shook as she took the cup and a few drops of water spilled on her skirt.

"Please continue, young lady." The sheriff returned to his perch on the edge of the desk.

Rose took a few sips of water. "My brothers were convicted of breaking and entering and attempted robbery. They were sentenced to seven years at the state prison. I was allowed to go in and see them at the county jail before they were transferred, and they were as belligerent as ever."

She heaved a sigh. "When I went to work that day, Mr. Griswold told me I no longer had a job. Even though there was no evidence proving I had anything to do with the crime, Mr. Griswold still believed I had helped my brothers.

"Later that afternoon, I went to a café and got a pot of chicken and dumplings to take to my brothers. I figured the food they were going to get in prison would be pretty bad, and I wanted to do something kind for them—to show them no matter how much I disapproved of what they'd done, they were still my brothers." Her throat began to burn, and she took a few more sips of water. "I took the pot of chicken and dumplings to the jail. The deputy on duty was drinking from a bottle when I walked in. He shoved it under the desk so I wouldn't see it, but I did see it. And then he wouldn't let me take the chicken and dumplings in to my brothers. He told me to leave it on the desk and he would take it, so I did as he said."

Reliving this nightmare made her chest ache. "I went back to the boardinghouse, but the next morning when I came downstairs, my landlady shoved a newspaper at me. The headline said my brothers had escaped from jail." A shudder rattled through her. "The sheriff came and started asking me a lot of questions about where I'd been that night, what was in the pot besides chicken and dumplings—things like that. He said my brothers had broken out of jail during the night, and his deputy had passed out after he'd tasted the chicken and dumplings. He accused me of putting something in it. I tried to tell him the deputy had been drinking when I walked in, but he didn't believe me. It was obvious he suspected I'd helped my brothers escape."

*God, please help me say this right. I'm telling the truth, but I can't make them believe me. God, I need Your peace.*

The assurance of God's presence fell around her like a distinct cloak of preservation. How many times had she read in Mama's Bible, "*The Lord shall preserve thee from all evil; He shall preserve thy soul*"? She sat up a little straighter. "After the sheriff left, the landlady told me I had to get out by the end of the week. Everyone at the boardinghouse was staring at me like they believed I was guilty. My boss thought I was guilty. The name of Fellrath was all over the newspapers. How was I ever to get another job or find a place to live in Raleigh?"

*You're doing fine. Just tell the truth.* She blinked. Did that come from Cullen?

She skittered her focus back to the sheriff. "I packed my things and left the boardinghouse very early the next morning. I walked to the train depot and bought a ticket for Hot Springs. It was as far as my money would take me, and it was a small town hidden away in the mountains. I thought it was safe from all those people who believed I was as guilty as my brothers." She dared to glance over at Cullen. "When I got off the train, I asked a couple of people at the depot if they knew where I might find work. I only intended to get a temporary job, make enough money to buy another train ticket to someplace farther away. A man at the depot said I might try inquiring at the Mountain Park Hotel for a job, so I walked to the hotel."

She tipped her head toward Cullen. "Mr. Delaney told me which door to go in, and to ask for Miss Templeton. When he asked me my name, I almost choked. It was unlikely anyone in this little town had ever heard of my brothers, but I couldn't take the chance. If I was going to start a new life, disconnected from my brothers' reputation, I had to change my name. My middle name is Rose, and my mother's maiden name was Miller, so I told him my name was Rose Miller. Over the months I've worked at the Mountain Park, I was Rose Miller, and nobody looked at me with suspicion or accused me of doing anything illegal." Her voice broke and she could no longer keep the tears at bay. "I had decided I liked it here. I have good friends where I work and I like my job. I don't want the job to be temporary anymore. I want to stay in Hot Springs. But then the robberies happened, and..." She was babbling, and she hoped her words made some sense.

"I'm so sorry, Rose." A hand touched her shoulder. She sent her glance sideways. Miss Templeton had scooted around sideways toward her. The woman had tears in her eyes, and her voice was barely above a whisper. "I didn't realize the hardships you've been through."

Rose's breath caught and she had to look away before she couldn't control herself any longer. "Three...or four days ago—I'm sorry, I've lost track of the days—I overheard the sheriff talking to Mr. Fairchild. He said the Fellrath gang were the ones who had committed the break-ins here in Hot Springs, and they had robbed banks, or something. I panicked. I had no idea my brothers were in this area. Then I was afraid they had found out I was here. What if they tried to see me? I thought I had no choice but to run."

She let her gaze slide back to Cullen. He leaned against the wall behind the desk, his hands shoved into his pockets, his eyes closed. Was he praying? For her? She hoped so.

"After two days, I realized I was doing the same thing I'd done when I left Raleigh. I hadn't done anything wrong. I wasn't guilty, but running made me look as though I was."

She'd done it. She got through her story. She silently thanked the Lord for His help. "So I came back to explain why I thought I had to run and to try to fix the wrong choice I'd made."

# CHAPTER THIRTY-TWO

Rose's story washed through Cullen in a wave of relief. After questioning Ned Fellrath for more than an hour last night, Rose's brother had already told him much of what Rose shared for the past several minutes. Cullen believed Fellrath's declaration of his sister's innocence. Not because he thought the outlaw was in the habit of telling the truth, but because he knew Rose. Her character had left an imprint on his heart. To hear her confirm her brother's story brought peace to his soul.

The thing that bothered him the most was knowing Rose endured so much all alone. The day he met her, she had no reason to trust him with her story. But as the weeks turned into months, he thought their friendship was growing. He wished she would have allowed him to share her burden. Disappointment raked him that she didn't view him as someone she could trust.

Rose stood, and he approached her. Her eyes filled with regret. "I'm sorry, Cullen."

The sheriff's office in the presence of witnesses wasn't the place to exchange what needed to be a private conversation, so he gave her a sad smile and touched her arm briefly, but said nothing.

Miss Templeton turned to Mr. Fairchild. "I'm going to take Rose over to have the doctor look at her foot, and then we will return to the hotel where Rose will rest for as long as the doctor thinks she should stay off her foot. When she is able, she will return to her duties."

A deep scowl twisted Mr. Fairchild's face. "I can't have the sibling of convicted thieves on staff at the Mountain Park. What if my guests find out she is Fellrath's sister?"

Cullen stepped in. "Wait a minute, Mr. Fairchild. You are being unjust. You're wrongly condemning Miss Miller like the people in Raleigh did. Rose isn't the one who committed the crimes. She is trying to start a new life here, and in my opinion, she has more than proven her character. What if your guests learn of the prejudicial and unethical firing of a hard-working, innocent employee? Don't you think that would leave them with an unfavorable feeling toward you and the Mountain Park Hotel?"

Miss Templeton lifted her chin. "Miss Miller is one of the best chambermaids I have. She has an extraordinary work ethic, she gets along well with her co-workers and motivates them to do their best. As Mr. Delaney has stated, she is a woman of character. She has risen above her circumstances and kept hold of her values. I, for one, completely understand why she felt justified altering her name. If you insist on terminating her, you will have more than one job vacancy to fill. I daresay half the domestic staff will quit."

Mr. Fairchild's face reddened and he sputtered, but he finally waved his hand in an exasperated gesture. "What about her name?"

Cullen shrugged. "What about it?" He turned to Rose. "Do you want to claim your original name, or do you want to continue to be known as Rose Miller?"

Rose's chin trembled and tears glittered in her eyes. "I've been Rose Miller to everyone here. Miller honors my mother, and her middle name was also Rose." She turned to Sheriff Harper. "If it's all right—I mean, if it's not illegal—can I keep being Rose Miller?"

The sheriff lifted his hands, palms up. "A lot o' folks use assumed names. You just can't sign any legal documents with that name. Other than that, use whatever name suits you."

Mr. Fairchild huffed his annoyance and stalked out the door.

Cullen turned back to Rose and Miss Templeton. "Now, what is this about Rose's foot?"

Miss Templeton's expression changed to one of concern. "She said she hurt it, but didn't say how. Rose?"

Rose sat back down on the chair. "I cut it pretty badly when I took my shoes off to cross a creek. When I came back last night, Cora sneaked down to the bathhouse and brought a basin of the hot mineral spring water up to our room to soak my foot."

Miss Templeton raised her eyebrows, but the corners of her mouth twitched.

"How deep is the cut?" Cullen stopped short of directing her to remove her shoe right there in the middle of the sheriff's office.

She lifted her shoulders. "It was deep, and there is a lot of bruising."

Miss Templeton *tsked*. "Come along, Rose. Let's get you to the doctor."

Rose twisted her fingers. "But I did want to see my brother. Which… You said prisoner, so that means you only captured one of them."

Cullen stooped in front of her chair and took her hands. "We arrested Ned." He wished he didn't have to be the one to give her sorrowful news. "Rose, Ned told us your other brother is dead."

She lowered her gaze and her fingers tightened. Her eyes squeezed shut for a moment and a tear slid down her cheek. "I guess I expected that would happen one day. Brock was the hot-headed one. I wish Mama and I could have made him listen. Sheriff, may I come back and visit Ned?"

Harper nodded. "After you see the doctor."

She stood and began limping toward the door.

"Wait." Cullen moved quickly to her side. "You're not walking all the way to the doctor's house."

"I walked for miles the last two days, and I walked here from the hotel." Rose's eyes reflected indifference and she gave a one-shouldered shrug.

Cullen shook his head. It was time for Rose Miller to realize her worth in his mind and heart. "Well, you're not walking to the doctor's office." Without another word, he scooped her into his arms.

Rose gasped and grabbed for his neck. Her arms reaching to hold onto him loosed an entire flock of eagles in his middle. If he'd known this was how it felt to have Rose in his arms, he would have done it weeks ago.

Harper snorted and released a "Ha!," and Miss Templeton squeaked a tiny, "Oh, my."

"Miss Templeton, would you mind accompanying us as chaperone?"

The woman's face flushed pink and her mouth formed an O, but she scurried to the door. She held it open and stepped aside. Cullen maneuvered sideways through the doorway with Rose in his arms.

Rose turned her saucer-eyed expression upward at him. Her cheeks reddened, and her lips gaped open and snapped closed as though she was trying to capture words. She finally reclaimed her voice and hissed at him, "Cullen! What do you think you're doing? Put me down this instant."

He grinned at her. "Nope."

With Miss Templeton only a step behind them, he gentled his words. "I listened to you, Miss Miller. Now you're going to listen to me, especially since you aren't going anywhere, at least for the time being."

She grimaced and hid her face against his shoulder. "Cullen, what is Miss Templeton going to think? This is highly improper. She's going to fire me on the spot."

Miss Templeton trotted a few steps and came alongside. "I think Mr. Delaney is a gallant gentleman." Her voice took on a bird-like quality, light and airy. "This is not at all improper since you have me as your chaperone, and I most certainly will not fire you. Now hush. Listen to what this young man wants to tell you."

Rose lifted her head. The shade of red on her cheeks deepened. "Yes, ma'am." She dipped her chin and pressed her lips together.

Cullen sent the housekeeper a broad smile before turning a more serious face toward Rose. "First of all, I want you to know how very disappointed I am at this whole situation."

He let her chew on that statement for a full minute.

"I'm sorry, Cullen." When she finally spoke, her tone was contrite. "I can't change the way things are. I can call myself Rose Miller, but I'll always be a Fellrath."

Is that what she thought? That he was disappointed in her lineage?

She cocked her head to one side, her brow furrowed. "If you were disappointed in me, why did you stand up for me to Mr. Fairchild?"

His heart fractured that she didn't expect him, or anyone who cared for her, to defend her. After hearing her story, however, he understood a little better. He had sisters, and he well remembered being their protector when they were growing up. Big brothers were supposed to protect their younger sister, but her brothers only brought anguish down on her. One thing was certain, however. He did not want her to view him as a big brother.

"Mr. Fairchild was being grossly dishonorable in viewing you as too undesirable to have in his employ. I could not stand by and see you treated so unfairly."

Her lips parted in preparation to reply, but he silenced her. "Shhh. I'm not finished."

She closed her lips into a pout, and it was all he could do to resist chuckling, but what he had to tell her came from the deepest part of his heart.

"Rose, it makes no difference to me who your brothers are. You have made very different choices than they did. I do not judge you or make assumptions about you the way the people in Raleigh did. I bear no prejudice against you because you felt the need to change your name so people wouldn't connect you with your brothers. I'm disappointed because you didn't feel you could trust me. People who care about each other trust each other. If you didn't feel you could trust me, maybe that was my fault. I didn't do a very good job of earning your trust."

They arrived at the doctor's house, and Cullen paused with one foot on the first step of the front porch. "I hope you will give me another chance to be someone you can trust."

Miss Templeton hurried past them and knocked on the doctor's door, but Cullen wouldn't budge until he'd heard Rose's answer.

Her eyes stared at his, and she *whooshed* an intake of breath. The tiny crease between her brows smoothed out as her features took on an expression of amazement. "You care about me?"

Cullen tipped his head back and released a soft laugh. "Oh, sweet Rose, I not only care *about* you, I care *for* you. In fact, I have—"

The door opened and the doctor's sweeping gaze took in all three of them. Gesturing to Rose in Cullen's arms, he nodded to Miss Templeton. "What seems to be the trouble?"

"I am Josephine Templeton. This is Miss Rose Miller and Mr. Cullen Delaney. Miss Miller injured her foot a few days ago, and it's very painful."

Cullen's insides squirmed in frustration. How was he to bare his heart to Rose when everyone kept interrupting?

As soon as Cullen put her down in the doctor's examination room, Rose missed his arms supporting her. She wished she knew what he'd been about to say. She watched as he pushed the curtain aside, sent her a lingering look over his shoulder, and then retreated to the outer area.

The doctor removed her shoe and stocking and scowled. "You should have come to see me sooner."

She didn't bother trying to explain to him why she couldn't. All she wanted was to get this over with so she and Cullen could continue their discussion. She clamped her teeth together and squeezed her eyes shut as the doctor cleaned the infected wound and put four stitches in place.

The doctor finished up and wrapped her foot in a clean bandage. Then he gave her some instructions and a warning to stay off her foot as much as possible until the infection was gone. She hobbled out to the waiting area where Miss Templeton sat just as Cullen came in the front door.

Once again, he scooped her up in his arms, but this time she didn't insist he put her down. She slipped her hands around his neck and interlaced her fingers. It was a good thing the doctor didn't take her pulse at that moment.

Miss Templeton assured him and the doctor that she would see to it Rose followed the doctor's orders, and she proceeded them out the door.

When Cullen stepped out to the porch, he smiled down at her—a different smile than she was used to seeing from him. "I got a buggy from the livery to take you and Miss Templeton back to the hotel."

"No."

Rose and Cullen both turned their heads toward Miss Templeton. The woman smiled. "It's a lovely day, and I feel like taking a walk."

Cullen started, "But I planned to—"

"Mr. Delaney, I choose to walk today." Miss Templeton was a formidable opponent. Her tone defined her unbending will. She tipped her head toward the conveyance. "You and Miss Miller take the buggy." Was that a twinkle in Miss Templeton's eye? She flipped her fingers in a dismissive manner. "And take your time." With that, the housekeeper descended the porch steps and headed in the direction of the hotel.

Rose exchanged a surprised look with Cullen. He settled her in the buggy seat, then he trotted around to the opposite side and climbed in. He tapped the reins on the horse's back and they moved out, but in the wrong direction.

Rose sat with her hands in her lap, calm and ladylike on the outside, but her insides engaged in a strange and wondrous dance. "The hotel is the other way."

When she peeked sideways at Cullen, he urged the horse to pick up the pace a bit. "I know. You heard Miss Templeton. We're taking our time."

If her heart beat any harder, he would surely hear it. He guided the horse out of town to a place where a bend in the road overlooked a mountain vista. The scenery was lovely, the sky cornflower blue, and the aroma of pine and hemlock scented the air while the song of larks and mockingbirds surrounded them. But how could she enjoy those things when all she wanted was for Cullen to finish saying what he'd started to say when he carried her to the doctor's office?

He halted the buggy and set the brake. "I have something to say, and I hope I can get it said out here with nobody to intrude or interrupt."

Her breath came in shallow gulps. Cullen took both her hands in his. "Miss Rose Miller, over the past five months, I first came to care *about* you. You needed a friend. After a while, I realized I cared *for* you, and those feelings of caring go deeper than anything I've ever known."

She bit her lip, aching for him to say the words she wanted to hear. Her hands itched to reach around his neck again, and she crossed and uncrossed her ankles.

"I wanted to make sure I say this right." He caressed the tops of her hands with his thumbs.

If he didn't say *something*, she wasn't going to be able to—

"Rose, I—"

"Cullen, I love you."

He threw his head back and laughed, then pulled her to him.

She snuggled against his chest. "I'm sorry I interrupted."

He leaned down and kissed her gently. "Sweet Rose, you can interrupt me to tell me you love me any time you want.

The End

# ACKNOWLEDGMENTS

Writing is a solitary profession in a lot of ways, but this writer has not ever written a book alone. Despite the many hours sitting at my computer with nobody for company or conversation, besides the cat, I've always had a cheering section.

Thank you to my writing buds, The Posse.

Kim Vogel Sawyer—who believed in me when I was first getting started.
Eileen Key
Margie Vawter
Jalana Franklin
Darlene Wells
Kristian Libel

Y'all have been so faithful to brainstorm, answer my techie questions, and give me honest feedback.

Thank you to my literary agent, Tamela Hancock Murray—you're the best! Thank you for your advice and mentorship.

Thank you to my sisters—Pam Bresee and Christine Lee. "Sisters" isn't the right label for these two ladies. They are Prayer Warriors!

Thank you to my Christian brothers and sisters, my church family—way too many to name, but y'all know who you are! Thank you for your encouragement.

# ABOUT THE AUTHOR

Connie Stevens lives with her husband of forty-plus years in north Georgia, within sight of her beloved mountains. A lifelong reader and lover of history, Connie began creating stories by the time she was ten. Her office manager and writing muse is a cat, but she's never more than a phone call or email away from her critique partners. She enjoys gardening and quilting, but one of her favorite pastimes is browsing antique shops where story ideas often take root in her imagination. Recently, Connie has stepped out by faith and launched her speaking and teaching ministry. Her published works include two Carol Award finalists, two Selah Award finalists, and an Inspirational Readers Choice Award winner. Connie has been a member of American Christian Fiction Writers since 2000.

Wings of Hope Publishing is committed to providing quality Christian
reading material in both the fiction and non-fiction markets.

Made in United States
North Haven, CT
17 November 2022

26862008R00148